T0160209

PRAISE FOR *The River Killers*

"Conspiracy is alive and well in Burrows's winning debut. There is plenty of technical detail for readers who love adventures like Sebastian Junger's *The Perfect Storm* or David Masiel's *2182 kHz*. Burrows's prose can be dense, but his ability to bring a mixed cast into the tale is stellar." —*Library Journal*

"Lovers of succinct dialogue à la Elmore Leonard and witty writing like Raymond Chandler's will be impressed by Burrows's style."
—*Western Mariner*

"A story that's bound to intrigue anyone who has made a living from fishing . . . The dialogue, filled with banter and smart-assed commentary, captures the rough-edged style of 1950s mystery novels." —*The Fisherman*

"Intriguing, insightful, and chock full of great humor."
—*North Island Gazette*

"A very good first book. Danny [Swanson] seems destined to return, which makes Burrows a writer to watch." —*Globe and Mail*

"*The River Killers* is engaging and informative . . . It's impossible not to be fascinated by the mess of fishing and fish stewardship."
—*Times Colonist*

THE FOURTH BETRAYAL

BRUCE BURROWS

TouchWood
Editions

Copyright © 2014 Bruce Burrows

All rights reserved. No part of this publication may be reproduced, stored in
a retrieval system, or transmitted in any form or by any means—electronic,
mechanical, recording, or otherwise—without the prior written consent
of the publisher or a licence from the Canadian Copyright Licensing Agency
(ACCESS Copyright). For a copyright licence, visit accesscopyright.ca.

TouchWood Editions
touchwoodeditions.com

LIBRARY AND ARCHIVES CANADA CATALOGUING IN PUBLICATION
Burrows, Bruce, 1946–, author
The fourth betrayal / Bruce Burrows.

Issued in print and electronic formats.
ISBN 978-1-77151-096-7

I. Title.

PS8603.U7474F69 2014   C813'.6   C2014-902767-2

Editor: Linda L. Richards
Proofreader: Vivian Sinclair
Design: Pete Kohut
Cover image: Island with trees—PhotoRx, istockphoto.com
Orca pod—Lazareva, istockphoto.com
Tanker—Pley, istockphoto.com
Illustration on page 87: Rebekah Pesicka
Author photo: Chris Black

 Canadian Patrimoine
Heritage canadien
 Canada Council Conseil des Arts
for the Arts du Canada
 BRITISH COLUMBIA
ARTS COUNCIL

We gratefully acknowledge the financial support for our publishing activities from
the Government of Canada through the Canada Book Fund and the Canada
Council for the Arts, and from the Province of British Columbia through the
British Columbia Arts Council and the Book Publishing Tax Credit.

The interior pages of this book have been printed on 100% post-consumer
recycled paper, processed chlorine free, and printed with vegetable-based inks.

This book is a work of fiction. Names, characters, places, and incidents are either
products of the author's imagination or are used fictitiously. Any resemblance to
actual events or locales or persons, living or dead, is entirely coincidental.

1 2 3 4 5 18 17 16 15 14

PRINTED IN CANADA

To all the dedicated Canadians resisting the desecration of our country by radical developmentalists dependent on foreign money.

OLLIE AND DOUGIE'S GREAT ADVENTURE

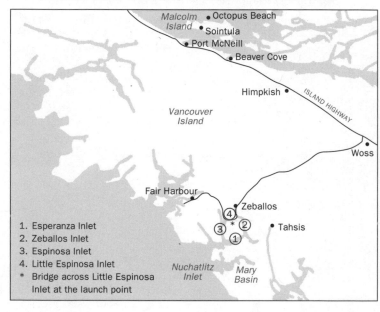

1. Esperanza Inlet
2. Zeballos Inlet
3. Espinosa Inlet
4. Little Espinosa Inlet
* Bridge across Little Espinosa
  Inlet at the launch point

One
1988

I was too drunk to be of any assistance to Dougie, who was puking copiously all over his brand-new running shoes. *Well*, I thought, *I guess he won't be getting laid tonight.* It was only when I tried to stand up and got no further than a wobbly kneeling position that I realized my prospects for sexual fulfilment were as dim as his. The girls would be *so* disappointed.

We had skipped the "dry grad" at North Island Secondary School, which resulted in the dry heaves at awkward locations and inconvenient occasions over the next two days. But prior to the penance, we had seriously enjoyed ourselves, watching the sun go down over Broughton Strait while quaffing deeply our drinks and thinking deeply our thoughts, on the eve of our entry into the adult world.

Doug Tarkenen and me, Ollie Swanson, had known each other for the entirety of our admittedly larval lives. Growing up among the 851 residents of Sointula had been a gift to us, for which our youthful oblivion precluded any thought of thanks. And whom would we have thanked? God was surely above gratitude, and Wilma Jarvenen, his local delegate, was too busy preparing for the rec committee's bake sale.

Sointula was settled as a Finnish utopian commune, socialist and free-loving, but the first settlers never attained their Republic of Rapture. Such a thing could not be built, only discovered, entrance granted with the passport of youth. And so we reveled in our own utopian republic with its unwritten constitutional guarantee—no fear and no fetters.

We were granted untrammeled freedom, the run of the town, at the age of four. Our parents could grant us that freedom because every adult in town was a surrogate parent, and even the older kids acted as big brothers and sisters, gently discouraging us from our more egregious acts of stupidity.

We built forts in the woods that no adult ever saw and created adventures that needed no adult's permission. Our scout troop went on camping trips more often than city kids went to the mall. We took for granted a natural splendor that was later packaged and sold to rich European tourists who seemed to need packaging in order to appreciate splendor. But for us kids, the ocean and the mountains and the forest and the bears and the deer and the fish and the whales were just part of our backyard.

And together, Dougie and I gloried in it. If Dougie wanted to chop down a tree, I would climb it first to enjoy the ride down. We scavenged wire rope from old logging sites to build zip lines and we built rafts from driftwood on the beaches. We built jumps for our bikes and raced go-carts down Boogieman's Hill and gloried in the crashes. We played Tarzan, swinging from branch to branch with ease. Unease and disease were strangers to us. Were we blessed with some ever-present, all-powerful analgesic? We must have been, because I can remember the falls and the collisions and even the damaged body parts, but not the pain. When did that change?

As teenagers we had the pick of highly paid logging and fishing jobs in the summers, and we bought pickup trucks before we were old enough to take our driver's tests. And because the natural speed limit on a gravel logging road is enforced by ever-present potholes rather than occasional cops, and because the density of vehicles per mile of road was about that of interstellar gas, and because all seven teenagers were always in one vehicle anyway, the possibility of a two-vehicle crash was remote. And vehicle-on-tree collisions at fifteen miles per hour have a low fatality rate, which explains the 100 percent survival rate for me and Dougie.

When all else failed, when the weather was too lousy for a real adventure, Dougie made up stories or retold the tale of some past escapade. He'd been a raconteur since I could remember. Lately he'd been writing stuff. The things he showed me were really good. He should be writing this story. I think at one time he meant to. But now I'll have to write it. So, in honor of Dougie, I'll throw in the odd bit of writerly descriptorama. "The evening sky imagined our fate." How's that?

And now we were emerging from the cocoon and we had plans. We didn't think of them as dreams and aspirations. They were things we would do, goals we would achieve. Work awhile. Save some money. Probably university for Dougie. Travel.

It was all so simple.

And one of the simplest things we did was embark on a trip to investigate whether Vancouver nightlife was any more exciting than Sointula's. It was.

We saved on hotel expenses by arranging a night in the drunk tank. It was upon awakening in that establishment that I discovered I had been tattooed: a badly drawn seine boat cruised the skin of my left bicep. Dougie, we discovered, had as usual been much more creative. His left buttock sported a Balinese fighting cock in full attack mode; the right buttock, a mirror image. The object of their aggression was evidently a large snake, which had been cleverly depicted so as to appear to be seeking refuge in a haven that I will leave to the reader's imagination.

They say youth is wasted on the young. But it didn't seem as though we wasted any of it. We extracted every precious nugget and converted each one into the currency of the future: stories, knowledge, strength, resilience. Maybe what we should have bargained for was prescience.

Two

Seventeen years later, when Dougie went missing, it was the first fleeting shadow that fell across the sunscape of my life. We had followed our master plan. Dougie was now working as a reporter for the *Ottawa Times*. My contribution to the master plan was my wife, Oshie, and our two kids, Daiki and Ren.

Dougie had phoned me just after the New Year. He talked in vague terms about this big story he was working on. He would only say that it was about corruption in government, but I could tell he was excited about it.

Then I didn't hear from him for a long time. I sort of knew he hadn't written anything for a while, and his monthly phone call was overdue, but in between driving my kids to soccer practice and overhauling the engine of the *Ryu II*, I wasn't really keeping track of time. Then Dougie's aunt Helga phoned. The annual birthday cheeseball she'd sent Dougie had been returned. I refrained from asking if that had meant an extra-dangerous cargo run for the ferry. She was also perturbed that he hadn't returned any of her phone calls. This triggered just a hint of unease, so I promised I'd e-mail him, reassured Helga that nothing could possibly be wrong and hung up.

His e-mail in-box was full. My unease increased somewhat. I phoned Dougie's editor at the *Ottawa Times*. Three months ago Dougie had taken a leave of absence to work on some important but rather vague "big story." They hadn't heard from him for a month. My unease now changed to concern that was edging closer to Helga's level of outright worry. Mind you, Dougie had taken up canoeing recently. Maybe he was just away on a long trip. Of course, it was possible he'd gotten lost. Where we grew up, if you were lost you just went downhill until you reached the ocean. In Ontario, if you went downhill long enough you'd end up on daytime TV.

Oshie came in carrying groceries. "I have to run out again, Ollie. Soccer moms meeting. Why don't soccer dads ever meet?"

"There are no soccer dads. We are all soccer moms now."

"Even Don Cherry?"

"He wishes he was. Hey listen, Oshie. Dougie's sort of missing."

"Sort of missing?"

"His aunt sent him a present that was returned. His in-box is full. His boss says he's on leave, but nobody knows where he is."

I had her full attention. She considered this information quickly but, I knew, completely. "Ollie, you better go look for him."

Spring break was over and the kids were back in school. If I had to go away, now was as good a time as any. So the next day I kissed Oshie and the kids goodbye and caught a flight to Ottawa. I tried to find an adult-sized seat—I was, after all, bigger than my dad, Big Ollie—but all the seats had been designed for kids or jockeys. After five uncomfortable hours of gazing down upon a beautiful and varied vastness, I landed at Macdonald–Cartier airport. Its international airport code is YOW, but it felt to me more like BLAH.

I took a cab to Dougie's apartment in the old neighborhood of Lower Town. After giving the driver a generous but apparently insufficient tip, I considered problem number one: access. Fortunately, a well-coiffed and well-dressed matron turned off the sidewalk and proceeded up the walk toward the entrance. I graciously held the door for her before following her into the foyer. We ended up in the elevator together, where we both succeeded in avoiding eye contact, and I got off before her, on the third floor.

Dougie's apartment was number three-five-one, and when I stood before the door I had reason to be thankful for all the cop shows I'd watched. The credit-card trick was easier than I thought it would be, and within twenty seconds I was inside Dougie's apartment. It was also, I soon realized, his home.

Just inside the door was the photo wall. I saw pictures of Dougie and me at our high school grad, Dougie's graduation from Simon Fraser University and lots of pictures of my wedding. There were a couple of really faded snaps of Dougie's father, who had died in the *Ocean Star* sinking in 1966, and his mother, who had succumbed to some unexplained illness two years later, and lots of pictures of Daiki and Ren. Dougie's aunt Helga, who had shepherded him through his teenage years, beamed from a framed eight-by-ten on the hall table. And pinned in the lower left corner, a curling, faded black-and-white, shot with a cheap instamatic, of Dougie pulling a log with a frayed piece of rope. In spidery handwriting, probably his mom's, was the caption "Dougie with his pet log." The memory ambled into my consciousness like an old friend you haven't seen for a while. The log wasn't Dougie's pet that day. It was a log and Dougie was a skidder. I believe I was a dump truck. Playing Machines was much more fun than Cowboys and Indians.

Dougie evidently had no female friends worthy of inclusion on the wall. No male friends either. No one at all from his Ottawa life.

As I continued into the apartment, I was unexpectedly perturbed by the sense of Dougieness that overcame more concrete sensations, like the musty air and the grittiness of dust everywhere. Dougie had definitely lived here, but he hadn't been here for quite a while.

The living room was obviously his office/work area. The computer stood on a long table against the windowed wall. Papers were scattered across the table and I examined a few of them—notes for stories and bits of research details.

I sat down at the desk in the corner, next to the TV. I opened and closed all the drawers. None were locked, so I went back to the top one for a detailed perusal. I found the expired insurance documents for a red 1999 Jeep. I assumed the current documents were in the Jeep. There were also some maps. I took them over to the table where I could spread them out.

They were all topographic maps of wilderness areas of Ontario. Many had lines drawn on them, presumably routes he'd taken, and printed comments, such as "Flooded in Nov.," "Bridge gone," "Huge trout," "Fucking flies."

On a map of Algonquin Park, next to Canoe Lake, he had written, "Okay to leave Jeep?" The question mark leapt out at me. He probably hadn't completed that trip yet. Maybe that was the trip he was on right now. Idiot! I'd have to give him hell for getting lost in Ontario scrub. Not even real trees, for Christ's sake.

I grabbed the phonebook next to the phone and looked up the number for the Ontario Provincial Police. It was now four thirty in the afternoon and I dialed quickly, hoping to get someone senior before they all left for the day. By the time I'd been routed through four different people, finally got Missing Persons and explained that I might have a friend missing in Algonquin Park but I had no idea when he'd gone missing, it was too late. But, displaying infinite patience, I managed to make an appointment to meet a Corporal Mayhew at eight thirty the following morning at the OPP detachment in Whitney, the closest detachment to the park.

Continuing my search, I opened the second drawer and found a key ring amid miscellaneous junk. One of the keys opened the front door. One looked like a vehicle ignition key, and the others were just so many small, jagged mysteries.

But I was feeling excited. I'd meet the cop in the morning. We'd go to Canoe Lake, find Dougie's Jeep parked somewhere, and the cop would declare him an official missing person. A search would be mounted, a sheepish Dougie would be found, and I'd get to razz the shit out of him.

Didn't work out that way. I rented a car, and after spending the night on Dougie's couch, I left his apartment at four in the morning. I sure as hell didn't want to be late for this appointment.

Heading west, I found my way to Renfrew and picked up Highway 60. The two-lane blacktop receded before me as the world revealed itself to a reticent sun. I was surprised by the amount of roadkill: skunks, raccoons, squirrels, and unidentified dead objects. Either there were a lot more animals in Ontario or they were stupider than their cousins in BC.

Billing itself as the east gateway to Algonquin Park, Whitney was well laid out in that Upper Canadian sort of way, and I had no trouble locating the OPP building. Unfortunately, I had made myself an early bird. Fortunately, I got no worm, but rather two cups of coffee and some pretty good corned beef hash.

Spiritually and bodily refreshed, I walked into the OPP building and asked to see Corporal Mayhew. Mayhew was, I'd say, six foot two and what you could call lanky. I almost expected him to drawl his words. I was disappointed. After I'd given a long explanation of who I was, who Dougie was, and why we thought he was a missing person, the corporal said, "That's not much basis to mount a full-scale search."

"Let's at least go out and look for his Jeep," I suggested. "I wouldn't have come all the way here if I didn't think this was serious."

He looked at me, probably appraising my reliability as a Missing Persons reporter. He must have appraised me favorably, for he stood up and said, "You want to ride with me or follow me?" I decided to ride with him and we left.

Continuing west on Highway 60 for about half an hour, we

turned north on Arowhon Road and followed it for about half an hour. Eventually, we came to the spot that Dougie had marked on the map, where the road crossed a narrow inlet at the northern end of the lake. It was an obvious canoe-launching spot. Mayhew pulled over and we got out.

We walked over the bridge and looked north to the head of the inlet, then south to where the expanse of Canoe Lake faded into the haze. The wind from the north chilled the back of my neck. There was sort of a cat road leading off into the bushes on the right. We followed it. About a hundred yards in we found Dougie's Jeep. I showed Mayhew the license number on the old insurance form to verify it. The doors were unlocked, typical small-town Dougie, so I got in and, using one of the keys I'd found, started it up. I shut it off and got out. We both gazed at the empty canoe rack.

Mayhew pulled out his cell phone and made a call. "We've got probable cause to assume there's a canoeist missing on Canoe Lake, possibly for over a month. Can we get a plane up? Okay."

He shut the phone off. "The plane will search until it's dark. But, as you can see by the map, Canoe Lake connects to a huge network of other lakes. Lot of ground to cover. We might as well head back."

Reluctantly, I agreed. There wasn't much we could do here without a boat, and even if we had one, the plane could cover the area faster. But it didn't have to. Just over a mile south they spotted a canoe, overturned and washed up against the beach. The plane landed, and they got a registration number off the canoe. Dougie had bought it over a year ago. They continued the search along the shoreline, looking for human traces: clothes, campfires, broken branches, anything. They found nothing.

When I left Ottawa I felt like a soldier abandoning his dead. I took Dougie's photo album, the only remnant of him I could salvage. It was inadequate. I was inadequate.

When I got on the plane back to Vancouver, I was numb. Halfway there the numbness had worn off like a dentist's freezing, exposing an array of painful emotions. Anger at Dougie for disappearing, at the searchers for not finding him, at me for letting it happen, plus grief, loss, and just a hint of puzzlement at how Dougie could have been inept enough to let this happen. By the time I arrived in Vancouver, I was just tired.

It was 9:00 PM when the cab dropped me at my front door. Oshie heard me and came out of the living room to greet me. As soon as she saw my face, she knew. She rushed forward to hug me. I hid my face on her shoulder and burst into tears.

"Ollie, Ollie, I'm so sorry. Baby, I'm so sorry." She hugged me tighter and sort of rocked me from side to side. After a few moments I raised my head and snuffled a bit and wiped my eyes with the back of my hand. Oshie pulled her sleeve over her hand and used that to help me dry my eyes. "What happened, sweetie?"

I took several deep breaths. "We just couldn't find him. He'd gone on this stupid canoe trip. We found his Jeep and then his canoe, but we couldn't find Dougie."

She didn't say anything for a while, just hugging me and using one hand to gently massage the back of my neck. "Come to bed, sweetie. You need some rest. It'll be better in the morning." But first I visited my kids' rooms and gave each of them a kiss as they slept.

In the morning we decided I would have to drive up to Sointula to deliver the sad news. Aunt Helga would be devastated. So would my parents, who considered Dougie almost a second son. I couldn't find the courage to phone first. I hoped I could muster some courage on the drive up.

At seven o'clock that evening I walked into my parents' house. My dad was home from his logging camp, sitting in his recliner, watching a hockey game. When he saw me, he gave me his big wide grin and stood up. "Hey, Ollie. Good to see you, son. What are you doing in this neck of the woods?"

My mother appeared out of the kitchen and gave me a sharp look. Somehow words formed themselves and came out of my mouth. "You guys know Helga was worried about Dougie. It looks like he's gone. Canoe accident."

"Shit! Fucking shit! That's a fucking shame. He was too good a kid for this fucking shit to happen." Big Ollie was a logger. He was used to losing friends. Hell, Sointula was a fishing-slash-logging village. Everyone had lost friends or relatives or both. That didn't make people less sympathetic to the loss, just less sympathetic to the circumstances.

My mother came and touched my arm. "You want me to come with you to Helga's?"

"Thanks, Mom."

As soon as Helga saw me, she knew it was bad. I told her quickly, and she looked down at her knitting and said nothing. Finally she looked up, sweet woman, and said, "Ollie, I'm so sorry for you. I know what Dougie meant to you, and you to him."

"We'll all miss him, Helga," I said. Declining Helga's offer of coffee, I handed her Dougie's photo album, then left her and my mom and went for a walk out on Kaleva Road.

When I got to Kemp's Beach, I went down to the water and stood there, looking across Broughton Strait to Vancouver Island. Tattered white clouds shrouded the mourning hills and the falling rain camouflaged my tears. After a while I became aware that I was shivering, so I began the walk back into town. The southeast wind pushed me gently from behind and the cold rain numbed my face but not the pain deep inside me. The evening sky imagined our fate.

Three
1989

It was the year after our triumphant grad party, and the party was most definitely over. We were back on the same beach, watching the same familiar sunset, the post storm number thirty-two, streaked with purple and gray and featuring increasing tones of threatening red fading to passive orange. We were almost as drunk as on grad night. But the metamorphosis from the cocoon had taken an unexpected turn. We weren't butterflies. We had become nineteen-year-old cripples, and we were feeling betrayed.

I had been working on a seine boat when my foot was crushed between the spoolers and the side of the stern ramp. It hurt, but being told it would never be normal hurt worse. Dougie had torn his back muscles carrying a tail block up a rock bluff. His steel-caulked boots had slipped on the rock, and the eighty-pound block on his shoulder overloaded his back muscles as the 9-1-1 center in his brain shrilled out its frantic "Don't fall, don't fall!" message.

Now we were using beer to wash down the painkillers and contemplating a bleak future. Dougie cursed as he tried to find a comfortable position leaning against a stump. He couldn't sit and I couldn't stand, but we were still chips off the same block. I used my crutch to drag the case of beer closer, took out two cans and tossed him one. "You on compo?"

"No. Soft tissue. If they can't see the injury on an X-ray, it doesn't exist. You?"

"Forty-seven dollars a day."

"What? You're supposed to get seventy-five percent of your lost wages. What's the crew share since you got hurt?"

"About twenty-eight grand. But compo has a way of screwing you. They average your fishing income out over three hundred and sixty-five days and then pay you seventy-five percent of that."

"Assholes."

"The best."

"What're you gonna do now?"

"Know any openings for a one-legged beachman?"

"No. How about a chokerman who can't bend over or lift more than his lunch kit?"

"Prospects are not good."

"Any ideas?"

"Legal or illegal?"

Dougie looked at me sharply. The guy he'd grown up with wouldn't have even asked that question. But I wasn't that guy anymore. "Drugs? You have to buy from one set of untrustworthy scumbags and sell to another bunch of untrustworthy scumbags. And the pension plan is weak."

"How's your current pension plan?"

"Don't throw away those beer cans."

"Actually, I've been thinking about something. There're risks, but you're not dealing with as many people as in the drug trade. Things would be way more in our control."

"I'm all ears."

I grinned at him. "Ever been to Esperanza in February?"

There was a pause while he made the necessary connections. "Knock over the cash buyers? Come to think of it, I'm surprised no one's done it before now."

The roe herring fishery had exploded in the seventies and early eighties. All the buyers were Japanese, because Canadian consumers had not yet warmed to, indeed, were distinctly cool to, the idea of eating raw herring eggs. At that time there were still lots of buyers, and there was intense competition among them. When the fleet was on the fishing grounds, packer boats representing the various buyers would try to entice the fishermen to sell their catch to them by offering the highest price. And they paid cash. The previous spring I'd been fishing in Esperanza, on the West Coast, and there had been twenty-three packers anchored up. Each one carried at least a hundred thousand dollars, some a lot more.

I crushed my beer can and opened another while Dougie pondered. When he spoke, he said what I knew he would. "I don't want to get caught and I don't want anyone to get hurt. But in principle? I'm with you."

A week later, the first southeast blow signaled the end of grace. The warm embrace of summer was withdrawn for the ministrations of a colder mistress. Dougie and I rented Pakolin's old farmhouse on Kaleva Road. It was a bit ramshackle, but cheap, and it was right across the road from the beach, which was handy for getting in the winter's wood.

Making wood, as they call it in Sointula, was slow going with two cripples. I could hobble around with a saw, but Dougie was limited to maneuvering his truck to pull the logs up the beach. Our buddy John, whose sister I had dated for a year and whose dad ran the fish plant where my mom worked part time, took pity on us and did the splitting and chucking into the truck. All we had to do was supply the beer and some good BS, start the occasional outrageous rumor and not remind John about the time he dropped an easy fly ball that allowed Port McNeill to win the Salmon Days tournament.

I shut off the saw and wiped wood chips off my face. Dougie was maneuvering his truck into position to pull up a big fir log. He got out of the cab slowly, with just the slightest grimace, and started pulling a rope out of the box. I limped over to the log. John put down his splitting maul and joined us as we strategized about the best methodology for the pull. Dougie pointed to one end of the log. "We'll grab 'er there. Put a double roll on it and it should swing and miss that rock."

John demurred. "I don't think it'll move without blocking it. Use the rock for a tail hold and grab the log right here."

Important decisions are best made by alcohol-soothed brains. Dougie passed out beers from the back of the truck. "Hey, did you guys hear that Tarmo is turning his net shed into a McDonald's?"

This was news to me, as was much of the output of Dougie's fertile brain. But the least I could do was reinforce it. "It's supposed to be finished by May 24, and Ronald McDonald is going to lead the May Day parade."

Back to Dougie. "Yeah, that's sure going to piss off the rec committee. Having a symbol of capitalist exploitation lead the celebration of our glorious Finnish socialist past."

John wasn't interested in the political implications, although others would be. "I know why the bastard did it. He had a bunch of yellow paint left over from painting his house. It'll be perfect for the golden arches."

I had a thought. "You know why they painted the arches yellow in the first place? So when people piss on them, it won't show up." Heads nodded as they internalized the answer to one of life's great mysteries.

The day passed slowly but pleasantly. We'd started with two dozen beer in the back of the truck and were pretty well honor bound not to quit until they were gone. Consequently, by four o'clock we had accumulated a fair pile of wood behind the house. By the time we dropped into the pub after supper, the McDonald's rumor had been Sointulaized. McDonald's was now going to buy the whole of Malcolm Island and turn it into a potato farm.

We were sitting at a table with Old Man Makela, and he was shaking his head as he considered the implications. "Golly, how did they find out we grow big bodaidoes here? A turist musta told 'em. Never shoulda let those turists off the ferry. Never shoulda had the ferry in the first place. Ruined the place. Never woulda happened in the old days."

Wilma Jarvenen came over to our table; she had that six-rum-and-coke look in her eye. "We just had an emergency joint meeting of the rec committee and the preschool mothers. We passed a resolution against clowns in the May Day parade."

"But Wilma, does that mean the regional directors won't be in the parade?" She glared at me and huffed away to a less flippant table. Nevertheless, I was impressed. The two dominant political forces in Sointula had united to repel the foreign foe. United we stood; divided we'd never get a decent ferry schedule.

The talk soon turned to more pleasant matters. The upcoming herring season, though still months away, was a popular topic, and the signifiers were all good. The quota had just been announced and it was fairly high, and the yen was strong. Or weak. Whichever translated into a good price. Soon we had produced a collective vision of punt loads of herring being exchanged for huge wads of cash, and floatplanes flying in with suitcases full of fresh money. It was agreed that a guy would have to have lots of plastic baggies to keep the cash uncontaminated by herring slime. Dougie and I exchanged brief glances.

After a couple more pints, it was time for the meat draw. Anticipation grew into excitement until the crowd buzzed with an Oscars-night-like frenzy. We all squinted at our ticket numbers as Walter, our MC for the occasion, afflicted us with the compulsory corny jokes before announcing the lucky ticket numbers. By the time we left an hour later, Dougie and I were packing four pounds of bacon, a bag of lamb chops, and a huge pork roast. What a night!

The next day I dropped into my folks' place for coffee. My dad, Big Ollie, was away in camp, tenderly ministering to ten-ton machines that ate forests. Occasionally an inkling of concern about that would flit across my consciousness. But what the hell, I wouldn't be looking for a logging job now.

The kitchen smelled like chocolate-chip cookies, and I realized why I had picked today for a visit. Thursday was cookie day. My mom glanced at me while she poured me a cup of coffee, added honey and set it in front of me. "How're things going? How's your foot?"

I took a cookie. "It's getting better, but I'll never play midfield for Canada."

"What a disappointment. Especially after getting cut from your high school team."

"I might have been a late developer."

"You are. But not at soccer."

I took another cookie. "Anything happening at the fish plant? I need gainful employment."

"They're laying off the salmon crew. But I've got a better idea. Your *mummu* has had this nice young girl helping her around the house, what they call assisted care, but the girl is getting married and moving to Port Alberni. The pay's not great, but you'd enjoy it."

"Are you suggesting I look after old folks for a living? I'm not a nurse."

"Ollie, you've always enjoyed hanging around the old-timers. And a lot of this job is just keeping company with them. Besides, your mummu needs someone."

I took another cookie. "I'm not trained. What if someone has a heart attack?"

"You don't have to be a doctor. I think you need a first-aid course, but you've already done that. Most of the work is just cleaning and helping out around the house. You'd be helping your own mummu. Ollie, it's useful, valuable work."

I took my last cookie. "Who do I talk to?"

"Sylvia Tanner at the health center."

"I'll go see her." I took two more cookies and left.

Sylvia was a briskly capable woman who was related to me by marriage. Many people were—related to me, that is, not, unfortunately, briskly capable. "Your mom said you'd be coming by."

"I'm not sure I can do this."

"Ollie, I've known you all your life. You can do this. You'll be working with four seniors, all of whom you know and one of whom is your own mummu. You'll be helping them out with chores they have difficulty with, just like you've always done."

"Do I need training?"

"You've already got your first-aid. I'll work with you for the first two weeks just to get your feet wet."

"When do I start?"

"Be here Monday at nine. And Ollie, you're going to enjoy this."

I headed back to the farmhouse to give Dougie the news. As I drove along Kaleva, I watched a line of angry gray waves punishing the rocky beach. An anxious flock of driftwood made its way toward the high-tide line, shepherded by eagles who dipped and soared with commendable purpose. I felt better than I had in a long time. The evening sky imagined our fate.

When I walked into the kitchen of the farmhouse, I discovered that Dougie did not share my mood. He was standing by the window with a glass in his hand. There was an open bottle of vodka on the table.

"Dougie boy. What's up?"

He continued staring out the window. "I spent all morning stacking wood."

I looked out the window at the woodpile. There was a row of maybe eight chunks of wood, with four or five more forming the second row and three on top of that. "You know what? We should convert the spare room to a sitting room. That way we could sit and look out at the water instead of a bunch of trees. Bloody Finns built all their houses backwards."

"Hey, Little Miss Sunshine! I'm not interested in your fucking redecorating schemes. My back hurts and I'm broke and useless and I want . . . you know what I want? Revenge. Somebody stole something from me. I'll never get it back, but I want to hurt the fucker who took it."

I poured a glass half full of vodka and looked in the fridge for mixer. There wasn't any. "Let's talk about the Esperanza thing."

"That's a pipe dream."

"No, it's not. We haven't had much of a chance to talk about it because we've been moving and shit. But we've got about five months to put together a plan, buy supplies, maybe rehearse."

"We're broke. How are we gonna buy what we need?"

"I start work on Monday. And you know what? Tomorrow we're gonna take a little road trip. Zeballos. Scout things out a little bit." I walked up to him and raised my glass. He tried to stay angry, but I knew I'd won him over. I'd played my role, suggesting a simple plan, and now his mind was racing, filling in details, constructing an edifice of plot and narrative, telling a story.

He clinked his glass against mine. "Here's to happy endings."

The next morning we caught the eleven o'clock ferry to Port McNeill. In those days you could drive up at five minutes before eleven and still get on. It was blowing thirty and raining, so we sat companionably in the cab of Dougie's truck and watched the windows steam up. I handed Dougie a tape and he slotted it into his deck. Soon Doug and the Slugs were animating the truck's cab with the cheerful boppiness of "Makin' It Work." The freedom of the highway loomed pleasantly. That, and the tunes, and our insulation from the cold and wet outside the cab of the truck, buoyed my spirits.

"Hey, Dougie, I've been thinking about you being so pissed off the other night. Your back is going to get better, partly at least, and you're less of a cripple than I am. But regardless, they haven't damaged your mind. You can still think and talk and argue and go to university and learn things, maybe write stories. So you can't run around and be a bush monkey anymore; the choker-setting profession can get along without you. And guess what? You can get along without it."

"Yeah, you're right. But it still pisses me off. When I got hurt I lost some freedom. I've got less options than before. Same as you. And here's the deal: we were supposed to get compensated for that. That's why they call it Workers' Compensation. But we didn't get compensated, we got fucked. Somebody has to pay for that."

"Well, look on the bright side. We're on our way to Zeballos. Woo-hoo!" The ferry pulled into Port McNeill, and we drove off and up the hill to the Island Highway. The rain was still falling, but the trees on both sides of the highway sheltered us a bit from the wind. We headed south toward the Zeballos turnoff.

Zeballos, population 189, maintained a precarious beachhead at the end of Zeballos Inlet, one of the branching arms of Esperanza Inlet. It was a potential base from which to launch our operation, a sea-to-land transition point that was as close as you could get by road to the herring grounds.

Dougie drove carefully on the rain-slicked pavement, no more than twenty miles per hour over the speed limit. I replaced Doug

and the Slugs with *Let It Bleed* and by the time Mick was inform-
ing us that sometimes we could get what we need, we had reached
the Zeballos turnoff. Dougie turned right and we had another
twenty-five miles to go, which took us three times as long as the
first twenty-five. After a challenging but scenic drive we pulled into
the former gold-mining town. It sure as hell didn't look like it had
ever seen much gold. Maybe a few bicuspid fillings, but observation
of the denizens of the local coffee shop suggested not.

There were four muddy pickup trucks parked outside the
Zeballos Hotel. Three of them had large but friendly dogs woofing
at each other from their respective boxes. Inside the coffee shop were
four of the above-mentioned denizens and the missing dog. The four
humans wore ragged Stanfields with cut-off sleeves and clutched
cups of steaming coffee. They woofed at each other companionably.
*Joe's machine. Broke. New cut block. Yarding downhill. Hoe chucker.
Can't keep up. Rigging slinger. Asshole.* The dog at their feet regarded
them with tolerant affection.

The waitress poured us coffee, gave us menus and looked at us
expectantly. We had, I figured, about thirty seconds to order before
she'd start tapping her foot. Under pressure, we made our decision
decisively: two baron of beef sandwiches with fries, to be washed
down with the best house lager. We lounged back in our chairs and
sipped beer contemplatively until the waitress brought our food.
I watched in disgust as Dougie poured vinegar over his sandwich
as well as the chips. "You abuse your taste buds like Jimi Hendrix
abused his entire body."

"Jimi's body abused him. I'm sure it wasn't his idea to aspirate
vomit. Healthy vinegar use clears the mind, cleanses the body and
improves physical response."

"Have you considered using it as a colonic? I understand it
opens the third chakra, which Western medicine refers to as the

sphincter." I was never entirely sure how serious Dougie was about being serious, and he was never entirely sure how serious I was about not being serious.

After lunch we wandered down to the government wharf. We surveyed an impressive gaggle of boats: trollers and gillnetters, small tugs, crew boats, herring punts, and a few small open skiffs half sunk with rainwater. The fleet was remarkable for its variety of form and similarity of decrepitude. There were no hulls sleek and shiny, no polished wood or chrome, nothing that would do over eight knots, nothing that might challenge the segregation of this nautical ghetto.

Dougie interrupted my ruminations. "This place is too busy."

"There's no one here."

"But someone could appear at any moment to bail out their boat or check the lines or something. We don't want to be leaving or returning from a criminal enterprise and risk being seen."

"Maybe we should launch from Little Espinosa. It's about as isolated as you can get. Let's take a look."

We left town via the dilapidated wooden bridge that ran north toward Little Espinosa Inlet and Fair Harbour. Six miles and fifteen minutes later we were at the bridge that crossed over the inlet and saved the logging trucks from having to traverse all the way around the head.

We stopped and got out of the truck. The tide was flooding, and water boiled through the constricted passage under the bridge. There was neither sight nor sound of other humans. During active logging you could expect a bit of traffic during the day. A school bus ran from Zeballos to Fair Harbour and back. But at night this road would be as deserted as a pregnant mistress.

On the south side of the bridge a boat ramp led down to the water. We walked down to the shore and looked out the inlet. It ran due west for a couple of miles, then turned south for about the same distance before it joined Espinosa Inlet proper. From that junction it was about four miles to the mouth of Esperanza Inlet and then maybe thirteen miles around the corner to Mary Basin. That would be our route to and from the treasure trove. It was all sheltered water except for the stretch that ran around the headland between Esperanza and Nuchatlitz Inlets. We would need to pick a weather window, but we didn't need a lot of time. A half hour tops to traverse the headland, two or three hours to strip the fleet of its riches, then head back into sheltered waters and run for the launch point at Little Espinosa. The worst-case scenario would be to rob all the boats and then have the weather come up and trap us in Mary Basin. It would be painfully embarrassing, more likely just painful, to be trapped in a small bay with our multitudinous and unforgiving victims. Fishermen are known less for turning the other cheek than for exposing it.

I bent down to pick up a good rock and skipped it toward Japan. Dougie started a similar motion but aborted it with a grimace of pain. After breathing deeply for half a minute, he spoke. "This is a perfect place to launch a Zodiac. Get here after dark, say nine o'clock, head out and be back by 4:00 AM and safe somewhere before daylight. Use the bypass road so we don't even have to get close to Zeballos."

I smiled. At the day, at the scenery, at the fact I'd gotten at least nine skips, and at this glimpse of the old Dougie. He didn't have exactly the same sparkly-eyed boyish enthusiasm. He was more restrained, but, I knew, none the less determined. We were big boys now, playing for big stakes. But at least we were playing.

Four

After giving Helga the bad news about Dougie, I returned to Vancouver and began to deal with the banal details of death. I phoned Dougie's landlord and arranged for his few possessions— computer, TV, assorted furniture, and a dirt bike he'd kept in the apartment's storage compound—to be put into storage. His clothes could go to the Goodwill. His Jeep had been towed to a compound, and I paid the storage fee for three months. I knew Dougie had a will and I was the executor because he'd gone through that process just after I'd made my will and made him the executor. This was shortly after I got married and became a responsible person.

But before we could deal with the will, we had to go through the emotionally and bureaucratically confusing process of having Dougie declared legally dead. Emotionally confusing because all I really wanted was for Dougie to be alive, but I was going through a process that would make him dead. Bureaucratically confusing because it was, *ipso facto*, a bureaucratic process.

When I'd phoned Dougie's boss at the *Ottawa Times* to tell him what had happened, he'd foreseen the hassle I was about to go through and given me the name of a good lawyer. Stacy Smith and Sons were now gathering affidavits—from the OPP, the search and rescue people, Aunt Helga, me, Dougie's editor. When the lawyers had all the information, they would go before a judge and make an application for a declaration of death.

But that would take awhile, for which I was glad. Because I wasn't looking forward to going to Aunt Helga, who I presumed was the beneficiary, and explaining to her how Dougie had managed to accumulate all the money he had left her. Therefore I was more than a little puzzled when I finally got to see Dougie's bank records. He had a balance of some eighty-seven thousand dollars. The rest had disappeared in four very large withdrawals spaced over the previous year. What the fuck was that all about? Had he bought some luxurious retirement home somewhere? Or several? Or had he made some huge donations to a worthy charity to assuage his middle-class Canadian guilt? That was more likely. But I was severely ill with curiosity to know where the money had gone.

The missing money plus all the other details of death were affecting me badly. I didn't notice it but Oshie did. She suggested a holiday. "Summer vacation's coming up," she said. "Let's take the kids on a car trip."

I could swear I stood a little straighter as the burden of Dougie's death was at least temporarily displaced. I had a sudden thought. "I've been thinking that I'd like to get Dougie's Jeep. Why don't we fly to Ottawa, do the tourist thing and then drive home in the Jeep?"

Oshie's smile showed her approval. The kids were ecstatic, especially Daiki, who had just covered Canadian government at school. "Ottawa. Cool! Can we go to Question Period?"

Ren chimed in, "Yeah, I've got lots of questions."

Don't we all, I thought.

The kids enjoyed the plane ride almost as much as a ride at the PNE. I remembered my first plane ride, and some of my other firsts. When, I wondered, did I stop having brand-new experiences? And then I realized I hadn't. This was the first time I'd taken my kids on a plane ride. Second-hand firsts were as good as, maybe better than, first-hand firsts.

We did indeed go to Parliament Hill and take in Question

Period. It was a typically rancorous and raucous debate, and Ren observed that the Honourable Members "weren't using their inside voices." Oshie assured him that it was sort of like a play. "Who's the hero?" he asked.

"No one knows," she said. "There may be no heroes, but there're lots of villains to make up for it."

He considered that briefly before asking where the washroom was.

We spent a whole day at the National Gallery, which featured an exhibition of Norval Morrisseau. The kids loved it. He should have done a children's book. Then we did a gallery tour that presented a history of flora and fauna in Canadian art.

The next four days were a blur: Aboriginal culture at Turtle Island, a ride on a historical steam train, rock climbing, laser tag, water parks, a reptile zoo, and thrills and chills at the IMAX theater.

Staid old Ottawa even produced some scandalous excitement while we were there. They had a murder, possibly the first one since D'Arcy McGee was shot. And this one had political ramifications as well. The dead man was Gerry Steadman, a rich guy with vague connections to the Alberta oil patch. He had been a huge donor to the Canadian Alliance and now the Conservative Party. After buying himself insider status, there had been a rumored falling out, and then his bullet-holed body was found in a suite at the Château Laurier. Several high-level Conservative operators were now "helping police with their inquiries." Juicy stuff, but it seemed as foreign as a Hollywood scandal to us.

Finally, all citied out, we collected Dougie's Jeep and began to follow the sun toward home. The first time we stopped for gas, I noticed the Jeep had duel gas tanks. When I went to fill the back tank I discovered a rounded piece of wood rammed into the filler pipe. A flash of memory. A surge of supposition. *Wow, do you suppose?* But I couldn't check my hunch with the kids around. It would have to wait until we were home.

Driving from Ontario to BC is a lot like eating one of my aunt's chocolate-chip cookies. There's the occasional good bit, but way too much filling. And most of the unnecessary filling occurs between Winnipeg and Jasper. However, we saw lots of giant stuff, hockey sticks and Vikings and dinosaurs, and the kids were suitably impressed. And they were awed by the drive through the Rockies. Then we were following the mighty Fraser River as it crashed impatiently through the Fraser Canyon. Then we were home, carrying sleeping kids from the Jeep to their bedroom.

I hugged Oshie as she straightened up from tucking Daiki into bed. "That was a good idea," I whispered. She kissed me and led me by the hand toward our bedroom.

The next morning Oshie took the kids over to visit her parents. I wasted no time in crawling under the Jeep. Sure enough, the rear gas tank sported a large patch of duct tape. I removed it, revealing an eight-inch-square hole. I reached in and after some feeling around was able to remove a cardboard box that held a number of microcassette tapes like business guys used to use for dictation.

I made absolutely sure there was nothing else in the gas tank, then jumped in the Jeep and drove to the Steveston mall. There was a large generic electronic-appliance store, and when I showed the clerk one of the tapes, he supplied me with the appropriate player. Some atavistic urge for caution made me pay with cash, and I drove down to my boat to do the listening.

On board the *Ryu II*, my apprehension vanished. I took a beer out of the fridge, plugged in the cassette player, inserted the tape marked number one and sat down at the galley table to listen. It was not unexpected to hear Dougie's voice, but it somehow startled me anyway, and not just because his voice sounded strange, sort of like he was acting a part.

Dougie: Jesus, Cliff. You played those guys like a cheap violin.
Cliff: It's what we do, sir. We have to be good. We're selling warm shit, and the opposition is selling truth and beauty. We don't want to be condemned to perpetual fourth-party status so we learn to make false statements, misquote, dissemble, misrepresent, fudge, fabricate, fib, and prevaricate. Our guys are mendacious, disingenuous, and dishonest. They are adept at demolishing straw men, conjuring up phony enemies, constructing invalid syllogisms, and deflecting cogent criticism. Joseph Goebbels is our God and the big lie is our sword and shield. And the truth? It can't set you free if it's buried in bullshit. [There was an expansive chortle and a long inhale and exhale. I could picture Cliff puffing on a large expensive cigar.]
Dougie: It's a form of creative genius.
Cliff: Why, thank you, sir. Not many people understand as well as you do.

I had to stop the tape before I vomited. It was almost like watching an old girlfriend in a pornographic movie. Dougie was obviously conning the guy, but still.

I couldn't listen to any more right now. I suddenly longed to see Oshie and the kids. As I drove home I wondered who the hell Cliff was, exactly what story Dougie was working on that would have led him into Cliff's company, and why Cliff felt comfortable talking as openly as he had to Dougie.

Back home, I was just in time to heat up some soup for lunch while Oshie did the grilled cheese sandwiches. As we sat down to eat Oshie gave me a quick kiss and said, "Somebody phoned for you, Ollie. A reporter at Dougie's newspaper. He wants you to phone him. I wrote everything on the board."

After lunch I perused the whiteboard I'd screwed to the wall by the phone. The marker dangled by a string. Messages are important to a self-employed fisherman, and as toddlers Ren and Daiki had occasionally sabotaged the answering machine. In Oshie's almost calligraphic script was written "Phil Davis" and an Ottawa number that was different than the one I'd used previously for the *Ottawa Times*, but I figured it was probably the guy's cell. It was after five Ottawa time, but I figured reporters are never off duty. I pressed the appropriate buttons on the phone.

A brisk voice answered. "Hello. Phil Davis here."

"Hi. It's Ollie Swanson in Steveston."

"Hey, thanks for calling. I worked with Dougie, and I was really sorry to hear about his accident."

I puzzled over how to respond to that, and finally I said, "Thanks. I'll pass that on to his aunt, and if there's a service of any kind, I'll let you know."

There was an awkward pause. "Actually, there's something you could help me with. Dougie and I were working together on a story and now, with him gone, everything's sort of up in the air. When you were going through his belongings, did you see any notes or materials of any sort?"

I said cautiously, "What sort of story were you working on?"

"Political corruption. The usual sort of thing. But on a really big scale. High-level people."

I tried to buy some time. "I'm going through some of his stuff now. If I find anything, I'll call you."

He was persistent, as I suppose good reporters are. "Dougie told me he recorded a lot of conversations. Secretly. Have you found any tapes?"

I found it difficult to tell a direct lie, and besides, why should I? This was a colleague of Dougie's, and Dougie would want the story to get out. "Yeah, I found some in his Jeep, but I haven't had a chance to listen to them yet."

"Terrific. Can you mail them to me?"

"Not until I've listened to them."

He pushed a bit. "Actually, they're the property of the newspaper."

I dug in. "Actually, that's not known at present. As executor of the estate, I have a legal responsibility to dispose of his property according to Dougie's wishes."

The reporter became more conciliatory. "You're probably right. But if they're what I think they are, I know Dougie would want me to have them so the story can get out. I'll tell you what: I'll fly out there and we'll listen to them together. See you soon." He hung up.

Shit! I wanted to listen to the tapes privately, mainly because they were my last link with Dougie. And this asshole, as I'd unconsciously categorized Mr. Davis, could be here as early as this evening.

Oshie was looking at me anxiously, and I realized she could read my inner turmoil like a large-print book. "What did you find in the Jeep, Ollie?"

Mentally, I scurried around like a mink in a trap, until I realized with a surprising sense of relief that I would have to explain . . . everything. "Daiki, why don't you take Ren to the park? And if you can find six different kinds of berries, we'll have some chocolate ice cream." Their eyes lit up, at the idea of the challenge, I hoped, but probably at least partly at the thought of the ice cream, and they were gone within minutes.

Oshie regarded me patiently as I took a bottle of Pinot Noir out of the fridge, opened it, took our two favorite handmade wine goblets out of the cupboard and sat down across from her at the table.

"Honey, I wasn't always the wise, sensible man that you married. Years before I met you, Dougie and I did something that seemed like a good idea at the time, but was actually, I guess, sort of stupid, but also, at that time of my life, kind of exciting."

Half an hour later the wine was finished and so were all of Oshie's questions. She grasped my hand across the table. "I didn't marry a wise, sensible man. I fell in love with an impetuous romantic who would do just the sort of thing you've described. And all these years, I've felt just the faintest hint that there was something about you I didn't know. I understand why you didn't tell me, but I'm glad I finally know." She gave my hand a gentle squeeze.

I leaned across the table and kissed her. When I'd expressed my feelings satisfactorily, I sat down. "I don't know what the hell to do with this Phil Davis," I said. "He's a reporter and I'm not, but I'm hesitant to give him those tapes."

"Go down to the boat and listen to them. Then you'll know what to do. But take a taxi. As a wise and sensible man, you'll realize you've had a bit too much wine to drive."

Five

1989

On the Monday morning after our trip to Zeballos, I showed up for work and Sylvia beamed a congratulatory smile. She gave me a brief introductory lecture and told me the names of my four "clients." When I absorbed that basic information without asking her to repeat anything, she almost wriggled in ecstasy. Expectations were obviously low. A decade later I might have suspected gender prejudice, but it didn't occur to me then. She was just a nice lady who was giving me "positive reinforcement." We jumped in her car, though *jumped* is a bad word choice: I'd lost my jumping ability and I'm not sure if Sylvia ever had any. We got into her car and set off for Old Man Ahola's place.

He lived in a weathered two-story house in the middle of a field off Kaleva Road. It was the most perfectly proportioned wooden structure I'd ever seen. If I could paint, I'd paint it. It needed paint, but that's not what I mean.

Inside, the old man sat at his kitchen table and gazed out at his back field. "Jesus, Penti. If the kitchen was facing the other way you'd have a beautiful view of the Strait. See the boats going by, gorgeous sunsets, whales, everything."

"There's lots of water around here but not much grass. And you don't have to worry about grass getting nasty and sinking the house. That's why I like looking at grass. What are you doing here?"

"I'm your new homemaker."

"Not as cute as the last one."

"That's your opinion."

"Most people's, I imagine."

Sylvia intervened. "Ollie can give you a hand with more of the heavy stuff, getting wood, moving furniture, and that sort of thing."

"I don't move furniture. Everything's in its proper place."

"Well, at least I can give you crib lessons."

He snorted. "Come by tomorrow and you can give me a lesson. Nickel a point and the loser calls the winner Your Majesty for a week."

Sylvia and I made a strategic withdrawal. As she backed out of the driveway, I reassured the two of us. "I thought that went well."

Our next stop was the Widow Hardy's place. She lived next to the breakwater in an old float house that had seen most of the central coast before being retired in Sointula. It sat on a concrete foundation now and seemed glad of the stability. As did the widow herself, who weighed over two hundred pounds and couldn't move far from the oxygen tank that assisted her breathing. But she was inexplicably cheerful and greeted us warmly. "Ollie, your mummu said you'd be coming around. How are you? You're still limping a bit."

"I'm fine, Grace. The foot's getting better all the time."

"And Dougie? I worry about him. He's too much like his dad."

"You mean his ears stick out?"

"Don't sass me, Ollie. I mean, he takes things too seriously, like his dad. I remember when his dad resigned from the credit union board because they gave a loan to Risto Saranen after he fished during the 1928 strike."

"That's not serious. Somebody else sliced Risto's purse line."

"You know what I mean. Dougie needs you to make him laugh."

"It's nice to have a purpose in life. And what can I do to keep you out of trouble? What's her curfew, Sylvia?"

"It's 9:00 PM. And you'll have to watch her. She's been sneaking out lately."

The Widow Hardy chuckled and the conversation turned to the seniors' bake sale the next day. We left soon after and walked three houses over to Sam Sjoberg's house. He was a typical old Finn: joyfully pessimistic and militantly independent. We convinced him to tolerate my visits twice a week and then set off for my mummu's neat little cottage.

Sitting at her kitchen table, her face illuminated by late-morning light through the window, Mummu could have been my mother's older sister instead of her mother. Only the stiffness of her movements betrayed her body's betrayal. She beamed us a smile that outshone the Pulteney Point lighthouse and waved her hand over an array of calories that could have powered an icebreaker. "Ollie, I know you young singles never eat properly. Help yourself."

I resisted saying that I was supposed to be the helper, not the pampered guest, and constructed a snack of pickled dog salmon on cream-cheese-smothered pulla bread. Sylvia opted for the blackberry pie, and while we masticated, Mummu meandered through a long story about curing my grandfather of pneumonia with regular infusions of salt fish and potatoes. When I'd balanced my diet with a large slab of lemon meringue pie, I asked Mummu about her schedule for the afternoon. "I've got bingo at three, but before that I need to go to the Co-op and post office. Would you mind driving me?"

I again resisted explaining reality, which was that I was getting paid to do those sorts of things. Somehow I knew that my reality would need to conform to that of my clientele if I was going to keep them happy. And their reality was probably that they were helping me. I was, after all, physically unfit for a real job. I said I'd come back at two, and Sylvia and I took our leave.

"You can begin to see what the job's all about now, helping them around the house, driving them around, and mostly being good company."

"While appearing grateful that they're putting up with me."

"Ollie, I knew you'd get it. You were always such a wise child."

"How come I'm such a stunned adult?"

Sylvia declined to answer, for which I was ambivalently grateful. Two hours later, I picked up Mummu and drove her downtown, where we flew the coop. Not flew, exactly, because shopping took second place to socializing. We cruised the aisles in the company of others equally concerned about the spotted bananas and poor condition of the apples. There were, however, UNVs—unidentified new vegetables—in the produce department. Tarmo informed us it was all the doing of the new manager. "She's from down island. Uses an umbrella. Lots of fancy ideas."

We ran into my cousin, Danny Swanson. He was two years younger than me, in his last year at high school, and one of the few sure bets to graduate. He was a bright kid, successfully camouflaged as a typical local haywire. "No school today?"

"Pro-D day."

"So lemme guess. You're shopping for legal stimulants so you can go home and study for eighteen hours straight."

"You're a mind reader, Ollie." He grinned at me like we were both at a great party and we needed to acknowledge the absolute fucking purrrfection of the zeitgeist. I didn't want him to know I was leaving the party and soon the beer would run out and the girls would go home.

"Drop by some night. I want to hear what your plans are."

"Sure thing, Ollie. See you, Mummu." He gave her a kiss on the cheek and drifted off in the direction of a shapely female vision who looked like someone I'd dated, only better.

At the checkout counter I was in mid-flirt with the cashier when a headline in the *North Island Gazette* caught my eye. *Regional district bumps head.* Evidently, the manager had been fired. There was no mention of anyone losing consciousness. I bought the paper to give Dougie a laugh. The seventy-three cents I spent had an unexpectedly salutary effect, as the Help Wanted ads revealed that the *Gazette* was looking for a reporter. Not, unfortunately, a headline writer, but reporting was right up Dougie's alley. And a Dougie engaged in gainful employment was a Dougie easier to get along with. I made a mental note to apply for my cherub wings.

When I showed Dougie the ad, he feigned indifference but said he'd go up to Port Hardy and talk to them. He gave away his excitement, though, by cracking a bottle of Koskenkorva. As the level of spirits fell in the vodka bottle, they rose in our hearts. We were soon engaged in full-on planning of The Project.

"Assuming the *Gazette* hires me, we'll have two incomes, although I know they don't pay much. But we can think about buying equipment. We need a Zodiac, and maybe a ninety-horse. I've got my uncle's old shotgun, completely unregistered. We've got vehicles. What else?"

"We can't use our own trucks in case they're spotted. I thought we could get an old beater, make sure it's reliable, stash it in the Nimpkish dump and go from there."

"That'll work. There's something else we've got to talk about: level of violence. We're obviously not going to kill anybody, but how far are we prepared to go? Say some company guy refuses to open the safe or tell us where the cash is hidden. What are we gonna do? Can we, say, shoot him in the foot?"

I reacted with a grimace. "Jesus! Feet are sort of close to my heart. Not because I've got short legs, but because I've got a long memory. Even if it was a less personal appendage, I couldn't pull the trigger. Could you?"

"No. So I guess it's all threats and tough talk. Sort of like American diplomacy."

"Well, they occasionally back up the tough talk with B-52 bomber ordnance."

Dougie responded, "Twelve-gauge shotgun ordnance works better as a threat. You can't shove a B-52 bomber up someone's left nostril. The more visceral the threat, the less chance you'll have to follow through on it."

"Visceral? Is that, like, really, really vicious?" Dougie deadpanned me with a quick glance, which I ignored. "You realize that some of our potential victims will be well known to us and vice versa. We'll have to be well disguised, including voices."

"Come on," he said. "Our real victims will be drinking sake in Tokyo nightclubs. The people we'll be dealing with are mere surrogates. If we see anyone familiar, just talk slowly and loudly, like you're trying to explain something to a foreigner."

Dougie got the job at the *Gazette* and the quality of the reporting went up immediately. Political machinations at the regional district meetings became understandable, almost interesting. Sports stories carried more quotes from the players; the business stories, less. Cultural events were never referred to as such and consequently were enjoyed more, although the court reports were still the highlight of the paper. Headline writing remained problematic. Eyebrows were raised when RCMP *Corporal Michelle Roberts reveals bust* was followed by *Disappointment for Alert Bay seniors*.

The job was great for Dougie, though. He was busy, running all over the North Island to the various communities and their various events. And he was telling stories. As he constructed stories about loggers losing their jobs due to US trade sanctions, and fishermen losing their jobs due to US violations of the Pacific Salmon Treaty, balanced with stories of fall fairs and victorious hockey tournaments, we were both working on our own not-for-publication story.

Our physical conditions were improving along with our financial conditions. I could walk with no limp, although I wouldn't beat anyone in a forty-yard dash. Dougie was down to eight or ten Advil per day and could do light lifting if he was careful.

Our hard-earned dollars were soon sufficient to allow for a trip to Vancouver and the purchase of a twelve-foot Zodiac with a ninety-horse Merc outboard. We also lashed out three hundred dollars on a 1979 Ford F-150. The mechanic we persuaded to do a complete engine overhaul wondered why we wanted to spend an additional two hundred and fifty dollars on such an old truck. We didn't enlighten him.

We got a one-day insurance permit and headed home. I drove what we optimistically referred to as the getaway vehicle (GV), with Dougie following in his slightly less battered pickup.

We stopped in Nimpkish to stash the GV at the renowned dump. Nimpkish is a logging camp just north of the Zeballos turnoff on the Island Highway. In the golden era of logging, its dump was famous as a cornucopia of still-usable appliances and vehicles. Loggers didn't throw away slightly damaged trucks anymore, but our old GV was still the most battered vehicle there. The scattered metal carcasses brought to mind the sarcastic Ford backronym, "found on road dead" and the corresponding expansion of GMC, "generally made crappy." There were no other makes in the graveyard, an exhibition of vehicular apartheid that no tribunal would ever address. We blocked the truck and removed the two rear wheels as well as the battery, to ensure the truck's stationary status, and headed north again.

Our stash for the Zodiac was truly ingenious. I'm not saying that just because it was my idea. We took it to Coastwise Marine in Port McNeill and told the owner we wanted to sell it. As expected, he declined to buy it outright but offered to sell it on commission. He told us our asking price was way too high, but we informed him the market would rise to it. He shrugged, and as we drove away, he was moving the Zodiac to a remote location on his back lot.

It was with a sense of great accomplishment, coupled with the usual homecoming mood boost, that we drove onto the ferry to Sointula. We were home in our proudly dilapidated house by four thirty. It was almost dark. A southeast gale was rising and the air was heavy with the coming rain. The evening sky imagined our fate.

I built a fire while Dougie did something with potatoes, cheese, and mushrooms. By the time they had congealed into an amazingly palatable concoction, the fire had grown enough to cozy the room. I opened a bottle of a local vintage, the 1989 Crazy Ray's Tractor Gas, and we sat down to *pommes de terre avec* stuff from the bottom cupboard.

The wine had an interesting sort of what-the-fuck note to it. Dougie sloshed a bit on his potatoes in lieu of vinegar. We were, of course, due to our socialist upbringing, firm believers in second chances, so I opened another bottle. The fire was roaring now, doing battle with the roaring of the wind outside. So far the forces of good, or at least of comfort, were prevailing over the chaotic void.

"Have we missed anything?" I looked at Dougie inquiringly.

"Dunno. I think we've covered most of the bases. But it's just like fishing. We know things are going to go wrong, so we have to be smart enough to deal with them."

"You're right. But with fishing we've got generations of experience to fall back on. We're stepping outside our boundaries here."

"More like we were forced out. But the truth is, I've wanted to go outside for a long time. I'm glad you thought of this, Ollie. This is better than when you used to row us out in the fog. Ten years old and completely lost, but we always found our way back. We've got a compass inside us, Ollie. If we trust it, we'll be all right."

I wanted to pray that he was right but couldn't summon up an appropriate god. There was no doubt, though, that there's nothing worse than overplanning. So we didn't.

Six

The late-afternoon sun burnished the river with a golden sheen as I walked down the dock. I stood for a moment beside the *Ryu II* and lifted my face to the sun's warmth. With my eyes closed, I listened to the gentle lapping of small waves and the drone of a passing tug. I could hear voices from the other side of the breakwater. They were unintelligible but comforting. A shadow passed over my closed eyelids and there was a momentary coolness. I opened my eyes to find the world still there, which shouldn't have surprised me and didn't.

I climbed over the rail of the *Ryu II* and entered the familiar galley. I put an Etta James CD in the player, got a beer from the fridge and sat down to examine the box of tapes. There were eleven of them and I figured they were each about an hour long. I felt a surge of anxiety as I realized I wouldn't be able to listen to them all before Phil Davis arrived.

Each tape was numbered, but some had written titles as well: "The Setup," "Personnel," "Betrayal One," "Finances," "Betrayal Two," "Betrayal Three," and "Future Policy." I slotted "The Setup" into the player and sat back to listen.

As I sipped my beer, the voice I recognized as belonging to Cliff pontificated over the unmistakable clink of ice cubes in a glass. "I left Hill and Knowlton in '68. They were goddamned good at the game and I learned a lot. But I had some ideas of my own and I wanted to express myself, know what I mean? Wanted to keep more of what I earned too. Those bastards made millions,

I mean literally millions, and they paid me like some chickenshit copywriter.

"Anyway, I took a few guys with me, recruited a few others and set up shop. We got a bit of the election work that year. The big guys got most of it and fucked it up. Imagine letting Robert Stanfield lose to a long-haired French Canadian hippie. And Medicare! If we'd had a shot, we could have smothered that baby. Oh well, no one gets to play on the first line right away."

All this was sort of interesting but somewhat repetitive. I fast-forwarded, only to hear more of the same corporate history, although Cliff's words grew a little more slurred as the tape went on. Dougie would interject with the odd question, always in the same adulatory tone, which would have disturbed me had I not been swaddled in the comforting womb of my boat with sufficient beer near at hand. The tape ended with roughly five minutes of silence, which obviously meant the meeting was over and Dougie was devoting one tape to each meeting.

I skipped to "Finances." Cliff again: "There was way more propaganda money available in the States, but by the mid-'70s, Canadian business was getting worried. That goddamn Trudeau was talking about democracy in Ottawa and Dave Barrett was actually trying to implement it in BC." And so on and so forth.

"Betrayal One" was a self-congratulatory explanation of how Cliff and company had orchestrated one of the greatest swindles in Canadian history, the splitting off of Landcor Developments from Continental Railways. Not long after Confederation, the Canadian government had granted the railway millions of acres of timberland, including the mineral rights, in return for which Continental agreed to keep the railway running efficiently in per-petuity. Continental's people backed this up by solemnly crossing their hearts and hoping to die. Bravely tempting fate, they later sold both the land and the mineral rights in a sweetheart deal that benefited all parties except the Canadian public.

Then, stripped of all the assets that made it viable, Continental Railways struggled to run an efficient and safe operation. According to Dougie's later research, they operated so efficiently that they had over a hundred derailments and collisions during the next few years. Jesus! If that was betrayal one, I couldn't imagine betrayal two.

As it turned out, I *could* imagine the second betrayal, since I was the victim, along with most of the other fishermen on the BC coast. Fish were once a common property resource, owned, like all natural resources, by the people of Canada. You could buy a license that gave you the right to fish, but you didn't own the fish until you actually caught them. That all changed when the Department of Fisheries and Oceans introduced Individual Transferable Quotas, ITQs, which allocated a certain amount of fish to each fisherman before he or she had even caught the fish. These ITQs were certifiable property rights that could be bought and sold. Most of them ended up in the hands of corporations, who then leased them back to the fishermen. The poor saps ended up paying over half of their income in lease fees. I'd always thought that DFO was too stupid to have organized this massive transfer of wealth. The tape made it clear that Cliff and his cronies and a couple of captive bureaucrats had engineered the whole swindle under the cover of "conservation measures."

By this time I was hungry. The oil stove was turned off, so I phoned for a pizza. When it arrived I opened another beer and ate half the pizza while listening to "Future Policy." This time the non-Dougie voice was not Cliff. The new voice was less avuncular, articulated a little more precisely, sounding sort of academic. But Dougie was still in character, ego stroking and asking questions.

Dougie: I really admire the way you guys have pulled together some useful, sort of redistributive policies.

Other voice: Redistributive is a good word.

Dougie: And not only developed the policy, but the implementation has been beautiful. You've done some amazing things.

Other voice: Well, thank you. We have had some successes.

Dougie: But honestly, there must have been a few projects that went sideways. Slippage, fog of war, and all that.

Other voice: Oh yes, of course. The best-laid plans, etcetera. Our West-Coast salmon initiative hit some snags. We tried to introduce genetically engineered salmon into the ocean. Phase one went well, but the second mandate was a bit of a debacle. Personnel problems, really. Still, we managed to insulate ourselves from the fallout.

Dougie: If I'm going to work with you on areas of common interest, my clients really need to be assured of anonymity. There must be complete separation of our . . . what shall I say . . . support activities and any sort of fieldwork.

Other voice: Of course, that goes without saying.

Jesus! What sort of cover had Dougie put together for himself? He was being accepted by these power brokers as someone of the same rank, a player of equal stature.

It was eight o'clock. My cell phone rang and I flinched guiltily. That changed to irritation as I wondered why the hell I, who had committed only one teensy-weensy major theft in my life, should feel guilty in the face of larceny of this magnitude. I answered my phone.

"Ollie. It's Phil. I'm at YVR. Where can I meet you?"

I was surprised that he was at the airport already. "Take a cab to the Steveston Hotel. I'll meet you in the pub." I broke the connection and phoned a cab, then sat for a moment and considered the current state of affairs. These tapes were dynamite. The story that Dougie was planning to write, based on these tapes and whatever other evidence he'd managed to accumulate, would blow the neoconservative ship right out of the water. All I could hope for was that Phil would do as good a job, or almost as good a job, as Dougie would have done. I would give Phil copies of the tapes and keep the originals, mainly so I could listen to the rest of them. A honk alerted me that the cab had arrived. I hid the box of tapes in the locker under the bench and went to meet Phil.

When I walked into the pub, it was easy to identify Phil. He was the only guy I didn't know. Also the only guy wearing a suit. It was dark and wrinkled and probably not an Armani. He was sitting at a table in the corner, and a waitress followed me as I walked over to him. We shook hands and did the "Hi, Ollie, Phil—Hi, Phil, Ollie" routine, and I sat down. Phil had dark, heavily gelled short hair on top of a slightly puzzled-looking face on top of a stocky, serviceable-looking body. The waitress waited expectantly and I ordered a cold Lucky. Phil said, "Maybe I'll get Lucky too" and winked at the waitress. She rolled her eyes and retreated toward the bar.

"Ollie, I'm glad to finally get to meet you. Dougie told me a lot about you."

"Really?" I felt like saying, "Did he tell you how much I dislike urban posers?" But that would prove nothing except that I was developing a bit of a dislike for this guy. So I murmured noncommittally and took a swig of beer.

"So you're a fisherman, eh?" Phil continued the charm offensive.

"Yeah, right." And I felt obligated to explain a bit about shrimp fishing and how it differed from other fisheries and so on and so forth. By this time the waitress was back, wondering if we wanted another beer.

"I'm always good for seconds," Phil said archly.

"Are you flirting with me?" she asked, puzzled.

"Sweetie, if I was flirting with you, you'd have your clothes off by now." He looked at me with the impervious satisfaction of the truly insensitive. The waitress looked at him with the wonderment of a kid at the zoo. She left. I tried not to look at the ceiling. "Small-town girls, eh?"

"Yeah, small-town girls." I was beginning to feel a sense of desperation. "What I thought about the tapes is, we'll make copies, I'll keep the originals, and you can have the copies. You'll get a great story. From the bits I've heard, it's dynamite stuff."

"I'm right with you, man, right with you. I even brought a high-speed duplicator." He gestured toward a tote bag on the chair beside him. "Only thing is, I'll need the originals. Legal reasons, you know. We could easily get sued over this stuff."

I couldn't see anything wrong with that. The waitress returned with two more beers and left quickly. I raised my bottle to Phil. "Deal."

The fascist dance beats of the background music were really starting to irritate me. I drained my beer. "We can get a cab outside. Let's go."

Phil left his beer, grabbed his bag and followed me out into the warm evening air. I knew the cabbie, so I just smiled at him and waved toward the breakwater, and we headed in that direction. "So this is your boat, eh?" Phil said when we got to the *Ryu II*.

I felt like saying, "No. It's a B-flat reciprocating effluvium." But I just said, "Yeah, it's my boat." And we climbed on board.

We entered the galley and I flicked on the lights. Phil marveled at that. "You've even got electricity on here."

"All the bells and whistles," I said.

Phil put his tote bag on the galley table and took out a dual tape recorder. "This little baby can duplicate an hour-long tape in ten minutes." He looked at me expectantly.

I lifted the seat cover and took out the box of tapes. "Let's do these in order. I want to make sure I get the labeling right on my copies."

"Good plan." I handed him tape one, and he inserted it in the left-hand deck, a blank tape in the right-hand deck, set the toggle switch at 6X and pressed Play and Record. The machine whirred away for about ten minutes while we stared blankly at each other, then clicked to a stop. Phil took out the original tape and pressed Play on the right-hand deck. Dougie's voice came out loud and clear.

"It works," Phil said. He took out what had been the blank tape and handed it to me for labeling. I passed him tape two, and he began the process all over again. Bored, I wandered up to the wheelhouse to listen to the radio. "I'll label them for you," Phil called.

"Thanks," I called back. I turned on the VHF and put it on Scan, idly hoping to eavesdrop on some conversations. Tugboat skippers were chattering away on channel 8, coastguard announcements were coming through on channel 16, and sporties were nattering to each other on channel 6. I turned to channel 78A, which was used by a lot of fishermen. I listened to the usual litany of complaints for about half an hour before I heard a familiar voice. Drago Vukovitch ran an Option B trawler, and he was bringing a load of live sole up the river to sell at the Steveston fish dock. He was talking to his buddy on the *Pearly Mae*, and when the conversation lagged I butted in.

"Drago, don't tell me you've actually got some fish on that old bucket. I thought you didn't like getting scales on your rails."

He chuckled. "Ollie Swanson, they never should have let you escape from Sointula. You deserve life on that rock, along with all those communist Finns."

We continued in this vein for a while, and other familiar voices chimed in with stories and reports and reminiscences and whatever-happened-to-old-whoevers. Brian DePaul butted in and tried to convince me that I owed him twenty bucks. I replied that I couldn't be speaking to Brian DePaul on the *Sea Hound* because my ugly-boat alarm hadn't gone off. Before I knew it, almost two hours had passed. I turned off the VHF and went back to the galley. Phil was just labeling the last tape. "If you want to call a couple of cabs, Ollie, I think we can say that we're finished here. It'll take me a few days to listen to all this, and when I'm finished I'll call you."

I yawned and pulled out my cell phone. Phil pointed at a box of tapes and mouthed, "Yours." I nodded as I ordered two cabs.

When Phil was in his cab, just about to pull away, he grinned at me through the window and shot me with his thumb and index finger. *Jerk*, I thought.

But I didn't know the half of it.

The next day when I went back to the boat to listen to the rest of the tapes, I discovered that they were all blank. I double-checked them with an audio technician, and he confirmed that the tapes had never been recorded on. Phil had scammed me. The only tape I was left with was tape one, which he'd really recorded just to prove to me that everything was working. Good thing I'd slipped it into my pocket instead of leaving it on the table.

When I got back to the house I was in a foul mood, which was lessened only slightly when I saw my cousin Danny drinking a beer at my kitchen table. He grinned a hello at me, but he could read me almost as well as Oshie. "What's the problem?" they said almost simultaneously. I told them the story. And because Danny had worked for DFO, I emphasized the bit about the West-Coast salmon initiative going awry.

That struck a nerve. "Those bastards!" he said. "I always knew the orders to transplant those mutant salmon into the ocean came from higher up, someone outside DFO." When I looked puzzled, he sketched the events that had led to him being pulled from the waters of Georgia Strait the previous fall.

Oshie said, "It sounds like Ottawa is a seething mass of corruption." Neither of us denied it.

"Do you have any idea who it was on that last tape you listened to?" Danny asked.

"No. But I'd recognize his voice again. And it shouldn't be too hard to identify Cliff."

Danny nodded. "I've got a pretty good idea already that it's Cliff Ernhardt of Ernhardt and Associates. They're the number-one sleaze spinners in Ottawa. Sort of our version of Hill and Knowlton."

"Well," I said, "I'm going to phone the editor of the *Ottawa Times* and give him shit about how Phil has acted." But of course Phil didn't work at the paper. They'd never heard of him.

The three of us looked at each other. Oshie spoke for all of us. "What now?"

I was pacing the kitchen, working off a combination of anger and embarrassment at being conned by a dimwit like Phil, and a sort of budding excitement at being involved in something important, the retrieval and resurrection of Dougie's story. "The first thing I'm going to do is track down Phil, get the tapes back and give them to the guys at the *Times* so they can write the story. I want to see these scumbags exposed, naked, on the front page of every newspaper in the country."

Oshie said, "They're obviously really worried about the story getting out. They went to a lot of trouble to get those tapes."

Danny looked serious—I would have said worried if I didn't

know that the only thing he worried about was marine biodiversity. "Cliff Ernhardt thinks of himself as a really powerful guy, but he's just the mouthpiece for the backroom boys who like to think of the nation's business as their business. This little stunt of grabbing the tapes was child's play for them." He thought for a moment. "Ollie, are you sure that Dougie's death was an accident?"

I was shocked. But the more I thought about it, the clearer it became that some very powerful people had had an extremely powerful reason for wanting Dougie dead. But still, we were talking about Ottawa, not New Jersey. "Let's not get all carried away with conspiracy theories," I said. "Lots of people fall out of canoes and drown. Experienced people. Look at Tom Thomson. Same damn lake, for Christ's sake."

Danny grinned. "Maybe this powerful cabal didn't like the direction Canadian art was going in."

"Yeah," I replied. "So they killed Tom Thomson to clear the way for faded watercolors on really big canvases. The bastards!"

"I just want you to keep your wits about you as you go charging around Ottawa. You're still a small-town kid, Ollie."

"I've lived in Steveston for ten years."

"A teeming cosmopolitan metropolis, to be sure. Do you lock your house?"

"This is a quiet street."

"Lock your boat?"

"I used to, until I lost the key."

"Your car?"

"Sometimes."

Danny looked at Oshie. "You can take the boy out of the small town, but you can't take the—"

"Heart out of the tree," Oshie finished.

Danny refused to be puzzled. "So there you go, Ollie."

"We've got a few weapons on our side," I said.

Danny looked at me. "Such as?"

"Time and money. I was going to take this season off anyway. And I've got enough money to buy or bribe the odd informant." When Danny looked at me quizzically, I added, "Shrimping has been really good the last few years."

"And my aunt left me some money," Oshie chimed in. And then looked away quickly before her face could give her away.

"And we've got you, Danny," I said. "You know your way around Ottawa. And now that you're a private consultant, you know a wider range of people. And because you had the good sense to marry a cop, we've got access to the RCMP if we need them. By the way, how is Louise?"

"Actually, that's what I came to tell you. She's been promoted to second in command of the Richmond detachment. We'll be almost neighbors to you."

"Congratulations! That's great news." Oshie was really enthused about the idea of having more family close by.

"I'm meeting her for lunch, so I should get going. Ollie, don't make a move without talking to me."

"Okay, cuz."

When he'd gone Oshie came over and hugged me. "Do you feel bad about not watching Phil more closely when he was duplicating the tapes?"

"I don't know. He could have done it with me right across the table from him. All he had to do was pretend to press the Record button. All the other moves were the same as for tape number one."

"And you had no reason to distrust him."

"But I do now," I said. "So what's my plan?"

Oshie started enumerating on her fingers. "Unfortunately, you'll need to go back to Ottawa for all of this. Step one: talk to Dougie's editor. He may have helpful information. And check Dougie's work computer. Step two: check all of Dougie's stuff in storage. His personal computer, papers, books—did he have a camera? Step three: when you have as much background info as possible, contact Cliff Ernhardt to see if he's the guy on the tapes. Step four: if Ernhardt is the guy, find out who his close associates are so you can meet them and identify the unknown voice. You'll need some sort of cover for that. I wonder how Dougie did it. And step five: find Phil Davis and get the tapes back." She paused for a second. "One other thing. You might want to contact that OPP cop who handled Dougie's search and give him a heads-up that there's a chance the disappearance wasn't an accident. Just a chance, mind you. Something he can keep in the back of his mind in case anything strange comes up."

We stared at each other while I digested all this. "Not exactly my household to-do list," I said. "I've never done anything even remotely like this."

"Ollie, in your job you operate independently. You assimilate information, form strategies and then catch things."

"Oshie, I catch shrimp, for Christ's sake! I outsmart crustaceans. Now I'm going up against some of the smartest, smoothest operators in Canada."

"Dougie did it."

I stopped myself from saying, "And where's Dougie now?"

That evening I phoned Danny. "I'm flying to Ottawa tomorrow. I'll need to talk to Ernhardt and a lot of his high-powered friends. Do you think if I took a few boxes of shrimp—humpbacks, of course—it would give me access to their hallowed halls?"

"Worth a try. If that doesn't work, being a newspaper reporter is a good cover. You can ask lots of questions. People may not answer, of course, but they won't question your right to be there. Talk to

Dougie's editor. He might even be able to give you some help. And Danny, trust no one. If you need backup, I'm there in a flash."

"Okay, cuz. I'll keep you posted."

Ren and Daiki were running around in their pajamas, and I watched them as they alternated between chaser and chasee. I'd always been the chaser. I hoped to keep it that way.

Eventually they slowed down, and I caught them and put them to bed. They insisted on a story, so I sat on the floor between their beds and regaled them with the Finnish version of the Paul Bunyan stories: A skipper dropped his anchor, but it wouldn't hold because there were so many halibut on the bottom. Then a giant halibut took the anchor like a fishhook and towed the boat all the way from Cape St. James to Knight Inlet. It was way too big to pull onto the boat, so they took it to the boatways at Minstrel Island. The crew managed to pull it up on the ways, but it was so big it sunk the island.

Eventually the children's eyes shut and their breathing deepened, and I stole out of the room. I poured myself a glass of wine and went out to sit on the front porch, waiting for Oshie to come home from her art class.

It was almost full dark, and I counted all the porch lights up and down the quiet street. I knew nearly everybody on the street and they were all decent people. I was about to venture into an area where I didn't know anyone and many people were not decent. As I pondered that, the air cooled and the shadows deepened and the evening sky imagined our fate.

Seven
1990

On a miserable afternoon in mid-March, I caught the four-thirty ferry and drove to the Nimpkish dump. It was dark when I got there. I took the getaway vehicle's two rear wheels out of the box of my pickup, bolted them on, jacked the truck down, hooked up the battery and was relieved when the engine started at the first turn of the key. Leaving it to warm up, I hid my truck behind an old skidder, climbed back into the encouragingly smooth-running GV and left.

I drove straight to Coastwise Marine in Port McNeill and around to the back of its unfenced storage yard. Our Zodiac was, not unexpectedly, unsold, and grunting softly, I pulled it into the box of the GV. Thence to Beaver Cove and a secluded beach, where I launched the Zodiac and ran it around to Octopus Beach, on the unoccupied north shore of Malcolm Island. Mounting the prestashed bike, I rode into Sointula and entered the pub at 8:00 PM.

Dougie was there and we played pool and drank—less than normal, but enough not to be suspicious. We stayed until the last ferry had left, and having thus established an alibi we hoped we'd never need, we left in Dougie's truck.

Back at Octopus Beach we clambered down the steep bank and were away in the Zodiac by nine twenty-five. At nine fifty we arrived at Beaver Cove, and the two of us had no trouble dragging the Zodiac up the beach and loading it into the GV. We now faced a two-hour drive to the launch point at Little Espinosa, and my nerves vibrated more tautly with every minute. The reality of what we were doing, two middle-class, small-town kids committing a major felony, soon to be pointing a gun at people and uttering grievous threats, began to sink in, and my stomach took a moral position of queasy nausea. My hands tightened on the steering wheel and I glanced at Dougie. The dim lights of the dashboard showed only that he was staring straight ahead, features obscured. Neither of us spoke.

By the time we got to the launch point, the weather had eased somewhat. The rain had stopped and there were breaks in the clouds. We never saw the moon, but enough light filtered through that the hills showed black against the sky. Fortunately, that was all we needed for navigation, because charts in an open boat with any kind of a breeze were a pain in the ass. Within minutes we were skimming over the flat, black, inscrutable surface of the inlet, and I felt calmer.

There was only a light breeze, but we were doing about twenty knots and the wind chill became our sole focus. We huddled behind the windscreen on the console and donned our ski masks earlier than intended. There was only the roar of the outboard and the rush of cold air as we hurtled forward, and the blackness, which constantly receded from us like a reluctant lover.

An hour later we were at the mouth of Esperanza Inlet, and the Zodiac hurdled the troughs between low swells as we rounded the headland into Mary Basin. As soon as we saw the lights of the anchored boats, Dougie slowed to an idle. It looked like a small town had grown up on the waters of the anchorage. There were fifty or sixty anchor lights, although the majority of them would be gillnetters. It would not be difficult to differentiate the fifteen or so larger hulls that were our targets: the packers.

It was just past midnight when we became criminals. At this point I sort of went on automatic pilot. Dougie told me later it was the same for him. It was almost as if we were outside of ourselves, watching ourselves do things in a dream. The first packer we came to was recognizable by silhouette alone. Long and low in the water except for a high bow, the *Eastern Express* was an ex-minesweeper. It was built of wood because wood doesn't set off mines—but it doesn't prevent robberies.

We idled up to it and bumped gently against its port side. I climbed quietly over the rail, carrying a duffel bag empty except for several rolls of duct tape, and secured our bowline. Dougie joined me on the deck, carrying his uncle's shotgun, and we locked eyes for a second before moving toward the galley.

I eased open the top half of the galley door and leaned in for a look. They had left one light burning above the oil stove. I knew the boat had a crew of four. The skipper had a stateroom behind the wheelhouse, and the deckhands slept down below in the fo'c's'le.

We snuck up to the wheelhouse first, in order to disable the radios. This was accomplished by simply cutting the mic wires and stowing the mics in my bag. We kept our eyes open for handheld radios and discovered two being charged. There were no unoccupied chargers, so we were sure we'd got them all. And now to wake up the captain.

This was ratcheting things up a notch, since we were now dealing with another human being. I knew who the guy was. He'd been pointed out to me in a bar, but I was fairly sure I'd never been pointed out to him. And even if I had been, I hadn't worn a ski mask in the bar, and he sure as hell wouldn't be able to recognize me by body type alone. I realized nervousness was making me over-rationalize things.

He woke as soon as we opened the door to his stateroom, and

when he saw the shotgun he knew exactly what was going on. No words were needed or spoken as I taped his arms behind his back and led him back to the galley. The deckhands were slightly more vocal when we woke them, but a long gun wielded by a faceless man can be a bit of a conversation dampener.

When they were all safely taped up and seated with the galley table blocking any desperate lunges, I said what they all knew they'd hear.

"Where's the money?"

"We don't carry any cash. The company just gave us a checkbook."

There was a TV bolted in the corner just above their heads. Without a word Dougie blasted it. The sound in the small galley was shocking. The cathode ray tube imploded with an echo of the shotgun blast, and bits of glass and plastic showered down over the cowering bodies. Dougie shoved the barrel of the gun into the captain's throat. "There's one loaded barrel left. Where's the money?"

"Cashbox. Under that bench."

I pulled the cushion off the forward galley bench and removed the wooden top. There, in the traditional grocery storage space, was a locked gray steel box.

"Key?"

"The jacket hanging in my room. Left-hand pocket."

I got the key and opened the box. It contained a lot of money. I took the money and left the box, making a mental note to maintain that order of operations. "We're leaving now. If we hear any noise or see anyone waving or trying to attract attention, we'll be back."

We climbed back into the Zodiac and headed for our next victim. "Figure anyone heard that shot?"

"The cabin would have muffled it pretty good. Anyway, it could just as well have been a drunken deckhand throwing seal bombs."

I nodded. We'd both been there, done that. The next packer, the *Red Dragon*, had a party going on. There was a guy on deck taking a leak. We came alongside, and I asked him if they had a spare hydraulic fitting, a number twelve female swivel. He must have thought my ski mask was for the cold.

"Hang on, I'll ask the chief."

We followed him into the galley, where there was a poker game in progress. Dougie produced the gun and I pushed Mr. Helpful down onto the bench so that he was behind the table with the others. We were looking at four moderately drunk, semi-irritated people, but I did a quick search of the boat just to make sure we had everyone.

"Where's the money?"

"We don't carry any cash. We're dealing with all company boats."

Another TV bit the dust. This time the cash was hidden in a bag in the engine room. I got grease on my hands as I was climbing back up the ladder.

That night we killed nine television sets. On three occasions we were given the money solely on the basis of our ferocious manner. Not bad, I thought, for two guys who cringed at the Punch and Judy violence of professional wrestling. When we left the last packer, we took a prisoner with us. We also took its skiff, which we towed a couple of miles north before placing the prisoner in it and instructing him to row back and release everyone we'd tied up.

Having thus engineered time for our getaway, we ran for home. I couldn't believe it. We'd pulled it off! Almost. Almost home and dry. Another half an hour and we'd be back at the launch point.

When the outboard quit, my heart stopped as well. After the constant roar there was only the soft swish of water slipping beneath us as we coasted to a stop. Dougie and I stared at each other, an unspoken "oh fuck" hanging between us like a flashing neon sign. We began a frantic diagnostic scramble.

I checked the gas tank and hose while Dougie flipped the engine up and checked the water intake. An instant before panic completely overwhelmed us, we solved the problem. The plastic ring holding the kill switch in the run position had vibrated out. I improvised a solution by cutting a piece off my Sointula library card. When the engine roared back to life it was the sweetest thunder imaginable.

Blessedly soon we were back at the launch point. Stiff with cold, it nevertheless took us only a minute to load the Zodiac, our gear, and the well-stuffed money bag into the GV. Then we were away on the last leg. Not far now, not far, damn it.

We reversed the order of operations that had got us to the launch point, restoring the GV to its resting spot at the Nimpkish dump, putting the Zodiac into my truck, and then running it back to Malcolm Island to drop Dougie off. I returned to Beaver Cove, and by the time I dropped the Zodiac back at Coastwise Marine, dawn was threatening the darkness of the eastern sky.

I drove to a secluded logging road and succeeded in getting a bit of sleep before it was time to catch the 4:00 PM ferry back to Sointula. Camouflaged among all the commuters, I kept my head down. After disembarking in Sointula, I turned right and drove fast. Kaleva Road led me home like a gentle river. The evening sky imagined our fate.

Dougie had set the table with an unopened bottle of vodka and a spring salmon stuffed with onions and wild rice. There were baked potatoes wrapped in tin foil and peas in a colander. Dougie stood at the table like a host welcoming a long-absent friend. Without a word, he opened the vodka, poured two drinks and handed me one.

"What are we toasting?"

"Success."

"How much success?"

"One million, six hundred and forty-seven thousand, seven hundred and ten successes."

My triumphant yell could have been heard all the way into town. We smashed our glasses together and hugged each other, heedless of the spilt alcohol. "I can't believe we did it. We actually pulled it off. Two hicks from the sticks pulled off the biggest heist in BC history."

"Who you calling a hick? The important thing now is not to act like a dumb hick. We both keep our jobs for now. Maybe next year I'll enrol at SFU. But no brand-new trucks and no buying rounds at the pub."

"You never bought a round in your life. And I love my old truck. But a year or so from now, I'd like to put a down payment on a boat. Everyone will think I borrowed the money from my folks, and my folks will think I got it from Mummu but they'd never ask."

By the time the food and the alcohol were finished we were drifting in a glorious haze of plans and promises and pontifications. "Hey, Dougie, this reminds me of our grad night. God, that seems ages ago. Well, we've really graduated now." Another clink of the glasses and slack-jawed grins.

Morning brought a mood that was slightly less celebratory, but a mere headache couldn't completely dampen the lingering sense of triumph. As I sipped coffee and admired the view of our woodpile, I turned my mind to a problem that many people would love to have. What to do with one million, six hundred and forty-seven thousand, seven hundred and ten dollars? Or more specifically, where to hide it so it would be reasonably accessible but safe. I didn't want to lose our hard-earned money to sleazy thieves, fire, or even nest-building squirrels.

When Dougie got up, I waited until he had a cup of coffee firmly gripped in both hands. "Dougie, it's about time we put in a bodaidoe patch."

He looked at me blankly. "Huh?"

"We can't put our money in the credit union. Next best? The potato patch. Individually wrapped bundles of fifty grand. When we need some cash, just dig a few bodaidoes."

"We won't be here forever. What happens if the next tenant decides to do some gardening?"

"We'll be here for at least a year. After that I'll come up with another brilliant idea."

"I'm sure you will. Hey, let's listen to the news."

Dougie turned on the CBC news and we discovered we were headliners. The announcer's comfortable CBC voice, usually staid to the point of tedium, what I referred to in my very own mind as a stadium voice, displayed just the faintest tremor of excitement. Reminiscent of when they'd covered the Queen's last visit. *Armed thieves have raided the West-Coast herring fleet and made off with well over a million dollars. RCMP are searching for leads.* I think they were shocked that that much money had been in the possession of a few grubby fish boats.

And they continued to be shocked over the next few days as the RCMP failed to discover any leads. It was as if the thieves had disappeared into a black hole. There was speculation that the heist had been pulled off by Japanese gangsters. That would explain the lack of local leads.

The next day I had to go to work. My first stop was Old Man Ahola's place. As I bustled unnecessarily around his kitchen, he looked at me suspiciously. "You're acting like a dog in a rabbit field. What's up? You finally got a girlfriend?"

Christ! Was I sending out signals? "Yahoo! I pulled off a huge score and now I don't have to worry anymore?" I tried to dampen my tail-wagging vibe. "No one special. I don't want to make any of them jealous."

"Heh heh heh, right. Hey, what about that robbery on the West Coast? I knew that was going to happen sooner or later. Where else in the world would you find millions in cash with not an armed guard in sight?"

"Sounds like an easy score, all right. But they'll screw up. Somebody will talk to somebody and the cops will hear about it. Loose lips screw up the best-laid plans."

"You're probably right. Still, I sort of hope they get away with it. Nobody got hurt but a bunch of rich businessmen who've been stealing from people like us for years."

I agreed with him but thought it wise not to say so. I left the old man sitting at his kitchen table, his still-active mind immersed in plans his body had no chance of implementing. My next client was Mummu. As I walked up to her house I could see water dripping from her eaves troughs. Probably clogged with leaves. My afternoon was now accounted for, but I wanted a chat first. I knocked on the door and entered to find her at the sink, doing dishes. "Mummu! Sit down. I'll do those."

"Don't be silly. I'm perfectly capable. Besides, I need something to occupy my time. But I'll let you make coffee and we can have some lunch." Five minutes later we sat at the table with fresh mugs of coffee and plates of smoked dog salmon on rye bread. I munched and sipped happily but gradually became aware that Mummu was doing neither. She was staring at me.

"When your father was your age, he was courting my daughter. Your generation seems hesitant to get on with life, like you're waiting for training or something."

"There're more choices now, Mummu. More decisions to make.

My dad had to decide whether to log or fish. And it wasn't hard to choose. If the fish were running, you fished. If they weren't, you logged. And you didn't need three certificates to do either one."

"Maybe things were simpler then. Getting a job was easy, and it didn't really matter what you did. Your job wasn't your career. Your family was. The job was just a way of feeding the kids and keeping a roof over their heads."

"I'll get there sooner or later, Mummu. Dougie and I are saving up a bit of a grubstake and then we'll head for Vancouver. Try our luck in The Big Smoke. Maybe I'll meet a nice girl. One that I haven't known since being in diapers."

"That may have been your most attractive age, Ollie. But don't worry. I've got the pictures to show to any girl you bring back here."

· "Do you want to see me back here or not?"

She smiled and patted my hand. "You'll be back, Ollie. You'll be back when you decide to be happy."

I cleaned up our lunch debris, hugged Mummu and wandered out to her yard just as her whist pals arrived. As I leaned a ladder against the eaves, her words rattled around my brain for a while, finally etching themselves in the important-things-you-need-to-remember cortex. *Life. Do you live it, or does it live you? Am I just a long-lived sockeye salmon with no choice but to return to his home waters? Or can I deny my biological destiny? Do I want to?* When I philosophized this to Dougie, his answer was simple.

"Salmon have two biological imperatives: spawning and death. You only have one. And it's not spawning." That seemed a bit unfair. Drink in hand, I wandered out to the porch. A flock of Canada geese were commuting from their work in Rough Bay to their home in Kemp's Beach. The southeast wind gusted threats like a belligerent drunk. The evening sky imagined our fate.

Eight

As I sat on the plane, I tried to remember Oshie's instructions for recovering Dougie's stolen tapes. I rehearsed her step-by-step instructions and did my best to enjoy what I told myself was a delightful airline breakfast consisting of some sort of brown stuff and something beigey and kind of yellow. My friends the Rockies were hiding under a fluffy blanket. By the time the blanket disappeared, so had anything worth seeing.

As I waited impatiently for five hours to pass, I couldn't help but pat the inside breast pocket of my jacket, which contained an envelope of two hundred one-hundred-dollar bills. If I had to bribe someone, or pay for some information, I wanted to be prepared. I knew it wasn't enough to buy a politician, of course. Well, maybe a Conservative senator.

I took a cab from the Ottawa airport to the Hotel Chateauvert. When I was as ensconced as one could be at a big city hotel, I decided to play a long shot. Would Cliff Ernhardt's home number be unlisted? It was not. So, assuming the guy was at work, I dialed the number. Bingo! The answering machine answered with the unmistakable warm and friendly voice that I'd heard on the tapes. Progress had been made.

Then I set off to do some errands. I had a 3:00 PM appointment with Lou Bernier, the features editor at the *Ottawa Times* and the man who had been Dougie's boss.

But I had something to do first before I formally burst onto the Ottawa scene. I expected, intended actually, to stir up a bit of a tempest. And when things got really stormy, I wanted a snug little anchorage somewhere hidden away from searchers and seekers.

I'd Googled Ottawa rooming houses, so I took a cab into the Little Italy district. The houses were a bit on the shabby side but struggling to remain respectable. I got dropped off at Rochester Street and walked three blocks to 953 Adele Avenue. I rang the bell and when a chubby little bald guy came to the door, I said I'd like to look at the basement suite he'd advertised. He smiled and nodded and asked me to wait a moment while he fetched the key. He then led me around to the back of the house to the suite's entrance. I noted that there was access to the back alley. Excellent. He led me inside, and I pretended to inspect everything thoroughly. After that charade I said I'd take it and gave him three months' rent and a phony name, and I had my little hideaway. I told Bert, the landlord, that I was going out of town for a few weeks so wouldn't move in right away. That was hunky-dory with him, so I waved goodbye and walked back toward Rochester.

I got to the *Ottawa Times* building just before three and didn't have to wait long before being shown in to Lou Bernier's office. He rose to shake my hand and said, "Mr. Swanson, I recognize you. Dougie had a picture of you and your wife on his desk." He was a small, trim man, maybe fifty years old and neatly dressed in sports jacket, pressed flannel trousers, shirt, and tie. I didn't know if that was old school or new school for a newsman. Maybe they didn't have schools.

He sat down and gestured me into a chair. "As Dougie's friend, you appreciate how really unfortunate his accident was. But we'll miss him too. He was our best reporter. He had a real future ahead of him."

"He left a bit of a hole, all right. And, of course, he left a lot of loose ends that I'm trying to tidy up. What can you tell me about the story he was working on?"

"Just the broadest outline. Political corruption, financial skul-duggery at the highest levels. It's an old story, really, but as long as they keep doing it we have to keep writing it."

"I found some tapes of conversations with heavy hitters like Cliff Ernhardt. I'm guessing that Dougie recorded them secretly, and also that he had devised a really good cover, because I don't think these guys realized they were talking to a reporter. They were far too open about what they were doing. Any idea who or what Dougie was posing as?"

"No, but a good reporter can get people to reveal some pretty dark stuff, especially if he does the Pierre Berton thing. You know, 'I'm writing history and you're in it.' Very often ego trumps self-preservation."

"Maybe, but Dougie sounded to me like he was playing a role. There was at least one other voice on the tapes aside from Ernhardt. A real player, someone with tremendous influence and connections and, I suspect, a colleague of Ernhardt's. Who does Ernhardt run with outside of the PR arena?"

"There's three types of major players in this town. There's the spin doctors, of whom Ernhardt is the best, there's the bagmen, most of whom I know and can introduce you to, and then there's the fixers, the guys who put the deals together. They're the ones that really run the show, but they stay in the shadows."

"I see. Well, here's my plan, Lou. I want to pursue Dougie's story. The stuff I heard on those tapes was explosive. If I can pull it together, will you run the story?"

"Absolutely. Provided you can provide sufficient verification."

"Second question. If I can claim to be a reporter for the *Times*, it would make everything a lot easier. Is that cool with you?"

He leaned back in his chair. "Give me some time to think about that one. I've got cousins back in Truro that are fishermen. It's not so much that they ignore rules. They don't really realize that there are rules. And if something gets in between where they are and where they want to be, there's often collateral damage. But maybe you West-Coast fishermen are a little more, uh, restrained?"

"Lou, restraint is my middle name." I thought about telling him how often I'd been restrained, but somehow that didn't strike the reassuring tone I was looking for. "Think it over and I'll call you tomorrow. This could be the story of the decade."

"And there's an interesting angle you may not be aware of. Have you heard of Gerry Steadman?"

The name rang a bell. "The guy that was murdered, right? Some big-time operator from Alberta."

"That's right. And he was tight with Ernhardt and his crowd until there was some kind of split. The cops have been talking to Ernhardt and some of his friends, and rumor has it that Ernhardt is starting to feel the heat. I'd be curious to know if Dougie had any material—notes or photos or tapes—that sheds light on the relationship between Steadman and Ernhardt."

"There's nothing here in the office? I presume he had a computer here?"

"We've been through it file by file. And there's no paperwork either. Don't forget, he'd been on a leave of absence, working entirely from home."

"Right. I'm going to go through all his stuff with a fine-tooth comb. I'll keep you posted."

As I descended in the elevator, I thought about this new angle. If this murder was somehow linked to any of the people that Dougie had been talking to, it put things in a whole new light. Ernhardt was undoubtedly feeling pressure and that might give me some leverage to pry something out of him. But how to approach him? I needed more background information—and some credentials courtesy of Lou Bernier. As it turned out, I provided my own credentials.

It was only four so I grabbed a cab to the storage facility holding all of Dougie's possessions. I found the correct container, unlocked the door and walked in. I looked around at not a lot of stuff: boxes of paper and books, a desktop computer plus a laptop, a filing cabinet, a few pieces of furniture, and, leaning against a wall, Dougie's yellow Yamaha dirt bike. *Well*, I thought, *at least I won't have to take cabs anymore.*

I started with one of the cardboard boxes full of papers and notebooks. There were printouts of all the stories Dougie had written, bundled up with the relevant notebooks and associated documents. The first box contained nothing related to the current story. Neither did any of the other boxes.

He must have had notes, I thought. *Where the hell are they?* An image of Phil Davis, notorious tape thief, crossed my mind. If they'd wanted the tapes, presumably they'd want any other incriminating stuff as well. Which meant they might very well try to search Dougie's stuff just as I was doing. However, they obviously hadn't found this place yet, because the computers were still here. I strapped Dougie's laptop to the pannier on the back of the dirt bike, wheeled it outside, locked the door of the container and rode well over the speed limit back to the hotel. I left the bike in the hotel's underground parking, leaning in a corner inaccessible to four-wheeled vehicles.

Back in my room, I looked through the Yellow Pages for private-investigation agencies. I picked one that didn't use the word *discreet* in its ad, because I thought that at a good agency, discretion was a given.

I phoned Capital Investigative Services and explained that I had rented a storage container to store some valuable stuff, I had reason to believe it might be broken into, and therefore I wanted it watched, starting now, and if it was broken into, the perpetrator should be discreetly followed to his lair. I gave them my credit card number, and they assured me they would get right on it.

Pleased with myself, I phoned home and had a diverting conversation with Ren, who had just mastered bike riding, and with Daiki, who had discovered the wondrous world of Sherlock Holmes, and finally with Oshie, whose voice negated the miles between us. I told her of my progress and she was pleased. I told her I missed her and she reciprocated. Then I said goodbye, and contact with my extended self came to an end.

I phoned room service and ordered a clubhouse sandwich and two Heinekens, then plugged in Dougie's laptop while I waited. He had told me his password years earlier, and I had no trouble remembering it. Kaleva capers.

When my food came, I ate while searching through Dougie's files for anything connected with the story he had spent the last three months of his life working on. There wasn't a goddamned thing. I checked his e-mail. Nothing from Cliff Ernhardt, Gerry Steadman, or any other name I recognized. I wondered if any had been deleted. I wondered how you would tell. I wondered if it was bedtime. At least I had an answer to that.

The next morning I had to drink four cups of coffee before I judged it was a reasonable time to phone Lou Bernier. When I got through to him, he had good news. "Ollie, I'm taking a risk here, but I want Dougie's story. I'm going to team you up with one of our young guns, kid by the name of Alex Porter. He'll pose as an intern, so the two of you have an excuse for appearing together. But in reality he'll be calling the shots. You okay with that?"

"Lou, that's great. Thanks. I'm too restrained to say anything more." I'm sure he almost chuckled.

"Just remember, you're representing me and the *Ottawa Times*. And any breach of good journalistic practice could queer the story. Now, Alex will be here about ten. Why don't you come down and meet him?"

"I'll be there."

I hung up and referred to my to-do list. Then I phoned Corporal Mayhew of the OPP. When he came on the line, I said, "Hi, it's Ollie Swanson. You assisted me with the search for my friend, Dougie Tarkenen."

"I recall that. How can I help you?"

I phrased my words cautiously. "Without sounding alarmist, I just wanted to make you aware that there may, just may, be more to Dougie's disappearance than a typical canoe accident. He was working on a big story for the *Ottawa Times* that would have exposed some very important people. They are worried enough that they stole some of Dougie's tapes that I'd found. And the same people Dougie was talking to may be involved with Gerry Steadman's murder. I'm just telling you this so that if you come across anything connected, you'll know what to connect it to."

There was a pause. He spoke hesitantly. "There was something a bit strange. After you left, the canoe was taken to the SAR compound in the park. We had to do something with it, so it was left there with other miscellaneous stuff and then sort of forgotten about. One night a warden got back from a patrol a little late and surprised a guy, he thought, trying to steal the canoe. The guy ran off, and when the warden took a closer look, he saw that the guy had been unscrewing the boards that form the seats. It was if he was looking for something. Anyway, he phoned me and I went down there and took all the boards off, but there was nothing underneath but the Styrofoam that provides flotation."

"That fits," I said. "Someone is desperate to find any material that Dougie had accumulated to support his story. I'm back in Ottawa now, looking into all this. You can reach me at the Hotel Chateauvert."

"Thanks for the tip. I'll keep in touch. And I'll pass your name on to the team investigating the Steadman murder. Don't be surprised if you get a call from them."

"Okay, Corporal. Thanks for your help."

I hung up and considered. I seemed to be in a race with Phil Davis and whoever he worked for to find material that Dougie may or may not have hidden. Surely, you'd think, I would have the advantage because of my knowledge of Dougie and his habits. But I seemed to be missing something.

By then it was nine thirty, so I grabbed my jacket and headed for the *Ottawa Times* building. I eschewed the bike because I planned to end up at the storage container and pack some stuff back to my hotel. I took a cab, and during the ten-minute ride I wondered what Alex Porter would be like.

He was twenty-six years old but looked nineteen. He was a big kid, but he had sort of an earnest stoop that made him look very nonthreatening, like he wanted to be your friend. He wore glasses and dressed nerdishly, which probably worked to his advantage. He didn't have an office, just a desk in the chaotic newsroom, so we went out for coffee and a chat.

Seated across from one another in a coffee joint that refused to serve a plain coffee, Alex looked at me nervously. "I know everyone says this, but I was really sorry to hear about Dougie's accident. He helped me a lot when I was a complete greenhorn. I wouldn't have got as far as I have without his help."

"He was a good guy. I'd love to finish his story for him. But I'm having a hell of a time finding the work in progress or whatever you'd call it. After finding those tapes, I haven't found anything else at all."

Alex nodded slowly. "You'd think there'd be something, notes or a journal. Dougie was meticulous about stuff like that. We'll have to think that through."

"Tell me, were there people he hung around with—girlfriends, men friends, anybody he was close to?"

Alex shook his head. "He wasn't really close to anyone, as far as I know. He wasn't unfriendly, but he was totally committed to his work. I was probably as close to him as anyone."

That was pretty much what I'd expected to hear. "So anyway, tell me about the Steadman murder. I haven't really been following it."

He leaned forward. "Okay, Steadman was sort of a shadowy figure. Not a lot is known about him. He had what is euphemistically called a consulting business in Calgary, but he wasn't from Alberta. We're trying to trace his roots.

"Whenever he came to Ottawa, which was a lot lately, he took a suite at the Château Laurier. He'd entertain Ernhardt and all the big Conservative Party wheelers and dealers. The rumor was that he represented offshore interests, and he splashed a bit of money around. The political whores were circling like hungry sharks, to mix a metaphor. At 9:00 PM on July 3, he phoned room service for a bottle of wine. The waiter took it up and heard a loud argument going on. He recognized Steadman's voice but not the other. He knocked. Steadman came to the door, took the wine, tipped the guy and closed the door. The waiter never really saw the inside of the room.

"In the morning, room service took his breakfast up at eight, standard arrangement. Knocked, no answer. Opened the door and saw Steadman lying on his back in the middle of the room, blood on his shirt, apparently dead. The gun was just inside the door, probably dropped there by the shooter as he left.

"The cops were called and staff interviewed. Someone had seen

Cliff Ernhardt walk into the lobby around eight the previous evening. He admitted he went up to see Steadman but said he left at eight thirty. The investigation continues. It's hot and it's juicy and lots of big names are running scared."

"Why?"

"Because Steadman was greasing palms, apparently to pave the way for some legislation he wanted. Anything of that nature that comes out during the investigation would be political dynamite. It could influence the next election."

I thought things over for a moment. "If Ernhardt did it, what's his motive?"

"I don't know, but these guys deal in some serious payola. Whenever you've got that sort of loose change kicking around, you've got a motive for all kinds of things."

I thought some more. "If Ernhardt shot Steadman, he'd have powder residue on his hands. Surely the cops could rule him in or out."

Alex nodded approval. "Ernhardt just happens to belong to the Royal Reserves Shooting Club. He'd been potting targets the morning of the murder."

"Okay, here's what I've got: one of the two voices on the tapes, aside from Dougie's, was Ernhardt. We need to identify the other voice. And there could be others as well. I didn't listen to all of the tapes. Which is why we have to get them back. And the OPP officer who organized the search for Dougie told me that someone tried to mess with his canoe, apparently searching for something. What I would recommend is that we go out to the storage container where all Dougie's stuff is and start going through it. I started yesterday but didn't get very far."

He nodded. "Let's take my car."

As we drove out to the storage compound I explained that I'd arranged to have it watched. "Let's see how good they are." When we got out of the car and approached the container, I couldn't see any watchers. Either they were very good or complete frauds.

Inside the container, I gestured at all the stuff. "Yesterday I went through all those boxes. Nothing. There was a laptop, which I took back to my hotel. Nothing. We'll take the computer when we leave, but in the meantime, why don't you start on the filing cabinet and I'll start tearing the furniture apart looking for something he might have hidden."

Alex was agreeable so we commenced. I found nothing, but Alex found a couple of things. Jammed in with a folder of household bills was a handwritten note from Cliff Ernhardt to Gerry Steadman.

> Mr. Steadman:
> I dropped by your hotel today, mainly to thank you for your incredible generosity. Unfortunately, you weren't in. I've left this note at the desk in the hope that you receive it before four this afternoon.
> My wife and I are having cocktails at fourish and would be extremely gratified if you could drop by. There will also be some other interesting people that I think you should meet.
> Thank you again for your support. There are never enough resources in the struggle to preserve the capital that this country needs as we go forward.
> Regards,
> Cliff Ernhardt

"Well, that's something," I said. "Dougie managed to show a link between Ernhardt and Steadman."

"Yeah," said Alex. "But why isn't there more?"

I shrugged. Ten minutes later Alex came across a handwritten journal. He looked through it for a minute or so and then handed it to me. "You should look at this," he said. "It seems sort of personal."

I looked at the first page. It was definitely Dougie's careful script, formed under the strict attention of Miss Prendergast back in Grade 3. The first paragraph was a little chilling.

The story is coming together, but my enthusiasm wanes. These people are such slimeballs, but why is it me who has to deal with them? I feel like a washroom attendant, knowing every day that he has to go out and deal with shit. I'm so tired.

I put the journal in my pocket. I would go through it later. After another hour we had looked at everything and found nothing else of interest. I picked up the desktop computer. "Let's go back to my room and go through this."

Half an hour later I was hooking up the desktop computer to the television in my room when the phone rang. It was Capital Investigative Services, reporting that two men had entered the storage container using a key, spent two hours and twenty-seven minutes inside, left with a computer and were now in room 842 of the Hotel Chateauvert. "You're very good," I said.

"I suspected it might be you," Mr. CIS said. "We should talk about our ongoing surveillance. Right now we have two watchers, each taking an eight-hour shift during the day, and a team of two at night. It's expensive. A cheaper option would be to attach tracers to some of the items inside, and if they're taken we'll know exactly where they end up."

"Thanks for the option," I said. "Carry on with the current plan for now and I'll let you know if I want to change."

Alex and I turned our attention to Dougie's computer. Two hours later we had found nothing of interest and I was starving.

"I need food. But before I pass out, where can we take this, plus Dougie's laptop, and find out if anything important has been deleted? I'm thinking particularly of e-mail."

Alex nodded. "There's a really reliable outfit that we use. The cops have used them too. If there's anything retrievable they'll get it."

We left with the two computers and dropped them off at Custom Electronics. We instructed the technician carefully, then went to a pizza joint. I had the meat lover's special, Alex had the animal lover's special, and we split a half liter of merlot.

After the third piece of toasted animals on a crispy crust, I felt revitalized enough to talk. "I think we're making progress, Alex. We know a few things I didn't know before I came back here. But I'm a little perturbed that we haven't found any trace of the story. Dougie must have written large chunks of it. Where is it? If he hid it, why? I can understand not leaving it lying around on the kitchen table, but he seems to have buried it completely beyond reach."

Alex didn't have grease on his chin but dabbed it anyway. "I agree with you. It's strange. But maybe we'll understand when we finally find it."

I thought of something. "I suppose we should go through his clothes. I told his landlord to give them to the Goodwill. Maybe we can track them down." I phoned the landlord and he confirmed that he'd given the clothes to the Goodwill establishment on Elm Street. "Everything?" I asked.

"Yeah, everything. Wait a minute. I tell a lie. There were some things, a bunch of shirts that were too grubby to give away. They had paint stains all over them. I put them in a bag, and they may still be in the basement."

"Can we look at them?"

"Come on over. I'll try to find them."

I explained the mission to Alex and we used his car. Before I was ready for it, we were in front of the familiar apartment building, Dougie's last residence on this blighted earth. The landlord was waiting for us. "You're in luck. I forgot to throw them out."

We were standing in the basement, and he handed me a green plastic garbage bag. Feeling slightly uneasy, I dumped the contents onto the concrete floor. There were five or six T-shirts, all the type Dougie would wear, sporting band's logos or political slogans. One was typically Dougie. *You're only young once but you can be immature forever.* The odd thing was that every shirt had a bright red paint stain in roughly the same place, right in the middle of the front.

"Was he doing any painting?" I asked.

"Not that I know of."

"Okay if I take these?"

"Sure."

I put the shirts back in the bag and we left. "Let's check out the Goodwill. They might have some of his stuff left."

As it turned out, they hadn't even processed Dougie's things. When I explained to the woman what we wanted, and the date the clothes had been collected, she said, "Those will still be in the back room. We're *so* far behind. Not enough volunteers."

I asked if we could look at the clothes and she led us to the back room. As well as being in the back, the room was large and permeated with the smell of mothballs. As my sinuses threatened mutiny, we threaded our way through piles of fabric that sullenly hinted of stories for which there would never be an audience. We came to a rolling rack that stood beside three cardboard boxes. Even before the women consulted a tag on the rack, I recognized Dougie's office clothes hanging there. The jackets seemed naked without him.

"Thanks," I said to the lady. "I just want to go through the pockets. We're looking for mementoes for his relatives." She nodded and left. I started on the stuff in the boxes and Alex began working his way through the stuff hanging on the rack. After half an hour we'd discovered nothing except that, in contrast to his left-of-Karl-Marx political alignment, Dougie was a sartorial conservative. With one exception. As incongruous as peas on pizza, a package of three brand-new string ties was nestled in with Dougie's other accessories.

"Interesting," Alex observed. "People can be so contradictory."

The mothball atmosphere and universe of unoccupied clothing accentuated the strangeness of it all. String ties? Dougie had not been what one would call a fashionista. But string ties were to fashion what Cheez Whiz was to the world of gastronomy, and Dougie didn't even use ketchup, if you follow me.

"Why don't you drop me back at the hotel," I said. "I need a good night's sleep. We'll resume our investigative activities in the morning."

But I couldn't sleep. I lay in bed and read Dougie's journal. It frightened me, which was silly, because Dougie was beyond harm and beyond help. Perhaps I could comfort his ghost.

The journal was a series of undated entries consisting of random thoughts, scraps of poetry, and depressing quotations.

> *Pain comes from the darkness and we call it wisdom.*
> *It is pain.*
>
> —*Randall Jarrell*

> *It is difficult to get the news from poems, yet men die*
> *miserably every day for lack of what is found there.*
> —*William Carlos Williams*

How beautiful the body is; how perfect its parts; with what precision it moves; how obedient, proud and strong. How terrible when torn. The little flame of life sinks lower and lower, and with a flicker, goes out. It goes out like a candle goes out. Quietly and gently. It makes its protest at extinction, then submits. It has its say, then is silent.

—Norman Bethune

And Dougie's contribution: *Journalism is not poetry, but I wish it was. Even the exploration of the ugly should have an audience more appreciative than the five o'clock commuter.*

I flipped through thirty or forty pages of Dougie's writing. The last entry was:

Resolution is its own reward. Finish the job, tie up the loose ends, secure the deck. Pray the anchor holds.

Oh God, oh God, oh God. Dougie had been drowning, and I'd had no idea. When he'd phoned I'd chirped happily about Oshie and the kids and my wonderful fucking life and Dougie had been slipping slowly beneath the surface of a stinking cesspool.

Why hadn't I seen what was happening? This was my closest friend, almost a brother. More than a brother, because we never fought. And he'd been in pain and I'd failed to see it, failed to protect him from the bad things.

I went to the minibar and poured a vodka, waved a bottle of juice over the glass, sat down and berated myself for five minutes. Then I phoned Danny. Louise answered the phone. She was bright and cheerful. Danny came on and he was bright and cheerful. I blinked away tears and tried to suppress the sobs gathering in my throat.

"I've just been reading Dougie's personal journal," I told

Danny. "He was having very negative thoughts. He was depressed, and I don't think it was just a short-term thing. Did you see any signs of it when you were hanging around with him?"

"Not really. He was always working hard and sometimes he was pretty intense. But nothing twenty-six ounces of vodka wouldn't cure. You sound a little shaky. I think you've found Dougie's three-o'clock-in-the-morning journal. You know, the dark-night-of-the-soul thing. I'm sure Dougie wasn't like that all the time."

"Christ, I hope not. I wanted life to be as good for Dougie as he was for it. Know what I mean?"

"Yeah, Ollie. You two were really close, and I know you miss him, but don't let it become more than that. The best requiem you can produce is to finish that story he was working on. Okay?"

"Yeah, okay. Talk to you later."

I poured another vodka and offered up a toast. *Resolve to be resolute and resolution will follow. Long live the resolution!*

And the evening sky imagined our fate.

Nine
1991

Dougie and I followed our master plan to the letter.

In January we dug up the bodaidoe patch, threw our belongings into my truck and headed for Vancouver. We had enrolled at Simon Fraser University, so we rented an apartment in Burnaby.

My new brilliant idea for stashing the cash truly was brilliant. The auxiliary gas tank in my truck had developed a leak months before, so, ever safety conscious, I had stopped filling it with gas. It was the work of but an hour to crawl under the truck, hacksaw a six-inch-square hole in the tank and sluice it out with the garden hose. The cash almost but not quite filled the tank. Duct tape closed the hole, and our cash was now secure as long as no one stole my truck. That was laughably unlikely. Once a month I crawled under the truck, which struck no one as unusual because it was the type of truck that looked like it needed to be crawled under frequently, and removed fourteen thousand dollars. We each kept two thousand for living expenses and deposited five thousand in our new savings accounts at the Gulf and Fraser Credit Union. Thus we managed to launder one hundred and sixty-eight thousand dollars a year.

University was fun. There were girls everywhere. I studied them and Dougie studied journalism. Not to say that I took no interest in my courses. Margaret Mead's books about the sex lives of the Trobriand Islanders were revelatory, and I used her examples of unrestricted sexual mores in many attempts to talk girls into bed. Unfortunately, candy is dandy, liquor is quicker, and anthropology is neither.

A couple of other courses were interesting, but somehow not pertinent. The pertinent aspects of my life had been things like what time does the tide turn at the Glory Hole, and which way is that snag really going to fall? The kinship system of Basque sheep herders piqued my interest, but in a vicarious way. I wasn't personally involved.

However, I always managed to pass, and one night while we were celebrating one of my brilliant passes and another of Dougie's routine A-pluses, we added to our tattoo inventory. I opted for a heart with an arrow through it and the name of my one true love: Sockeye. Dougie wanted a portrait of George Orwell, "arguably the most important writer of the twentieth century." The tattoo artiste didn't have Orwell in his repertoire, so Dougie told him to just "do Hitler with a thinner face and looking a bit more English and a bit less German." Amazingly, the artiste got it pretty close, although I'm sure he didn't appreciate the irony that Orwell hated Hitler almost as much as he hated Stalin. And on a pennant around the portrait, Dougie's favorite Orwell quote: "All art is propaganda, but not all propaganda is art."

One night just before mid-term exams, I was drinking at the Princeton in hope of seeing someone from home. I ran into a dragger and he offered me a job and I took it. Draggers fished the year round, made decent money, and it wouldn't be long before I could reasonably claim to have saved enough money for a down payment on my own boat.

Dougie stayed in school because it was where he belonged. He lived and breathed ideas: the mechanisms of twentieth-century Western society, and how things connected. When I had a few nights onshore, we'd drink beer and eat pizza and Dougie would spill out his latest treasures from the castle of learning. "And when the US went off the gold standard, money became a psychological artifact. It only has value because we believe it does. It's like a quantum particle. It only achieves the parameters of existence if we observe it to. The universe exists because we think it. We're God, Ollie. Imperfect and lazy and selfish, but we're God." And I understood him. Because it was Dougie and he was almost my twin and his thoughts were at home in my brain.

Two years later I bought a shrimp dragger from Otokichi Tanaka, who lived in Steveston. Kich had built the *Ryu II* as a bigger version of the *Ryu I*, which he had built after being released from an internment camp at the end of the Second World War.

He was a very interesting man. He built boats with attention to line and shape, like an artist, which I guess he was. He was a small man who spoke quietly, and he was completely without bitterness.

His youngest daughter, Oshiro, was not. By the time I convinced her I bore no direct responsibility for anything that had happened during the Second World War, she decided I was worth marrying. My family was ecstatic, their joy dampened only by our decision to live, at least for the time being, in Steveston. Her family was noncommittal, their reserve tempered only by our decision to live, at least for now, in Steveston.

Dougie and I were the only guys at my stag. We decided against falling-down drunkenness and opted instead for only a few beers to wash down the powdered mushrooms, which were a gift from George in Mitchell Bay. When the hallucinations started, we were walking through Deer Park. I'd had the foresight to bring my camera and ten rolls of film, which I managed to use up while laughing hysterically at Dougie, who acted as my spotter. By the time we had focused down to shooting individual blades of grass, it was almost dark and I was out of film and we were hungry, so we retired to spend my last night at the apartment.

A year later I attended Dougie's graduation ceremony with my very pregnant Oshie. SFU graduations were a little more formal than our high school grad had been, the speeches a little less corny but just as meaningless, the graduates just as ignorant but in different ways.

I had brought a case of beer for old time's sake. After the ceremony we drove to the nearest beach to watch the sun go down. Oshie sipped fruit juice out of a bottle while Dougie and I drank beer. I clanked bottles with Dougie. "You've come a long way, baby. From unemployable small-time hick to honors graduate in English and Journalism."

"And a job as well. The *Vancouver Sun* is putting me on the police beat. Crime and punishment in Section B. You're doing pretty well too, Ollie. A wife who puts up with you, and family on the way. Finances okay?"

I put my arm around Oshie. "We're doing okay." At our wedding reception Dougie and I had had a serious talk.

"I know you love her, Ollie. And you're not going to want to have any secrets. But for my sake, please don't tell her." So I hadn't, and I felt a little guilty about it. But guilt is a given. It's happiness that is the variable, and Oshie and I had seized happiness like a sword from a stone.

So we lounged on the beach and bantered about single versus married life, and talked more seriously about Dougie's career, and about our child to be and our disparate familial communities.

Soon the sun was just barely above the horizon and its acutely angled rays turned the ocean to gold. The silhouettes of homewarding boats were arranged tastefully over the bay and the black vees of their wakes tied the whole picture together. *Nice job, God.* When the sun disappeared it grew cool and we went home. There were still four beers left.

Three years passed, as they do when you have children, in a blur of frozen moments. The birth of our first son, and not quite two years later, our second. Birthdays, Christmases, teeth falling out and coming in—milestones on the path of life. But they were markers left in the rearview mirror, guidance for whatever ghosts followed us. The road ahead was devoid of signs, but we navigated with the compass of confidence.

When Daiki was ready to start kindergarten, and Ren chaffing to join his brother, Dougie moved to Ottawa to cover politics for the *Ottawa Times*. He was really in his element now, tracing the lines of power, their sources and end points and intersections. I subscribed to the paper so I could read his stories. I got them two days late but that didn't matter, because all I cared about was sharing his thoughts. And his words came off the page like he was seated across from me. "Preston Manning criticized the Liberals today for catering to Quebec. It's unclear whether Mr. Manning is also against subsidies to other provinces, past or present." I could read Dougie's mind. *Canada subsidized Alberta for decades. At least with Quebec we get poutine and maple syrup. All we get from Alberta is oil-soaked birds.*

Not long after his move to our nation's soporific nerve center, Dougie ran into my cousin Danny, who had gone there to work for DFO. The two Sointulians produced a few tremors on the city's sin recorders, by virtue of staying out past nine and eschewing herbal tea as their libation of choice.

The two of them phoned me on my birthday and sang "Haaaapy Birthdaaaaay" loudly and badly, not that it's a melodic masterpiece at the best of times. Whoever wrote it made a concerted effort not to waste too many notes, and certainly not any good ones.

When I talked to them after the performance, I detected hints of disillusionment. Dougie and Danny both sounded just a little

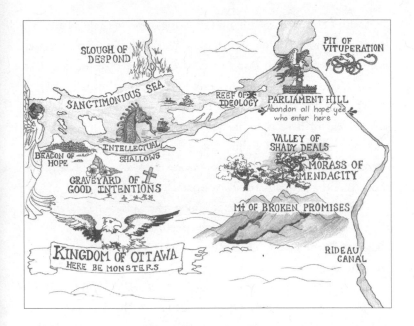

tired, a little less vital. Danny had gone back there to save the fish and Dougie was trying to save, I don't know, the nation's virtue or something. It sounded like progress was not being made. Pierre Trudeau had died and Preston Manning hadn't, and my friends talked as if the forces of darkness were gathering. I pictured a gargantuan vampire looming in the sky, sucking away their energy. But they were not completely daunted and we made plans to reunite in Sointula for Christmas. When I hung up, I hugged Oshie and went looking for Daiki and Ren to hug them.

Shortly after that, a present from Dougie arrived in the mail. It was a drawing, indicative of Dougie's mordant wit and, more disturbingly, I feared, indicative of Dougie's state of mind. It purported to be a map of Ottawa, done in an ancient cartographic style. And like those ancient maps, it more accurately expressed social attitudes than actual geography.

Oshie's family wasn't big on Christmas, saving their celebratory energy for Shogatsu, the Shinto New Year bash. So we packed two carloads worth of stuff into one car, remembered to include both kids and embarked on the day-long journey to Sointula.

The Christmas holidays in a resource town like Sointula always seemed less artificial than in the city. Fishing was over for the year and logging was usually shut down due to snow. No one had to decree that you got a few days off work. Everyone simply enjoyed the leisure that was a natural seasonal occurrence.

Families drove onto the back logging roads to select and cut their own Christmas trees, pastries were baked rather than purchased, and the bird of choice was often a wild goose instead of a tame turkey.

There usually wasn't a lot of snow, just enough to get the sleds out and make a few snowmen. The ice on Big Lake was carefully monitored until one of the elders declared it safe. If that didn't happen, there was always Malm's Pond, which was only two feet deep, so falling through the ice was half the fun instead of a potential tragedy.

It never occurred to Daiki and Ren to play the big-city sophisticates. They were having too much fun with their multitudinous cousins. The days were spent keeping one eye on the kids, visiting with old friends and family and slowly wading into the gentle current of small-town life.

Dougie and my cousin Danny were both home from Ottawa. Danny had cast off whatever malaise was afflicting him the last time we had talked. Dougie hadn't. Every time I saw him, his smile seemed a little forced, his attention not quite there. I knew we should get off alone together. I really wanted to, and I think he did as well. But it just didn't happen.

New Year's Eve, everyone was at the big party at the hall.

Dougie arrived drunk and never slackened in his valiant struggle against sobriety. After Oshie and I had exhausted ourselves with three dances in a row, she sat down to chat with my mom and I went looking for Dougie. I couldn't find him and the next morning he was gone. I regretted that for the rest of my life.

But in the meantime, life went on. And 2001 was a challenging year for Dougie. He viewed with distaste and trepidation the march of the right wing across the unsuspecting and undefended borders of Canadian civil society. But he had pledged allegiance to the journalistic code of "objectivity."

He complained about it every time he phoned me. "Jesus, Ollie. I'm supposed to be writing the truth, but every story has to have 'on the other hand' or 'opponents say.' If I was writing about the crucifixion, I would have to say 'Judas's alleged betrayal led to what some have seen as a crucifixion' and then do a follow-up on whether it was thirty pieces of silver or just twenty and whether it was a legitimate consulting fee."

I tried to console him. "Most people get it, Dougie. You keep writing the stories and they'll connect the dots."

"I don't know, Ollie. We live in a complex world and most people prefer simple. I should have been a sports reporter, or done Hollywood gossip. That's what people like to read, if they read at all."

Dougie was right. What was wanted was simple writing for simple people. After all, the Reform Party had mutated into the Canadian Alliance under the leadership of a man who believed the earth was only six thousand years old. It was enough to depress the Friendly Giant. But I had my family and fishing was good, so I turned a blind eye and ignored the writing on the wall and didn't pay attention and lived in my own world. I guess that makes me culpable as much as any cross-border shopping, CNN-watching Bud-swiller.

The year didn't get any better as it progressed; *regressed* is probably a more accurate word. The Summit of the Americas in Quebec City pounded several more nails into the coffin of democracy. Then 9/11: an attack on Americans by a religious thug in Afghanistan legitimized an attack on everybody by a religious thug in Washington, DC. The Liberal Party of Canada, as always, got things half right by keeping us out of Iraq but began our fatal involvement in Afghanistan. And to top everything off, the NDP in BC was defeated by a malicious weasel (I know this is unfair to real weasels) who was determined to transfer even more money from those who worked hard to earn it to those who didn't and were already rich.

In the spring of 2002, Dougie filed a series of stories about Stephen Harper becoming leader of the Canadian Alliance. And the following year he muted his outrage sufficiently that his editor didn't kill his story of how Peter MacKay became the leader of the Progressive Conservative Party—on the basis of a promise not to merge with the Alliance—and then merged with the Alliance. Dougie described MacKay as being "in quality, if not in quantity, the greatest liar in the history of Canadian politics." His editor changed it to: "The merger has led many observers to question Mr. MacKay's veracity." Indeed.

In 2003, thousands of Canadians were infected with avian influenza, and a year later the new Conservative Party of Canada was infected with Stephen Harper, who, in the only policy that Dougie and I agreed with, had once proposed the implementation of "a firewall around Alberta."

"Quarantine," Dougie said. "It's our only hope."

Dougie phoned one Friday evening and, in a laughing-to-keep-from-crying sort of mood, regaled me with behind-the-scenes stories of the Ottawa press club. One Halloween a well-known columnist decided to dress in drag. The costume featured a small compressed air tank that could be used to inflate the breasts. The columnist had the foresight to bring a couple of spare tanks, because even before the party, he amused friends in a number of bars by deflating and inflating his bosom. (The sophistication of our national capital is difficult to underestimate.) When he got to the actual party, security personnel inspected his purse and inquired as to the purpose of the air tanks. Our hero, at this point in the evening, was somewhat diminished in his usual verbal facility. After a few fumbling attempts at explanation he lost patience and screamed, "Tanks! Tanks for the mammaries!" The guard said, "I've never seen you before" and radioed for backup. The columnist, in a last desperate attempt to explain, opened the air valve too far and blew up both breasts. The guard dove for the floor, and the columnist's friends spirited him away before the situation deteriorated further.

I laughingly accused Dougie of making the story up, but he swore it was true and demanded to speak to Oshie. She steered the conversation to more important matters and elicited the information that Dougie did not have a girlfriend but he did have a canoe. Evidently, the need for wilderness therapy had become acute and he was spending weekends exploring Ontario's waterways.

Oshie passed the phone back to me and Dougie and I insulted each other for a while before making vague plans for a reunion and then saying goodbye.

The next year, 2005, Daiki turned ten and Ren was eight. My kids were growing up and I still didn't feel grown up. Maybe that's normal. But if I wasn't grown up, what the hell was I doing playing with the big boys? Couldn't that get a guy hurt?

And the evening sky imagined our fate.

Ten

When I woke up the morning after meeting with Alex and finding Dougie's journal, I didn't have a hangover. It had me—in a painful submission hold that felt like a raging full-body toothache. At least I knew it wasn't a stroke. Building on that bit of good news, I seriously considered getting out of bed. Twenty minutes later, I did so.

At approximately 07:10, investigative activities recommenced with three cups of coffee and other necessary nourishments. Subsequent to that activity I rendezvoused with my colleague at the establishment of Custom Electronics. We spoke at length with an employee who informed us of the following.

Regarding the computer tower: Over the past twelve months there had been some deleted e-mail that Custom Electronics had restored to a file titled "Restored e-mail." Regarding the laptop computer: Over the past twelve months there had been some deleted e-mail that had been restored to a file titled "Restored e-mail." We took possession of the two computers and returned to my hotel room.

I hooked up Dougie's computer tower to the television again and Alex booted up Dougie's laptop. I started scrolling through the file of deleted e-mail messages. Most were innocuous spam, but one leapt up and down and waved its arms at me. It was from Cliff Ernhardt, sent November 21, 2004.

> Mr. Tarkenen, Sir:
> I've been following your career at the *Ottawa Times* with some interest.

Your stories are consistently well researched and well written, and I think they, and you, deserve more attention than you've received.

There are a couple of emerging issues that I think should be aired out for the Canadian public, and I know you could do a good job of explaining all the ramifications.

Give me a call and perhaps we can get together.

Regards,

Cliff Ernhardt

I showed it to Alex and he reacted with a sort of familiar contempt. "That's what we call 'flashing the wallet.' He's got something he wants you to do or say, but he frames it like he's doing you a favor."

Still, I was excited. This could be the entrée to Ernhardt and his pals that I'd been looking for. "What do you say we call him up, tell him we've taken over Dougie's files and we'd like to meet him? Mind you, I'd like to get the tapes back first. I'm sure there's more dialogue with Mr. Ernhardt that I should hear."

Alex nodded. "I agree we really need to get those tapes back. I'm not seeing much of anything here."

I finished scrolling through the incoming e-mail, then clicked Sent. A pertinent address popped into view: Lou Bernier. I almost said something but bit my tongue when I read the title. *The Story So Far.* I quickly read the body of the e-mail.

What do you think of the story so far? Pretty explosive, eh? But I want to follow it to the end before we publish anything.

Don't lose that memory stick because it's the

only record. I don't keep anything on my computer
because I'm getting as paranoid as hell.

Doug

Suddenly I wanted Alex gone. There was stuff I had to think
about. Christ, there were emotions I had to feel, like betrayal,
anger . . . and fear. Lou Bernier had sworn he knew nothing about
Dougie's story. So he was playing some type of double game, and
Alex in all probability was his mole.

Somehow I pretended to attend to Dougie's computer for the
next twenty minutes. At last Alex stood up and stretched. "I don't
see anything relevant on the laptop. I need to put in some time at
the office. Call me if anything comes up or if you need anything."

At last he was gone, and I called room service for a printer.
When they brought one up, I plugged it into Dougie's computer
and printed off the e-mail. Then I phoned Danny. When I'd
updated him on everything, I almost cried into the phone. "Jesus
Christ! You can't trust anybody in this town. How did you stand it
here for six fuckin' years?"

"I'm tougher than you. And remember, I did warn you not
to trust anyone. But don't panic. We can play this to our advantage. You now have some leverage over Bernier. If he's sold out to
Ernhardt and company, and it looks like he has, we can threaten to
expose him. He's still a well-respected newspaperman, and exposure
would kill him. And if Alex is a mole, and he's probably at least an
unwitting one, we can use him to send false info."

"Bernier must have known we'd discover that e-mail. Why
would he claim to know nothing about the story?"

"Simple. He forgot about it. The important thing was that
Dougie told him he'd given him the only record of the story. When
Dougie disappeared, Bernier figured it was safe to kill the story,

which is probably what he's being paid to do. People always make little slips that eventually sink the ship."

After my conversation with Danny, I was slightly mollified but still uneasy. I wasn't used to living without trust. I was beginning to understand Dougie's paranoia and I felt deeply and painfully alone. So I called Oshie.

I unburdened myself and she soothed me and reminded me that I'd made considerable progress and I felt calmer and she told me about the kids and I felt warm and when I hung up I felt strong again.

I realized now that I couldn't trust Alex. I'd have to go over Dougie's laptop to double-check that there was indeed nothing on it pertinent to the case. There wasn't. You can't rely on people you don't trust to deceive you.

I paced around the hotel room for some time before a cunning little plan crept stealthily into my brain. I phoned Capital Investigative Services and spoke to the same gentleman I'd spoken with before. "You talked about planting tracking devices on certain items rather than continuing personal surveillance on the storage unit. Are they undetectable and are they reliable?"

"Completely," he assured me, "and extremely."

"Can you come to my room this afternoon and plant two devices inside a couple of computers?"

"I'll be there at two fifteen."

While I waited I watched a Jays game on TV. It was early in the game and the Jays sometimes won the first five or six innings. It was unfortunate and unfair that they were forced to play nine. I was glad when I heard a knock on the door because the Jays were up by four and about to bring in their best reliever. I knew they probably wouldn't get a save but more likely a steaming pile of what you would normally expect from a bullpen.

When I opened the door I met Jim Hernandez, junior partner in Capital Investigation Services. He was neat, polite, and exuded competence, and I knew that an hour after he was gone, I would have difficulty describing him. So I won't bother doing it now.

It took him about fifteen minutes to unscrew the backs of the two computers and install in each a miniature hockey puck that he assured me was a transmitter. When he'd closed the computers up, he took out a receiver and turned it on. Both transmitters were working. "How long will they last?" I asked.

"At least three months, probably longer in warm weather."

"Perfect. Tomorrow I'm going to phone you . . . no, better you phone me, just after twelve, and I'll tell you to reduce surveillance on the storage container to nighttime only. That's what I want my lunch date to hear, so you can ignore it. But if those computers move, I want to know, and I want to know where they end up."

He nodded, shook hands and left. I phoned a cab and took the computers, along with the bag of paint-stained T-shirts I'd gotten from Dougie's landlord, back to the storage container. Dougie's possessions looked lonelier than ever, so I left them some company.

I then made the mistake of going for seafood at the best seafood restaurant in Ottawa. The fish was overcooked and the potatoes were undercooked. Fortunately, the portions were very small. As I dawdled over one more glass of wine, I thought back to Jim Hernandez and hoped his equipment was as reliable as he was. And, despite a concerted effort, I realized I couldn't remember what he'd been wearing or much about his features.

First thing in the morning I phoned Danny. It was handy having a cousin with a cop for a wife. "I need a couple of things from Louise. I'm assuming you know her better than me, so I'll let you make the approach."

"Good planning, cuz. What do you need?"

"I need to know who's in charge of the Gerry Steadman murder investigation and then I need Louise to phone that person and explain that I'm known, you know, to the police. Not known to the police, but some of the police, like Louise, know me, you know?"

"And I guess you need this ASAP?"

"As ASAP as you can manage."

"Consider it done."

It was too early for a Jays game, thank God, but I managed to find a rerun of the previous night's Toronto FC game. You had to admire a city that, when faced with the challenge of naming its beloved football club, of stamping it with a moniker that would sum up the cultural identity of said city, of giving the warriors representing the city a title that they could wear with pride, a title with verve and dash that encapsulated the very character and unique aspirations of said city, came up with the name Toronto Football Club.

Their opponents were not very good but managed to stumble to three goals by halftime. The burning question seemed not to be whether Toronto would win, but if they would score a goal. I was glad when the phone rang.

It was a Staff Sergeant Carl Stala of the Ottawa City Police. "Mr. Swanson, a few days ago I had a call from Corporal Mayhew of the OPP about you. Fifteen minutes ago I had a call from Staff Sergeant Louise Karavchuk of the Richmond RCMP about you. I think we need to talk."

"Absolutely. If it's okay I'll come in this afternoon. But first, I'm going through all my friend's e-mail, looking for something from Gerry Steadman. It would be easier if I knew Steadman's e-mail address."

There was a long pause. Finally, "I guess that's not exactly classified information. It was Steadman1, the numeral one, at gmail.com."

"Thanks. I'll drop by around two."

Next, I implemented Phase II of my cunning little plan. I referred to it as Phase II rather than phase two because I was damn proud of it and, frankly, it was worthy of Roman numerals. I had realized that if I was going to continue to use the computers as bait, they would have to be of some interest to the bad guys. But now they would presumably know, through Alex, that there was nothing on them of interest except for one innocuous e-mail from Cliff Ernhardt to Dougie. I needed to change that.

I booted up the hotel computer and changed the date setting to November 28, 2004. Then I opened the mail program and wrote the following e-mail.

> From: Steadman1@gmail.com
> To: Dtarkenen@OttawaTimes.com
> Cc:
> Subject: Matters of mutual interest
> Mr. Tarkenen:
> I'm new in town and Cliff Ernhardt told me you were "the man" when it comes to savvy newspaper guys. I'd like to have a drink with you, maybe pass on a few tidbits that may be of interest.
> Cheers
> Gerry Steadman
>
> From: Dtarkenen@OttawaTimes.com
> To: Steadman1@gmail.com
> Cc:

Subject: Meeting
Sure. Friday at Sollie's. Say 6:00 PM. I'll have a table on the patio.

I then advanced the date one day.

From: Steadman1@gmail.com
To: Dtarkenen@OttawaTimes.com
Cc:
Subject: Meeting
Dougie:
It was great to meet you. As I said, I mainly wanted to give you a little background before you met Cliff. Cliff has a lot of irons in the fire. Don't get me wrong. He's a good guy, but he's a hell of a lot more complicated than I am.
Cheers
Gerry

I advanced the date two more days.

From: Steadman1@gmail.com
To: Dtarkenen@OttawaTimes.com
Cc:
Subject: Unmentionables
Dougie:
Cliff said something to me that rattled me a little bit. Drop by tonight and I'll explain it to you.

One more day ahead.

To: Steadman1@gmail.com
From: Dtarkenen@OttawaTimes.com
Cc:
Subject: Your worries
Gerry:
You're right. To hear Ernhardt come right out and say that is a bit disconcerting.
But don't worry. I've got records of everything you've told me and everything my informant has told me about Cliff, plus lots of juicy stuff from Mr. Fix It. It's all on my computer, but it's stealth filed so it should be secure.
I'll drop by again tonight.
Doug

I figured what the hell. Steadman was dead so he couldn't deny any of it. And when the bad guys got wind of the e-mail, they'd come after the computers like Bobby Hull coming down the wing: with *intent!*

Next I phoned Alex and made a lunch date to talk about this exciting stuff I'd found on Dougie's computer. I printed the whole correspondence, then met Alex at a deli just down the street from his paper. "It's a good thing we took the computers to Custom Electronics. Otherwise we'd never have seen this stuff."

Alex looked a lot less boyish and a lot more serious as he studied the printout. "How are we going to get at these stealth files? If Dougie knew what he was doing, he could rig virtual trip wires so unauthorized entry would destroy the files."

Before I could answer, my phone rang. It was Jim Hernandez. "Oh, hi, Mr. Hernandez. Listen, I can't really afford the full-meal deal on the surveillance. Let's scale it back to just nighttime, say, six at night to six in the morning. Right. Okay, thanks for calling."

I turned back to Alex. "I put the computers back in the storage container. They're safer there than in my hotel room. As for Dougie's stealth files, let me think about it. I know how his mind works—worked."

Alex said, "This looks like the beginning of a falling-out between Steadman and Ernhardt. It might relate to the murder. You should probably go to the cops with it."

"I'm seeing Staff Sergeant Stala this afternoon. You know him?"

"By reputation. Smart, hardworking, bit of a temper problem, which may have held him back a bit."

"Can he be intimidated?"

"Not so far."

"Can he be bought?"

"What currency?"

"Good point."

I paid the bill and we went our separate ways. I had time for a walk so I explored Ottawa while I thought things through. The story Dougie had been working on was serious enough to scare some heavyweight people. I could deduce that from the few tapes I'd listened to, plus the fact that they'd gone to a lot of trouble to steal them back. At least, it would have been a lot of trouble if I hadn't been so gullible. And somebody had been snooping around Dougie's canoe, probably looking for anything else that might be incriminating.

And one of the guys Dougie had secretly taped, Cliff Ernhardt, may have murdered some oil lobbyist named Gerry Steadman. I wondered if Dougie had met Steadman. And what the hell had Dougie done with all his money? Our individual shares from the big heist had been over eight hundred thousand dollars. It had taken a few years to launder it all into our bank accounts, but once invested in term deposits, the money had averaged about 6 percent interest over the years. I'd spent about three hundred thousand on my boat and my house and I still had almost eight hundred thousand. Dougie hadn't spent a nickel except maybe fifty thousand on his degree. He should have had over a million in his account. Had he given it away because he was depressed?

Perhaps the scariest thing was that Dougie had given at least the first part of his story to his editor, Lou Bernier, but Bernier denied any knowledge of it. Dougie had obviously trusted Bernier and been betrayed. Betrayal was rampant in this case.

At two that afternoon I walked into the downtown police building and asked for Staff Sergeant Stala. When Stala came out to greet me, I was surprised at how small he was. Maybe five foot nine and lightly built. But he had hard eyes and a permanent frown. He attempted to smile and almost succeeded. "Mr. Swanson, come into my office."

I followed him down a hallway, through a coffee room and into a windowless space that he apparently thought of as an office. He gestured toward a chair, and we sat down on opposite sides of a desk. "It's good to meet you, Mr. Swanson. Staff Sergeant Karavchuk assured me that you are not a typical West-Coast yahoo."

I nodded. "Not typical at all."

This seemed to reassure him. "I understand that your friend disappeared last February and you think there might be a connection to Gerry Steadman's murder."

"I wouldn't go that far. Dougie was connected to Cliff Ernhardt. He'd made surreptitious tapes of Ernhardt and some of his cronies for a story he was doing on political corruption. After Dougie's death I ended up with the tapes, and then they were stolen from me by someone I presume was acting for Ernhardt. But as of yet I haven't found any connection between Dougie and Steadman, although it wouldn't surprise me. Steadman was exactly the type of guy that Dougie was focusing on: big business reputation, big money, looking for political connections."

"And what was on the tapes?"

"I listened to six of them, and they showed clear evidence of influence peddling and general sleaze, but probably not outright criminality."

"And who was speaking?"

"Mostly Ernhardt, with Dougie asking the questions. And one other person I haven't been able to identify."

"Describe the person who stole the tapes."

"Five eight, stocky, dark hair cut short. Vague resemblance to Sylvester Stallone, but not as pouty, you know?"

"Doesn't fit anyone we've seen so far. So what exactly is your purpose here in Ottawa?"

"Long term: publish the story that Dougie was working on. Short term: recover the tapes."

"And how do you intend to do that?"

Trust no one. "I was hoping you could help me with that."

Stala stared at me. When he finally spoke, it was as though he were reading from a script. "If, in the course of our investigation, we come into possession of the tapes you've described, and if we determine that they are not relevant to our investigation, they will be returned to you."

"Thanks. That would be great. Um, is Ernhardt a suspect in Steadman's murder?"

"He remains a person of interest and is assisting us with our inquiries."

"What would his motive be?"

The frown on Stala's face progressed to a scowl. "We're considering a number of possibilities, none of which we're at liberty to discuss."

Trying desperately to keep any hint of sarcasm out of my voice, I thanked him for "all his help," promised to stay in touch and stood up to leave. He accompanied me back to the foyer, we shook hands, and I left.

As I walked back to my hotel, I thought how, in many ways, it had not been a good meeting. It had, in point of fact, been the very antithesis of a good meeting, a veritable train wreck, a massive-mudslide-causing-ancillary-flooding-that-destroyed-five-villages sort of meeting. I would have to have more meetings to practice my meeting skills. But as I regarded the harried, briefcase-toting denizens who rushed by me with eyes averted, I couldn't see anyone I'd really like to meet with.

And so I wandered, lonely as a cloud, all the way back to my hotel, where I wondered, thoughtful as a stone, what the hell to do with the looming evening. I decided to have a meeting with a clubhouse sandwich and a six-pack of boutique beer. I was masterfully in control and the meeting went well.

Then I returned to Dougie's journal. Reading sequentially now, halfway down page one, there was this:

I need to connect the dots to the formal party structures, libs and cons. They each have their own spin masters, bagmen, and fixers. But at the center of the power structure, the lines of force converge to a singularity, a black hole of evil that even Stephen Hawking would be unable to explain.

There were a couple of pages of similar forebodings, and then this:

The web of deceit encompasses the entire city. The web of deceit is the city. I live in fear of the spider, whose venom threatens democracy.

Following this was a rambling four-page quasi book review of *Man and Superman*, which concluded, *I agree with Shaw when he says, "We must either breed political capacity or be ruined by democracy, which was forced on us by the failure of the older alter-natives. Yet if Despotism failed only for want of a capable benevolent despot, what chance has democracy, which requires a whole popula-tion of capable voters?"*

Dougie had always had a taste for existential angst, but here he was poisoning himself. Had he forgotten that in Sointula, at least, there were no governance problems? Everything could be left safely in the hands of the preschool mothers or the rec committee. Surely we could scale up. I couldn't read any more so I switched on the news, only to see a series of earnest people deploring the sponsorship scandal in Quebec. Didn't they realize that politics was the art of the affordable?

After that I desired only darkness and dreams, a temporary gift of madness that was too brief a respite from belligerent reality. And the evening sky imagined our fate.

Eleven

Then followed two days during which absolutely nothing happened. I mean, nothing to do with the case. News broadcasts were not suspended or anything, and I'm sure events of some nature did transpire in various locations. But nothing happened that related to me, Ollie Swanson, and my mission of enlightenment or whatever it was.

My suffering reached a peak on Thursday evening, and I thought seriously about booking a flight home. But as they say in the fishing racket, "Stick and stay and make it pay." My patience was finally rewarded at five thirty on Friday. I was lounging on my hotel-room bed, going through the TV channels for the hundredth time, when Jim Hernandez from Capital Investigation Services phoned.

"Your computers are on the move."

My blood pressure surged. "Where are you?"

"I'm in the office, tracking the transmissions on a GPS. They're heading west from the storage park, toward the Overbrook area. I'll call again when they stop moving."

I turned off the TV and stood in front of the window, staring out at the city in twilight. After a while the lights seemed brighter and more distinct. I realized some time had passed and it was now fully dark. The phone rang again.

"The blips have stopped moving. They appear to be inside a house, 721 Belmont Street." There was a pause. "Are you going to call the police?"

"I don't think the police would be interested, Jim. I believe I know the perpetrator, and I should be able to deal with him with no problems. But if I don't phone you within an hour, you'll know I was wrong."

After I hung up I checked an online map and found 721 Belmont Street and noted that my route went right by Westbrook Mall. I retrieved my envelope of mad money from its hiding place in my good shoes, and divided the hundred-dollar bills into bunches of ten. Then I took the elevator down to the underground parking.

Dougie's dirt bike was where I'd left it. I mounted and took off for Westbrook Mall, where I found a sporting goods store and bought a forty-two-ounce Louisville Slugger. I then rode to within a half block of 721 Belmont and parked the bike between two cars.

I slid the handle of the bat up the right sleeve of my jacket and cupped the head in the palm of my hand. A quick walk-by reconnoiter showed 721 to be a small bungalow, almost identical to its neighbors. The lights were on but the curtains were drawn.

I walked silently up the flagstone path and then across the lawn to the curtained window. I could hear a TV but no other voices. A slight gap in the curtains gave me a narrow line of sight into the living room, but all I could see was the opposite wall. *Nothing ventured, nothing gained.*

I returned to the front door and knocked loudly. I stood with my back to the peephole and was pleased to hear the sound of a bolt being slid back and the door opening. I immediately spun and slammed into the door with my left shoulder. Being what my mother refers to as a "big-boned Swede" made the fact that the door was still on the chain irrelevant. The door crashed inwards, knocking whoever had opened it to the floor.

I took one more step inside and simultaneously kicked the door shut and slid the bat down my sleeve, so I could grip it firmly by the handle. Recognizing the person on the floor as my old friend Phil Davis, I gave him a tap of greeting on his kneecap. The way he screamed, you'd think I hit him hard. When his screams had subsided to groans, I initiated the conversation.

"Phil, buddy, good to see you again. What were you planning on doing with my computers?"

"Fuck you!"

I took a half swing at his other knee, sort of like a golfer hitting a short iron. But it was a forty-two-ounce bat and the knee is a very tender spot. Phil gasped and turned very white and arched his back in some sort of spasm. While waiting for him to recover, I reached into his back pocket and pulled out his wallet. It contained a driver's license and a private investigator's ID with the name Phil Trimmer.

"Phil, I'm glad your name really is Phil. You look like a Phil. About those computers?"

His eyes were squeezed shut and he spoke quickly, through a clenched jaw. "In the morning I'm handing them over to some techie guy."

"Name?"

"Pat. Works in a shop in Bytown."

"Who hired you?"

It was almost as if a pained look superimposed itself on his already pained face. "I can't tell you. Please . . . *oh fuck!*"

This in response to the gentlest of pokes to his left knee.

"All right, all right. Don't. Shit. Ahhh. Shit, fuck."

"You'll have to be a little more articulate, Phil. It's a simple question. All I want is a name. But"—and I waved the bat gently— "it has to be the right name."

"Cliff Ernhardt."

"Well done, Phil. We're making excellent progress here. Now, you might not know this, but the last time I saw you, you somehow screwed up the tape-copying deal. Inadvertent, I'm sure. But I do need the originals."

He was still speaking breathlessly, between groans. "Can't. Gave them to Ernhardt."

I decided to eschew the stick and employ the carrot. "How much did he pay you for that little caper?"

"Ten grand."

"Was it worth it?"

"No, Christ no."

"Well, maybe I can help make it up to you, Phil. Being the type of guy you are, and having access to that handy dandy little copier you had, I'll bet you couldn't resist making a set of copies for yourself."

He said nothing, only continuing to groan in pain. I took the envelope of money out of my pocket and three bunches of hundred-dollar bills out of the envelope. I removed the elastics and scattered the bills on his chest. "Where are the tapes, Phil?"

He continued to groan, but I could almost see the mental gears rotating with ill-meshed clanks and clunks. However, he continued to say nothing. Well, perhaps one should not be too dependent on the carrot. I cocked my wrists as if preparing for another swing.

"Backyard, backyard, Jesus. They're in the backyard."

"Now Phil, this is going to hurt me more than it hurts you, but I can't leave you alone. I'm going to gently drag you across the floor to the back door. Be brave and think of England." I gripped the back of his shirt and slid him as gently as I could across the floor to the back door. He groaned constantly but with no increase in intensity. I turned out the lights and opened the door.

"Where exactly?"

"Third tile, second row, as you're looking at it."

There was enough light to see a sort of paved patio. The tiles were foot-square concrete blocks, about ten rows of ten. I lifted the third tile from the left, second row, and discovered a shallow hole, and in the hole, a plastic baggie, and in the baggie, some tapes.

"Where's your tape player, Phil? I need to check these."

"Ernhardt took it back. Please, I wouldn't have hidden them if they weren't genuine."

That made sense. "See, Phil? That didn't hurt a bit, did it? Well, maybe a bit. I may contact you in the future with questions about Ernhardt. If I do, maybe we can accentuate the positive and eliminate the negative in the reinforcement department. What do you say?"

"Yeah, yeah, sure. Whatever."

I picked up my bat and left. I interrupted the ride back to the hotel only to ditch the bat in an alley. For the rest of the trip, I reflected on how easily violence had come to me. True, you could say that Phil had "deserved it," and I had acted with restraint, but surely those were the justifications of every torturer. The most disturbing aspect of it was that I didn't want to tell Oshie about it, and maybe that was the ultimate litmus test for wrongdoing.

Back in my hotel room, I phoned Jim Hernandez at Capital Investigation Services. "I talked to the guy who took the computers. Everything's fine. Thanks for a good job. If I need any more assistance I'll call you."

In the morning, Phil would take the computers to his techie guy, and he'd find nothing. But I'd found out that Alex, unwittingly or not, was a conduit of information that went through Lou Bernier to Cliff Ernhardt. That was, as they say, a situational advantage. Plus, I'd recovered the tapes. A celebration was called for, so I opened the minibar and ate what must have been a thirty-dollar bag of salt-and-vinegar chips. Then I called home.

Oshie's voice took me home like some wondrous teleportation machine. Instantly it seemed as if I was sitting across from her at our kitchen table, the kids' voices carrying in from the backyard. I could see her smile as she congratulated me on recovering the tapes and then frown just a little as she puzzled with me about why Dougie hadn't left notes for his story. Was it just his native paranoia that had overridden standard working practice, or had he left notes and I'd failed to find them?

We discussed this and more pleasant issues for too short a time, and then Oshie put the kids on the line. Daiki regaled me with the wonders of "Silver Blaze" and "The Adventures of the Lion's Mane." Ren informed me that he was the best hider of all his friends and we discussed the possibility of hide-and-go-seek becoming an Olympic sport. Regretfully—more regretfully than I cared to dwell on—I said goodbye to them all and was left back in my hotel room, alone.

I unpacked the tape player I'd bought and settled in to listen to more of Dougie's tapes. I'd listened to part of tape number one and all of five others. Deciding to plow through the rest of the tapes in order, I slotted in the otherwise untitled tape number one and fast-forwarded to where I'd left off oh so long ago, when the world was innocent and so was I.

The tape had started off with Cliff Ernhardt pontificating on the need for good right-wing spin doctors, and Dougie stroking him and urging him on. It continued in that vein and I really had to force myself to listen to it. In the end, it was a wasted effort in bile suppression, because I learned nothing new. I'd listened to tape number two, "The Setup," and tape number three was boring beyond belief. Tape number four was "Finances," which I'd also already heard. Tape number five, however, shocked me with a clue that would prove to be one end of the thread that unraveled this whole sad—no, tragic—story. Listen to this:

Cliff Ernhardt: I want to thank you so much, both on my behalf and also on behalf of my principals, for your generous donation.

Dougie: It was just a friendly gesture. And on behalf of my principals, we hope this is just the beginning of a long and mutually beneficial relationship.

Ernhardt: Well, a quarter of a million dollars is an *extremely* friendly gesture. And I can assure you and your principals that we are open to a continuing relationship.

Well, holy shit! I mean, *holy shit!* One question had been answered, namely, what Dougie had done with at least part of his money. But other questions had risen like zombies from the grave. Why? How? Who? What the fuck?

I paced the hotel room, completely oblivious to where I was. Or even, for that matter, who I was. I was conscious only of the tortured logic circuits of my brain as they arranged facts, asked questions, rearranged facts and reached conclusions that became new facts. Dougie gave a huge sum of money to a slimeball named Cliff Ernhardt. Why? Access. Access to what? To the machine behind Ernhardt, the would-be controllers of the political and economic agenda of the country. Because? He wanted a story, and the story presumably would have scandalized the nation. Maybe Ernhardt had tipped Dougie to a scandal that would have seriously damaged, maybe destroyed, the machine. And maybe, just maybe, the people who were the machine realized that Dougie was on the verge of destroying them. And so they destroyed him.

My brain stopped. It had spit out an answer and awaited new

instructions. Who or what would give it the new instructions? My other brain? *Stupid brain! Stupid brain!* I pounded the heel of my left hand against my head, then again, harder. Finally my logic circuits skipped ahead a bit and resumed activity.

The bastards. The dirty rotten bastards. The dirty rotten slug-fucking bastards. They most definitely would pay for this. They would regret the day they'd fucked around with Dougie Tarkenen.

At this point I realized that my hotel room was much too small for the magnitude of the pacing I needed to do. I grabbed my coat and went outside, where I could engage in a pace of epic proportions. It was dark and it was cold. I walked. I walked until it was less cold and less dark. I was conscious of not a single thought until I looked at my watch and saw that it was seven in the morning.

The neighborhood was one I'd never seen before. Down the block and on the other side of the street was one of those family-run coffee shops that caters to the earlier-than-normal working person. Warm and well lit, it drew me across the street and up to the slightly fogged glass door. I went in.

As the door closed behind me, I stood for a moment and savored the warmth and the smell of coffee. The place was surprisingly full of very, very pale faces, most of which were intently scanning the sports section of the *Ottawa Times*. In a booth eight down from the door, by the window, I spied a familiar face. At one end of the counter was a serve-yourself coffee pot. I poured a cup and approached my acquaintance, who was staring morosely out the window. As I slid in opposite him, I said, "Of all the coffee joints in all the towns in the world, I had to walk into this one."

Phil Trimmer startled and looked at me. Panic showed momentarily before he got himself under control. "What the hell do you want?"

"Phil, I thought at the very least I'd have bought myself some civility."

His eyes moved constantly around the café, either because he was afraid to look at me or because he was afraid of being seen with me or because for him fear was a character trait. "Look, I appreciate that little present you left me. I spent some of it on a wheelchair. But I don't think we should be seen together."

"You're probably right. But I may want to continue our business relationship. What's the best way to stay in touch with you?"

He looked at me for the first time. I could almost see the wheels of avarice turning behind his eyes. "I hang out at Big Frank's sports bar. Phone me there. If I'm not there you can leave a message. Say, 'Tell Phil to phone his mother.'" He stood and limped toward the door, not a wheelchair in sight. Some people were hopeless exaggerators.

I was aware of two burgeoning sensations: the glimmering of an idea and the pangs of extreme hunger. I dealt with the latter first. As the waitress refilled my coffee cup, I ordered a plate of corned beef hash with two fried eggs on top. Ten minutes later the hunger pangs were considerably weaker and the mental glimmering was considerably stronger.

I'd been searching for a way to approach Cliff Ernhardt. I could, of course, walk up to him and introduce myself as a friend of Doug Tarkenen and say I was hoping to finish the story that Dougie had been working on, the one that was going to expose Cliff and his friends to the whole world as dollar-addled rutting weasels, but I could see that that plan was not completely assured of success. Hmmm.

Then it hit me. A glancing blow that fortunately did no visible damage. Cliff Ernhardt was facing a murder charge, a situation that presumably made him feel vulnerable and thus less prone to completely rational thought. Suppose I approached him as a friend of Gerry Steadman who had information related to the murder, information that Steadman had given him that could clear Ernhardt or maybe implicate him further? I could decide which later. Why did I think I could get away with this? Because no one seemed to know much about Steadman, so I could easily be a friend from the old days. Besides, I didn't have a better idea.

Three hours later I found an intact payphone on Laurier Avenue and dialed Ernhardt and Associates. I introduced myself as Jimmie Johnson and said I wanted to speak to Mr. Ernhardt. Of course, he was in a meeting. "And what," the secretary enthused, "is this regarding?"

"Regarding the murder of Gerry Steadman. I'll phone back in an hour. Please make sure that Mr. Ernhardt is available."

I hung up and phoned Big Frank's sports bar. Someone answered and when I asked for Phil, I heard, "Phil, are you here?" and then, to me, "Who is it?"

As maternally as possible, I said, "Tell him it's his mother."

"Which mother?"

Somewhat less maternally, I said, "The mother that's going to cut off his allowance if he doesn't quit fucking around."

That message was apparently relayed because Phil came on the line. "What?"

"We need to talk. Be out front in ten minutes and I'll pick you up in a cab."

My confidence in Ottawa cabs was only slightly misplaced, and fifteen minutes later we picked up a disgruntled Phil Trimmer. "Son, it's been so long since we've had a nice visit. I thought we'd go for a walk."

"My legs are still sore."

"Exercise will do you good."

I paid off the cab in the middle of a busy shopping area and stood impatiently while Phil levered himself painfully out of the backseat. "How much longer are you going to play the sympathy angle?"

"Fuck you."

"That's better. You don't do the baby-seal thing very well. I want to talk about your boss. I understand Ernhardt is in the frame for Gerry Steadman's murder. What do you know about it?"

"Not a lot. Ernhardt had me do a background check on Steadman, but I couldn't find much. When Steadman got whacked it was a real shock. But I can guarantee you that Ernhardt didn't do it."

I leaned over so I could look directly into his face. "How can you be so sure?"

"Because Ernhardt is a bullshitter, not a killer."

Phil might lack character, but I felt he was a pretty good judge of it. "What have the cops got on Ernhardt?"

He shrugged. "Ernhardt was there the night Steadman was shot, although he swears he left him alive. But Steadman left some papers, documents of some kind, that point to Ernhardt. I've leaned on my usual sources at the cop shop, but they've got this locked up tight. No one's saying anything."

"What did Ernhardt tell you about Dougie Tarkenen?"

"He thought Steadman might be giving Tarkenen information. I looked into it but couldn't find any contact between them. How your friend got those tapes is a mystery. But Ernhardt was really worried about the tapes."

"How worried?"

"Look, I know your friend is missing, but like I said before, if Ernhardt's a killer, I'm a rubber ducky."

I placed my hands on his shoulders and gave him a gentle shake, which shouldn't have caused him to wince, but it did.

"This is important. Let's say you're right about Ernhardt not being a killer. But he played with some pretty heavy hitters and some of them might not have shared Ernhardt's delicate sensibilities. Any names come to mind?"

"No. These guys are legitimate businessmen, for Christ's sake. Well, mostly legit. I'm sure some of them have tax issues and some of the politicians may not have reported all their campaign donations. But that's business as usual in this town. Nothing to get all heavy-handed about."

I stared at the horizon as I thought this over. No conclusions were reached. "Okay, here's the deal. I'm going to approach Ernhardt, posing as a friend of Steadman's named Jimmie Johnson. I'm going to tell him Steadman gave me information that could clear Ernhardt or maybe put him more squarely in the frame. I haven't made up my mind yet. If Ernhardt says anything to you about it, like getting you to tail me or anything, I want to know about it. Right?"

A pained look disturbed Phil's countenance, which I would like to report was a departure from its normal cheery openness, but I can't.

"Jesus, Swanson! There are so many ways this could go sideways. I said he's not a killer, but the guy's facing a murder rap. You rattle his cage and all bets are off. And what if the cops find out? I'll be fucked if I'm going to stand up for you for obstruction of justice, or fraudulent impersonation, or whatever the fuck they want to make out of it."

"I thought we had a congenial employer-employee relationship. All I'm asking you to do is relay things to me. Things your ex-boss tells you that your new boss—me—might find useful. What's the problem?"

He grumbled and shifted from foot to foot and looked at the sky. Finally he said, "How much?"

I knew I had him. "Phil, I think you've seen that I'm a pretty generous guy. I'm sure we can come to an agreement on the value of anything you give me. You have my number at the hotel? Excellent. Now, if you'll excuse me, I have to make a phone call."

I left Phil to his equivocations and set off in search of another payphone. It took awhile, so my second call to Ernhardt and Associates was twenty minutes late. But maybe it was better if I came across as a little bit unreliable. In spite of my tardiness, I was quickly transferred through to Cliff Ernhardt. After some obsequious and unpleasant pleasantries, Ernhardt came to the point. "Mr. Johnson, I understand you have some information about the Steadman murder. Shouldn't you go to the police?"

"Of course. But the fact is, my information came from my old friend Gerry Steadman. It could help your case. And if you knew Gerry, you know he understood that information is never free. I feel I have to honor his memory by handling this the way he would have."

"You mean a *quid pro quo*. All right. I have some free time this afternoon. Why don't you come by my office?" He quickly realized the downside of that scenario. "Actually, it might be more, uh, relaxing if we met out of the office."

"Yeah. I'll meet you in the bar of the York Hotel. Tomorrow morning at ten." I hung up.

As I walked away I remembered something Dougie had once said. "The art of the hunt demands the appropriate camouflage." In those days he was referring to army camouflage gear that had been properly stained, bloodied, and broken in. The present situation demanded something different.

I headed for Harry Rosen.

Twelve

When I walked out of the store I was almost strutting. Resplendent, as they say, in a three-button houndstooth jacket setting off pearl-gray slacks, with the ensemble well accessorized by Italian loafers and a tie that didn't say "Fuck you" all over it. I had my old clothes in a bag and almost threw them into a trash receptacle before realizing that midnight would come to the ball eventually.

Back at the hotel, I approached the desk clerk and embarked on another scam. Where was this coming from? "Hi. I've got a friend coming in today and I said I'd get a room for him. Can I get a room for Jimmie Johnson for five days?" I pushed my credit card across the counter.

"Certainly, sir. Smoking or non?"

"Non. And by the way, his boss is expecting him today, and if he doesn't show he'll be in trouble. If anyone phones for Jimmie, would it be okay not to say he hasn't arrived yet? Just say that he's not in his room and you'll take a message?" I put on my most heartfelt look, which, I can assure you, is the very quintessence of heartfeltedness. "You wouldn't be telling a lie. He wouldn't be in his room. Unless, of course, he was, in which case you wouldn't say that."

The desk clerk gave me a resigned look, which I took as acquiescence. "Room 427. Would you like a key, or will he pick it up?"

"Maybe I'll take a key, and if I don't hook up with him, there'll still be one at the desk." I got another resigned look along with the key.

In my room, I carefully hung my new clothes in the closet and, resplendent, as they say, in my underwear, sat down to finish my homework. I needed to listen to the rest of the tapes before meeting Ernhardt. I needed anything on him I could get. The last tape I'd listened to was number five, during which I'd discovered that Dougie had given Ernhardt a quarter of a million dollars. But I hadn't finished listening to it. It was still in the machine, so I pressed Play. Ernhardt was still speaking. He had just told Dougie that he and his people, whoever they were, were open to a continuing relationship with Dougie and his people, whoever they were supposed to be. He continued, "And over the next few months, as we get a better understanding of your needs, we can begin to design a program to deliver certain things. And as expenses arise, we can discuss reimbursement, but please understand that ongoing program funding is even more important than specific expense funding."

Dougie: Of course. And what I think we need here, Cliff, is a two-pronged approach. We need to develop a regulatory regime that will give my offshore clients the access to oil they need, and more generally, we need to change the government here. They just aren't sympathetic to our needs. Have your people given any thought to that?

Ernhardt: Of course. Regarding the regulatory issues with getting oil offshore, we've been working for some time with some of your western colleagues, and we've made a lot of progress. You know, of course, who I'm referring to.

Dougie: Oh yeah, the pipeline boys. They're a well-organized bunch. The fact that they're supply side and I'm demand side means that really we're on the same side.

Ernhardt: As far as the upcoming campaign goes, my agency is preparing an ad campaign that will scorch the political earth. The Liberals won't know what hit them.

Dougie: All well and good, Cliff. But we outspent them last time and they still won. I think we have to deploy unconventional weapons.

Ernhardt: All right. This is absolutely top secret. For your ears only. We've got close contacts with our American friends, who are much more advanced in these sorts of techniques. They call it voter suppression. I prefer to think of it as democratic enhancement: making sure that the right people's votes really count by making sure the wrong people don't vote. But that can't leave this room for now.

Dougie: [Whistles] I'm impressed, Cliff. At the very least, I can tell my people we're putting our money on the right horse.

This was getting more interesting by the minute. Dougie was pretending to represent foreigners wanting to buy our oil. And the same clients were evidently already working with the pipeline companies. Who could they be? Europeans? Or one of the developing economies, India or an Asian nation?

The rest of the tape contained more of the same, but there was nothing important except that Dougie promised to deliver some more money. "The same amount as last time."

I'd listened to tapes six and seven, so next I slotted in tape eight, titled "Personnel." The familiar, offensively self-important voice emanated from the tinny speaker. "We like to think of ourselves as the armed services of the righteous right, capitalist soldiers fighting the good fight. And, like the armed forces, we're divided into different services. The land battle, if you will, is slogged out every day in the media. We have people in every newspaper and TV station in the country. They are either natural sympathizers or paid mercenaries."

Lou Bernier, the editor of the *Ottawa Times*, would be the latter, I thought.

Cliff went on. "I see the bureaucracy as an ungoverned ocean where all kinds of threats can arise, so we've got battleships to cover it. We have people at the assistant deputy minister level in every department in government. There were a lot of right-wing moles implanted at low levels during the Mulroney era. They've now risen to positions of authority. It was a couple of those moles in DFO that managed to privatize the West-Coast fishery. Occasionally we have to buy an ADM, usually after the fact, by letting him retire early and then giving him a lucrative job somewhere.

"And the air force, the high flyers, are the politicians themselves. They take a lot of nurturing. But it's understandable because there's a lot of casualties. And many of them are our guys, true believers, who deserve all the support they can get."

He chortled. "And, of course, then there's yours truly, who some would refer to as the minister of propaganda. But damn it, it's not propaganda if it's the truth. And if we say it, it's goddamn well the truth."

The sound of clapping, presumably from Dougie. "But what we want to know, Cliff, is who's in the war room? Who's putting pins in the map and issuing the final marching orders?"

"Let me get you another drink, sir." There was a pause during which clinking and pouring sounds could be heard, and a muttered "Thanks" from Dougie.

Ernhardt: Well, sir, we call ourselves the Committee. It's not what you would call an open membership. When a member dies, we have a long discussion and then inform the replacement that he's been selected. No one ever refuses. There are, of course, the money guys, four of them. We call them the bankers, but they're not real bankers, although one of them is. They're more like collectors, what the enemy press calls bagmen. There are seven members from the business community, representing broad sectors of the economy: energy, communications, natural resources, manufacturing, and so on. We have two ideas guys, both economists, and myself as an *ex officio* member. And, of course, there's the Chairman. [There was a pause during which ice tinkled in a glass.] I know you'd like to meet them, and of course they'd like to meet you. Perhaps after our relationship has become a bit more formalized we can have a little get-together with you and your principals.

Dougie: I'm looking forward to it, perhaps after we complete phase one of the action plan.

After listening to hours of this, I could not only read between the lines, I could hear the real words behind the spoken words. *After our relationship has become a bit more formalized* really meant "after you've given us another giant whack of money." *After we complete phase one of the action plan* really meant "once you've actually delivered on something."

After that, the conversation descended into a slag fest of the Liberal Party, the NDP, liberals in general, and especially "those liberal bastards at the CBC." Tape number nine was sort of a general mishmash of running political commentary, business types who could or couldn't be trusted, and a semi-autobiographical summary of the splendid and distinguished career of Cliff Ernhardt. I awarded myself a liquid medal, a double, actually, for remaining conscious through all of it.

I'd already listened to tapes nine and ten, which elucidated the betrayal of the West-Coast fishing community. I picked up tape eleven, subtitled "Betrayal Three." Even though I'd been jumping all over in the chronology of the tapes, I hadn't listened to this one yet. I'd been semi-consciously saving it, like the last chocolate almond in the box of assorted nuts. It turned out to be even more satisfying.

The first voice was Dougie's. "Good evening, sir. It's a pleasure to meet you again."

He was answered by the unknown voice I'd first heard on tape seven, talking about future policy. "And you, sir. Cliff has informed me of your generosity. But more than that, he's assured us of your reliability and, well, your compatibility. We're a pretty exclusive club. Now I don't want to sound snobbish, but we like to associate with like-minded people. And Cliff says your thinking is sound, very sound."

Dougie: Well, thank you. Just the way I was brought up, I guess.

Unknown voice: Now then, it's time to get down to brass tacks. Why don't you tell me a little more specifically about your needs, and we'll see if we can't put something together that'll keep your clients happy.

Dougie: Well, I'm sure you've deduced that I represent Chinese interests. And what they need is Canadian oil. Step one is to get approval to build the infrastructure that will deliver the oil to the West Coast. And I know the pipeline boys have made a start on that and we're happy to back them. As a matter of interest, what have you managed to do for them so far?

Unknown voice: [Chuckles] Oh, we've pulled together a couple of things. We've bought them at least two cabinet ministers in the present government. And if we can elect our man in the coming election, we'll have bought them a whole bloody government.

Dougie: Wow! I'm impressed. Really impressed. But there are limits to what politicians can deliver.

Unknown voice: These are all regulatory issues, and we specialize in those. There are underlying political and social issues, of course.

Environmentalists these days can create some real problems. But that aspect is more Cliff's department. So here's what we can do. The pipeline will have to go through an environmental review. We'll stack the review panel with business-development types. Then we get every ministry that has input into the review to give positive input. They will be told to be unable to see any problems at all. And I'm talking Environment Canada, Fisheries and Oceans, and, oh yes, Transport Canada, because I guess there'll be tankers involved. When the enviros complain, and this is Cliff's department, we'll simply call them radicals, operating on foreign money, trying to destroy jobs, anti-workingman, and so on and so forth. The usual message.

Dougie: There's a hell of a lot of bureaucrats that are going to be involved, from at least three departments. Are you sure you can keep them all under control?

Unknown voice: Guaranteed. They'll roll over like well-trained dogs, which most of them are. I'll make you a bet. When the environmental review panel delivers its final report, Environment Canada will have no objections, Fisheries and Oceans will have no objections, and Transport Canada will see no problems at all.

Dougie: Are you sure? When I was a kid, I fished on the West Coast. I'm not sure there's any safe tanker routes.

Unknown voice: I'm sure there's all kinds of dangers and risks. All I'm saying is that they'll be ignored. Will you take my bet, sir?

Dougie: [Laughing] Okay, what stakes are we talking?

Unknown voice: Do you have any other projects that you're working on?

Dougie: Well, I've got some clients that may get burned by the Gomery inquiry.

Unknown voice: I wouldn't cheat you, sir. That's already a done deal. We've designated one civil servant to take the fall on the government side and a couple of ad-company execs on the private side. Anything else?

Dougie: There is one other thing. My clients don't want to be just passive buyers. They want to develop equity, which means ownership of the resource. I can see problems there with Investment Canada.

Unknown voice: That's the simplest of all your problems. That board reports to me.

Dougie: In that case, if you can't deliver on a positive result from the Environmental Review Board, you have to get Investment Canada to approve Chinese investment in the oil sands.

Unknown voice: Interesting wager. I accept. And you, sir, if I deliver on my promise to control the Canadian bureaucracy, it means you lose the bet. So what will your penalty be?

Dougie: I don't know. What do you need outside of our existing arrangement?

Unknown voice: Well, sir, believe it or not, there are occasionally things, or more accurately, people, that can't be bought. This opposition is intolerable and unacceptable. It, of course, must be removed, which is the sort of operational skillset that we in Canada don't have a lot of expertise in. So, hypothetically, if we needed to call on you, or more precisely, your clients, in the sort of situation which may or may not occur, could we rely on them to take the sort of necessary, but purely conjectural, actions that I think you know I'm referring to?

Dougie: I believe that the sort of expertise you're referring to could be obtained.

Unknown voice: Excellent. That's gratifying to hear. And in a bet of this type, as I'm sure you can see, there are no losers.

Well, you couldn't call that uninteresting, an Ottawa power broker hinting at using foreign muscle to "remove opposition." I wondered if I could use any of this stuff to give me credibility when I met Ernhardt in the morning. Anything he'd told Dougie he had probably told Steadman, especially the stuff about the oil deal, since Steadman was from Alberta. And if I was Steadman's old friend and colleague, he could well have passed the information on to me. It was a gamble, but I needed some sort of bona fides. And if I could convince Ernhardt that I was in on the action, even on the periphery, who knows what information I might get from him?

I went to bed with my mind whirring at a zillion RPM. That soon changed to REM, but the dreams were fragmentary, unresolved, and strangely unsatisfying. I remembered only speaking to faceless people, trying to convey an urgent message but not having the words to do it. The faceless people disappeared and for some reason I was looking in a mirror. I realized that I was faceless too.

I awoke in time for the morning set, but soon remembered I was a long way from the Halibut Bank. I showered and had two cups of coffee while I previewed the looming meeting. Finally I donned my costume and left.

I walked into the York Hotel just before ten and found my way to the bar. The place exuded the sort of luxury and discretion demanded by wealth and power. I hoped Ernhardt would feel comfortable. I certainly didn't. There was a semi-private alcove by the exit that led to the lobby. I installed myself in a plush armchair and wondered how many nefarious deals had been completed here. When the waiter appeared I ordered a Vodka Collins on the rocks. "My name's Johnson. If someone asks for me, please show him over."

I was enjoying my second sip, trying to keep the ice away from my sensitive front teeth, when a man in an expensive overcoat approached the bar, said something to the waiter, glanced in my direction and then walked toward me. Ernhardt was not only well-dressed, he was well-shaved, well-coiffed, well-fed, and well-mannered. The sleaze was almost concealed.

"Mr. Johnson," he said, holding out his hand. "I'm Cliff Ernhardt."

I'd decided to play it tough, which saved me from having to shake his hand. I gestured with my drink. "Sit down." By the time he'd hung up his overcoat and sat, the waiter had come and gone and Ernhardt had a drink, which he used as a stage prop. He swirled the liquid in a confident manner, took a deliberate sip and considered the drink as if it was the only thing worthy of his attention. Then he looked at me.

"Why don't you tell me your story, Mr. Johnson?"

"Steadman and I go way back. We've been partners in a number of ventures and we've always kept in touch, sort of kept each other up-to-date on our latest deals. So when I found myself in Ottawa, I looked Gerry up. That was the night of July 3, the night he was shot." I took a ruminative sip of my drink and stared at the gilded ceiling.

Ernhardt asked anxiously, "What time were you there?"

"I guess I got up to his suite just before nine. We had a few drinks, shot the breeze. He told me about the deal you're working on with the pipeline boys."

Ernhardt relaxed a bit. "So you could give me an alibi. You can back me up that I was gone by nine o'clock."

I looked at him coolly. "Yeah, I could give you an alibi. If I said you weren't there at nine o'clock."

All the tension left Ernhardt's body. He looked like he was back on familiar ground, back in control. "How much do you want?"

I tried to sound disappointed. "Cliff, you misunderstand the situation. Money's not the object here. I'm a professional, just like you. And just like you, I deal in information and . . ." I waved my drink. "You know."

"Know what?"

"Access, Cliff. Access and information. These are the currencies we're dealing in here."

He thought that over. "Okay, what do you want to know?"

"For starters, what can you tell me about Doug Tarkenen, used to be a reporter with the *Times*?"

"Nothing. Never met the guy."

"Suppose I produce an e-mail from you, asking for a meeting with Tarkenen?"

"Big deal. I try and meet with all the press. I asked Tarkenen for a meeting. It never happened. He went missing or something, didn't he?" Ernhardt sounded awfully confident, almost like he was telling the truth.

I leaned forward and put both arms on the table. "I have good information that you had a connection with Tarkenen."

He spread his hands. "All right. I thought I had a leak somewhere and the leak went to Tarkenen. But I can assure you I never met the guy."

Again, Ernhardt's words had the ring of truth, more so than even a professional liar can achieve. I gambled on another tack. "I'd like to meet the Committee. I have a proposal."

Ernhardt leaned back in his chair. "Mr. Johnson, the Committee is not exactly the Wednesday-evening book club. These are important guys. Exclusive." With emphasis: "Very exclusive."

I leaned forward in my chair. "Mr. Ernhardt, I'm working on a hugely important play. I think it's very important to both of us." With emphasis: "Very important." I took a long sip of my drink. "Are you telling me that getting you off the hook for a murder is not worth setting up a fucking meeting?" I stood up and turned to go.

Ernhardt half rose while making placating gestures with every appendage he had. "Mr. Johnson, relax. I didn't say no, I just said it wouldn't be easy. Sit down. Let's have another drink." He waved for the waiter. By the time our drinks had been delivered, Ernhardt was much more his old calculating self. Coincidentally, I was Jimmie now. Or was it Jimmy? Definitely not Jimi. "Jimmie, like you say, we're both professionals, so let's approach this in a professional manner. How about the minute I receive assurances that you've told the police you were with Steadman from nine o'clock onwards and that I wasn't there, I'll be happy to introduce you to the Committee."

I thought this over. "Okay, Cliff, I believe we have the basis of a deal. Only two problems. I need some kind of guarantee that you'll come through on your end if I go to the cops. And if I go to the cops, there's the danger that I'll put myself in the frame because I become the probable last person to see Steadman alive. There are ways around that. I just have to get certain things in place. I'll give you a call tomorrow, and you be ready with some sort of guarantee for me." That nonsense about putting myself in the frame was just to buy some time. Asking Cliff for a guarantee was not. I saw that as a way to lever more information out of him.

Cliff pulled his wallet out and handed me a card. "That's a secure number. Anytime you call me, use that one."

I threw a twenty on the table and walked out before I'd have to shake his hand.

As I walked back to my hotel I thought over what I'd heard. I was sure I'd learned something, but I didn't know what. When I got to my room I phoned Big Frank's sports bar and asked for Phil. "Tell him it's his mother calling." When he came on the line, I said, "Son, kind of early to be in a bar, isn't it?"

"What can I say? I love sports."

"Great. Let's play Twenty Questions. When Ernhardt sent you

out to the coast to steal those tapes, what did he tell you about them?"

"Not much. Just that there'd been a leak and somehow that reporter had got hold of some tapes of revealing conversations."

That had probably come from Lou Bernier, Dougie's editor. "And who was on the tapes? Who was doing the talking?"

"I don't know everyone. You heard them. Mostly it was Ernhardt and Gerry Steadman."

I felt faint. "Thanks, Phil."

"That's only two questions."

"Game called on account of stupidity." I hung up.

Gerry Steadman was Dougie! I knew Dougie had been playing some sort of role, but it had never occurred to me that the role was Gerry Steadman. Now I understood the string ties we'd found when Alex and I looked through Dougie's clothes: just part of the costume if you're supposed to be an Albertan. As I continued to think it through, I could see that I needed to change a lot of my assumptions. It meant that Dougie had not disappeared on Canoe Lake or even been made to disappear on Canoe Lake. He had been shot to death in a suite of the Château Laurier sometime on the night of July 3. It took a long time for that to sink in. I had completely accepted the idea of him being drowned, accidentally or otherwise. Being shot to death seemed like a different movie altogether.

The question now became was Dougie shot as Dougie or as Gerry Steadman? If the shooter had knowingly shot Dougie Tarkenen, it was probably because his cover had been broken. My bet was on that scenario, but it was possible the shooter had thought he was shooting Gerry Steadman, because Steadman had somehow come to pose a threat to him. In any case, it was obvious that I would have to have another talk with Staff Sergeant Carl Stala.

But Jesus, there were pitfalls there. Stala would want the tapes. Could I give them to him? There was nothing on the tapes that Stala shouldn't know except that a lowly reporter had been handing out hundreds of thousands of dollars. It was part of an act, but the money was real, and it might come out that the total amount was a million dollars. I might have to lose tape five. Or could I hint to Stala that Dougie had once run a grow-op?

I phoned home. Cousin Danny first, because I wanted to talk to Oshie later, when the kids were in bed. "Hey, cuz."

"Ollie! How's it going? Any news?"

"Yeah. Yeah, you could say there's some news." I paused to collect my thoughts, or maybe out of sheer reluctance to say the words "Dougie was shot." Finally, I had to speak. "I know you still follow Ottawa events. Did you hear about the murder of Gerry Steadman?"

"Yeah, some big-time wheeler-dealer from Alberta. Shot in his suite at the Château Laurier."

"It was Dougie. Gerry Steadman was Dougie."

Silence. Then, "But Steadman moved in rarefied air. Reliable people tell me he was making major payoffs. Where did Dougie get all that money?"

"Cuz, when Dougie and I were young and foolish, we did something that was, strictly speaking, against the law."

It didn't take Danny long. "The cash-buyer heist. West-Coast herring fleet, 1990. You little fuckers. I knew it had to be fishermen that pulled it off. And now that I think about it, you and Tarkenen were crazy enough to think of it and smart enough to pull it off. So Dougie used his cut to get access to people he hoped would provide him with a major exposé. What did you do with yours?"

"I've still got most of it. But I think I might need to spend it on a conviction. Not one of my convictions. Someone else's conviction."

Danny said, "You know what, cuz? I think you need to come home now. Give what you've got to the local cops and come home. Oshie won't say anything, but this is going to scare the hell out of her. It scares the hell out of me."

"I'm going to talk to Staff Sergeant Stala first thing tomorrow. I might have to hang around for a few days just to liaise with him. But I won't be running around out in the open."

Danny exhaled loudly and I knew he was getting irritated. "Ollie, don't make me come back there and get you."

"Relax. There's just a few loose ends to tie up and then I'll be home."

I hung up and phoned Staff Sergeant Stala. I got his voicemail. "Hello, Staff Sergeant. It's Ollie Swanson. I've got some information regarding the Steadman killing. I'd like to meet with you tomorrow. Give me a call and let me know when would be convenient."

Then I started thinking about which tapes I could give him. Definitely not number five. It would be too difficult to explain how Dougie had come to possess all the money he was throwing around. But the tapes were all numbered. If I just took out number five, Stala, being a detective, would notice there was one missing. I would have to relabel them. But I couldn't just stick new labels over the old ones. Stala would probably pick up on that. I'd have to make a new set of tapes, excluding number five, and number them one to ten. So I gathered up the tapes and set out for one of those instant offices where they do copies and faxes and let you use their computers. When I found one, they were happy to copy the ten tapes I gave them.

When I got back to my hotel room, the message light on the phone was flashing red. Stala had called and said he'd meet me at eleven. I lay on my bed and thought things over. I was interrupted by a call from Phil Trimmer.

"Ernhardt had me follow you after you left the meeting."

"And did you?"

"Why bother? I know where you stay."

"Good point. Save energy. Just so you know, Jimmie Johnson is in room 427. Coincidentally, in this very same hotel."

Phil grunted and hung up. His phone manners were deplorable. I resumed thinking. Soon it was suppertime, and I thought all the way down to the lobby and into the restaurant. Of course, I had to stop thinking while I ate—New York steak, baked potato, Greek salad—but I thought all the way back to my room and right up to nine o'clock, when I phoned Oshie.

By now she recognized the number on call display. "Ollie, I was hoping you'd call. How are you, sweetie?"

At the sound of her voice, my personal gravitational field suddenly decreased by half. I hadn't realized the weight I'd been carrying. "Hi, honey. How are you and the kids?" This was banal beyond belief, but to me it was important beyond belief.

"Oh, we're fine. The kids got their report cards today. Ollie, they're doing so well. They're scholars. Just like their dad." When I stopped laughing, she continued, "And how are you, Ollie? Are you any closer to Dougie's story?"

"Well, no, actually. But I have found out some pretty important stuff." So I told her.

Her response was immediate concern for me. "I know that was an awful shock for you. But Ollie, you've already grieved once. You don't have to go through it again. Dougie would most certainly not have wanted that."

"I know, honey. But it was a shock. The only thing I'm feeling right now is anger. I have to make sure Dougie's killer is caught."

Her voice lightened a bit. "I know you do, Ollie. But you know what? Maybe you should take a bit of a break. You've been gone almost two weeks now and the kids miss you. Why don't you come home for a bit? If the police can't catch the killer without your help, you can always go back."

"Maybe you're right, Oshie. I'm meeting with the police tomorrow. After that I'll have a better idea where things stand. I'll call you tomorrow night." I hung up and tried to think some more, but I was all thought out. I brushed my teeth and went to bed.

As usual, I didn't get to choose my dreams. I was in the mood for a romantic comedy, but what I got was sort of a film noir horror show. I found myself in a miniature casino, watching two hooded figures throw dice. It was cold. I felt sick with apprehension, though I didn't know why. The gamblers were intent on their game, oblivious to the patients who crowded the hospital room where we now were. One of the patients began choking, and I knew she was dying. I asked the dice thrower to call a doctor, but he ignored me. Then a child reached out to me, eyes pleading for help. We needed a doctor, and I shook the shoulder of the dice thrower. He turned to me and I was shocked to see it was Dougie. He screamed at me to go away. "This is too important. I have to win this bet!" I wondered what they were playing for. In a rush, a scene passed before me that stretched from the sand beaches of Tofino to the barren cliffs of Labrador, with people working and playing and reading stories to their children. I startled to realize what the players were gambling for. I never found out who won.

Or even what the evening sky was doing.

Thirteen

About nine the next morning I let myself into Jimmie Johnson's hotel room and phoned the secure number Ernhardt had given me. When he answered, I said, "I'm supposed to see Stala this morning. I'm prepared to tell him what we discussed, but I need assurances that you won't stiff me."

Ernhardt sounded eager. "What can I offer you?"

"Give me the name of the person you've been dealing with on the pipeline side of things."

Now he sounded nervous. "Why do you want to know that?"

"Because if you stiff me, I'll go to the guy and tell him you're a fucking welsher and can't be trusted. You want me to talk to Stala or not?"

"All right. But you've got to promise me that if you ever approach the guy to make some kind of deal, and I'm not saying you shouldn't, but if you do, you've got to give me a heads-up first. Okay?"

I grunted.

"The guy's name is Tap Dickens of Crude Operations Inc. He's a hard-ass pipeline guy and he's liquid as hell."

"Okay, Ernhardt. We've got a deal. Don't forget your end." I hung up.

I was at the police station on the dot of eleven o'clock. I asked for Staff Sergeant Stala and was led into his office. Stala shook my hand while pretending he was glad to see me and then came right to the point.

"So Mr. Swanson, what have you got for me?"

"Two things. I recovered the tapes." I placed the copies on his desk. "And I can ID your body."

Stala's frown deepened. "We know who the body is. It's Gerry Steadman."

I shook my head. "I don't think so. Any chance I could view the body?"

"Sure, but is an urn of ashes going to be much help?"

I was shocked. "You cremated the body?"

"The body had been identified by hotel staff as Gerry Steadman. We'd done the autopsy and all the toxicology. We can't keep bodies in the morgue forever. Although we kept one small square of tissue for DNA analysis."

I told myself that ignorance was no reason for embarrassment, so I pressed on. "That was stupid, I guess. I don't know much about police procedures. Let's try this. Did the body have any tattoos?"

"Yes. Adolf Hitler, for one. We think he may have had some association with one of those Albertan white supremacist groups."

"It wasn't Adolf Hitler. It was George Orwell. And printed under the picture were the words, 'All art is propaganda, but not all propaganda is art.'"

His eyes widened just a bit and he hesitated before reluctantly accepting what I had been even more reluctant to accept.

"Okay," he said, "who was it?"

"My friend Dougie Tarkenen, the reporter for the *Ottawa Times*. He posed as Gerry Steadman, sort of a bagman-slash-lobbyist, so he could get some dirt on the gang that runs this town."

"And did he find any?"

"Some of it's on those tapes. The bulk of it must be contained in the story he was writing, which I haven't managed to find yet. I think someone found out that Gerry Steadman was really a newspaper reporter who was on the verge of writing a really damning story, and they killed him, Dougie, because of it."

Stala nodded. "That's certainly plausible."

"There's one other possibility," I continued. "The killer didn't know Steadman was a false personality and killed him as Gerry Steadman. But I think that's unlikely."

"Okay, Mr. Swanson," Stala said, "you've raised some very interesting possibilities. But before we get ahead of ourselves, we need to be positive that you're right about the identity of the body. Is there a next of kin who could ID the body from our autopsy photos?"

I shuddered. "His only living relative is his aunt Helga, but I wouldn't want to put her through that. If you don't trust me to make the ID, what about dental records? I could put you in touch with his dentist back home, but Dougie lived in Ottawa for six years. You should be able to track down his dentist here."

"We'll do our best, Mr. Swanson. Anything else?"

"Yes. There are at least two new avenues to pursue. First, I understand you have some material that Dougie left that implicates Ernhardt. If I could look at that material, I might be able to shed some new light on it, just because I knew Dougie so well."

Stala shook his head. "We've managed to keep that stuff out of the public eye up until now. That's important if we ever go to trial. I can't risk that evidence leaking to the press and becoming worthless at trial."

"Why would I do anything to jeopardize the case? Plus, I've just brought you your best lead so far. You were at a dead end, for Christ's sake."

He pondered this for a minute. "All right, you can see everything we've got. But God help you if there's a leak. What's the second thing?"

I knew this was going to be a tough sell, and I didn't really have an inner salesman I could call on. So I called on my inner fisherman and baited the hook. "Right now Ernhardt is the prime suspect. But there's fourteen of his close associates who also would feel a lot safer with Dougie dead. I don't know their names, but they call themselves the Committee. Ernhardt has offered to introduce me to them, but only if I deliver on something for him."

"What's that got to do with me?"

"Well, Ernhardt thinks I'm someone else, a guy called Jimmie Johnson. I contacted him as Jimmie Johnson and managed to convince him that I was an old friend of Steadman's and that Steadman had told me a lot of the stuff that he and Ernhardt had been talking about. And from listening to the tapes, I knew enough stuff to make myself convincing."

Stala looked at me like you would a strange and wonderful animal. "Man, you West-Coast boys are really something. You're like a race of natural-born con men."

I flushed. "I'm a fisherman, for Christ's sake. But you do what you have to do. And by doing what I've been doing, I'm giving you a chance to solve this case. A murder case. Plus political corruption on a huge scale."

"To tell you the truth, corruption cases don't interest me much. Hardly anyone ever goes to jail. At least with a murder case, if you nail the guy, you get to slam the door on him for a few years. But I can tell you want something from me. Spit it out."

"When I was stringing Ernhardt along, I told him I'd been having drinks with my old friend Steadman on the night of the murder. I was with him most of the night and Ernhardt was nowhere around. I said I'd tell you that, which would put Ernhardt in the clear, and in return he'd introduce me to the Committee."

"Let me guess. And so you want me to tell Ernhardt that this Jimmie Johnson came in and talked to me and put Ernhardt in the clear?"

"Why not? There's no law against a cop lying to a suspect. And who's to say you're lying? This guy Jimmie Johnson came in and told you something, and then you phone Ernhardt and tell him what Jimmie Johnson told you, and then Jimmie Johnson disappears." I spread my hands. "What could possibly go wrong?"

Stala rolled his eyes to the ceiling. "Man, you West-Coast boys are *deep*, I mean *deeeep*. I gotta get out there and drink some of that water." He reached for his phone.

"Wait! Are you going to phone him?" Stala nodded. "Okay, give me half an hour. Ernhardt's going to phone me right after you talk to him, and I have to be in the right place to take the call. Thanks, Staff Sergeant." I left quickly.

I got a cab back to the hotel and let myself into room 427, the room I'd rented for Jimmie Johnson. I paced around for about fifteen minutes until the phone rang. I picked it up. "Hello."

"You did a good job, Jimmie. I just talked to Stala. He's off my case."

"How did you find me here?"

"This is my town, Jimmie. If a sparrow falleth, I knoweth. Or something like that."

"So wheneth do I meet the Committee?"

"Every second Friday evening we meet at my place for updates and general discussions. The business is usually over by nine, and then we have a few cocktails. That would be a good time to drop in. Coincidentally, Tap Dickens is in town and he'll be there as well. And Jimmie, the Chairman is very old-school, very formal. You know what I mean?"

I knew what it meant: another visit to Harry Rosen. "I hear you, Cliff. See you then."

It was two o'clock Thursday afternoon. I figured what the hell, I might as well get the shopping out of the way. I got the same clerk at Harry Rosen I'd had before, and we had a jolly old time discussing appropriate evening wear. This wasn't England, so I assumed evening wear didn't mean tails. We decided that a dark business suit would fit the occasion. And what exactly was the occasion anyway? Initiation into a secret society or interview for a fraternity or prelude to a gang bang? The last thought worried me because I knew I wasn't part of the gang.

I picked out a dark blue suit and was measured extensively for the alterations. The measurer asked me if I "dressed right" and I said, "Of course I do." The ensemble was completed with a snow-white silk shirt, a maroon tie with beige stripes, and black brogues. They said the suit would be ready in a couple of hours, so I went for a walk, had a spicy hot dog from a sidewalk vendor and stopped at a newsstand to read the headlines in the scandal mags. My favorite was, *Chocoholic mom gives birth to sugar-covered baby!* I hoped she wouldn't lick it to death.

I went back to Harry Rosen and tried on my suit. It might be an overstatement to say I looked svelte, but I looked pretty damn good: like Mats Sundin on NHL awards night, only with more hair. They hung the suit in a bag for me, and I walked back to the hotel while I pondered my next move. I decided it was time to have a little talk with Dougie's editor, Lou Bernier. After I dropped off the suit at my room, I took a cab over to the *Ottawa Times* building.

While I was waiting to see Bernier, Alex Porter walked in. "Ollie, where've you been the last few days? I've been expecting you to call. Have you found any new leads?"

141

His anxiousness was a little off-putting. When I sort of hedged and danced clumsily around his questions, he gave me a baleful look before walking away.

When they finally allowed me into Bernier's office, he was signing papers his secretary placed in front of him while giving instructions on the phone and scrolling through e-mail on his computer. I wasn't impressed. Hell, I could simultaneously steer a boat, talk on the VHF and speculate about the price of shrimp. Finally the secretary left and Lou hung up the phone, although he didn't take his eye off the computer screen. "Mr. Swanson, what's up? Have you discovered anything about the story Dougie was working on?"

"Lou, what have they got on you?"

He looked at me for the first time. "I beg your pardon?"

"I had you figured for a straight guy. Dougie always spoke highly of you. Yet you've been leaking stuff to Ernhardt. And you killed the story Dougie wrote and lied to me that you'd never seen it."

His poker face fell away for a split second, but he quickly regrouped. "You've got a nerve, Swanson. Who the hell do you think you are to question my integrity?"

I reached into my pocket and took out a piece of paper. I placed it on his desk. It was the printout of Dougie's e-mail to Bernier, asking him what he thought of the story he'd given him in the form of a memory stick. It took Bernier three seconds to read it, and after those three seconds he was twenty years older. He sat slumped in his chair for what seemed a long time. Finally he mumbled, "Come with me" and walked out of the office.

I thought of Bernier as the enemy, but I just couldn't think of him as posing a physical threat, so I followed him. We took an elevator down to the parking garage and Bernier led the way to an almost new Japanese sedan. He unlocked the doors and we got in, and then he reversed out of the parking stall and squealed away toward the exit. We drove for about twenty minutes in complete silence, until we reached an area of upscale shops and condos. Bernier drove into a parking garage and parked. We got out; he locked the car and then led the way toward the elevator.

Up on the tenth floor, Bernier let us into a well-appointed if somewhat sterile condo. He paused for a moment in the hallway, as if to gather strength, and then walked into the living room. I followed. Bernier stood in front of the gas fireplace and pointed to a picture hanging on the wall above it. It was an eight-by-ten, professionally done photo of a woman in early middle age. She was what used to be called a handsome woman, with strong features and dark brown hair with a bit of a wave, and she gazed out of the photo with a confident and genial expression.

"My wife," Bernier said. "She died of breast cancer, May 17, 1996." He went over to a sideboard, picked up a bottle of scotch and looked at me inquiringly. I nodded. He poured two tall drinks, handed me one and gestured to an armchair while he sat at one end of a matching couch.

"Breast cancer," he said. "Sometimes I think of it as a human being, a thug like Saddam Hussein; stupid, brutal, powerful, cruel, implacable, unjust, capricious, malicious, malignant, *goddamn* cocksucking . . ." He stopped himself. "She was actually diagnosed in 1993. She went through a radical mastectomy, radiation treatment, and a full course of chemotherapy. Strong woman. Didn't complain once. I'd falter occasionally and *she'd* comfort *me*. Strong woman." He sipped his drink as he stared at something that didn't appear to be there. "We thought we had it beat. She was in remission for two years, and then it came back. Metastasized into her lungs. There's a lovely word for you.

Metasta-fucking-sized." He took another drink, more of a gulp this time.

"We knew it was a death sentence. For the first time in our married life, I had a hard time talking to her. It was like she was standing on the other side of a barrier. But that was me, not her. She didn't really change. Just accepted it and decided to live the rest of her life. Strong woman. I was absolutely terrified of the lung cancer. It's a terrible, awful way to die, not being able to breathe. We talked about ending it early but kept putting off the decision. In the end, she caught a break. The cancer spread to her brain and that's what killed her. Died in her sleep. Caught a break there."

I sat motionless, clasping my untouched and forgotten drink. Mercifully, Bernier didn't seem to expect any form of response from me.

"When the cancer came back, I got a bit desperate. The doctors couldn't do anything more than alleviate the symptoms, and they told us that. I started looking at alternative medicine, and there's lots of it around. It all costs money, though, especially if you have to fly to Mexico to get it."

I sat frozen, as if movement would have been a sign of disrespect, although Bernier seemed oblivious to me and just about everything else.

"Our circle of friends at the time was very supportive, and Ernhardt was one of them. The women would bring over food and the men would take me out and try to get me drunk, but I was in a fog. We kept spending money on dodgy treatments, and I knew in the back of my mind that I was outspending my income, but at the end of the month there was always more money in our account than I expected. But, like I say, I was in a fog, or acting like a football player with a concussion—functioning, but strictly automatic pilot, you know?"

I nodded, as if my participation was necessary.

"Anyway, one time Ernhardt took me aside and said not to worry about money. 'You get Patty anything she needs,' he said. 'Let your friends worry about your bank balance.' And I was happy to do that. I would have done the same if the situation was reversed. What are friends for?

"At the funeral, Ernhardt came up to me and said, 'Don't worry about paying the money back.' Everybody had been happy to help out. Christ, I didn't even know how much money it was. About six months after the funeral, we ran a series of stories about how an insurance company was ripping off consumers, refusing to pay claims. Turns out it was one of Ernhardt's clients. He phoned me up. 'Lou, can you lighten up on that story a bit? I'm not asking you to kill it, just try not to make my guy out to be such a criminal. He's just a businessman, trying to make a living.'

"How could I refuse? I rewrote the article and the reporter almost quit. The next time, he wanted me to actually kill a story. 'Lou, we've been through so much together. We were there for you, buddy. I know Patty appreciated what little help we could give. Now this is my hour of need. I need help, buddy.' How could I refuse? But once you kill a story, you've crossed a line. He knew he had me. A year later I had to fire a reporter because Ernhardt told me to."

His drink was empty by this time. He looked at my full drink and got up to pour himself another one.

I cleared my throat. "What exactly did you tell Ernhardt about those tapes that Dougie made?"

"Just that Dougie had taped some conversations that might be a bit incriminating. Dougie could be very persuasive. He had a knack for getting people talking, especially if it was over drinks."

"Did Dougie ever talk to Gerry Steadman?"

"Don't know. Don't know if they ever met."

So now I knew that Dougie had never told Lou that he was posing as Steadman, maybe because of journalistic ethics. And because Lou didn't know, Ernhardt didn't know. I was the only one who had made the connection between Dougie and Gerry Steadman. "Lou, did you read Dougie's story?"

"Oh yes. And what a story. Well-researched, well-written, well-organized, well-documented. It would have been a huge sensation."

"Does Ernhardt know about the story?"

"Not the details of it. I try to convince myself that I might even run it one day."

"Lou, I need that story."

"What, and let you scoop me?"

"Lou, you're never going to run the fucking story." I decided to play it the Cliff Ernhardt way, tighten the screws until you get what you need and ignore the screams. "Lou, what do you think happened to Dougie?"

"He drowned in Canoe Lake?"

"You don't think that's a bit too much of a coincidence? Dougie writes a story that'll rip the Committee to pieces, maybe put a lot of them in jail. Ernhardt would do anything to kill that story. You know he would. And the only way to kill that story was to kill Dougie."

"You're jumping to conclusions."

"I wonder if the police would agree with that. I wonder if that story contains any clues that would shed light on his death. And I wonder if they might not like to see that story. And I especially wonder if they would consider it obstruction of justice to conceal that story."

Lou Bernier in his prime would have laughed and told me to fuck off. But this Lou Bernier was old and tired and sick at heart.

He walked over to a rolltop desk and unlocked a small drawer. He took out a memory stick and tossed it to me.

"I don't know how this is going to play out, Lou. But I'll do my best to cover your ass." All the way back to my room I tried to convince myself that those words made up for what I'd done.

And the evening sky imagined our fate.

Fourteen

I phoned Oshie and told her I had some things to do the next day and if nothing dramatic happened I would fly home the day after. That would be my twelfth day in Ottawa. It would be one day too many.

The next morning I phoned Staff Sergeant Stala and made an appointment to see him at ten thirty. Then I inserted the memory stick into the computer and began to read Dougie's story. There wasn't a lot that was new to me having heard the tapes. But it was better organized, with lots of background research and references to other related stories. To the uninitiated, it would be explosive. Careers would be ruined and charges would be laid. It provided ample motive for murder. I had just come to the end of the first installment when it was time to leave to see Stala. I wondered if Dougie had written an ending, or if the ending was still up in the air, or if there even was such a thing as an ending.

On my way to the police station, I stopped at an electronics shop and made three copies of the memory stick. When I was ushered into his office, I gave one of them to Staff Sergeant Stala. "That's the story Dougie was working on. I've only read the first part, but it's explosive. Definitely a motive for murder."

"Where'd you find it?"

"Dougie had given it to someone for safekeeping and they kept it safe." Stala gave me a look but said nothing. "I was hoping I could get a look at the material you found at the murder scene. Also, I was wondering about the time of death. Do you have an accurate estimate?"

"Analysis of his stomach contents puts it at around 9:30 PM. But that could be plus or minus an hour or so." He got up and went over to a filing cabinet and took out a file folder and a cassette tape. "This tape"—he waved it at me—"was found at the scene along with some documents. It just happens to be a duplicate of tape ten of the bunch you gave me. By the way, all the ones you gave me are duplicates as well. Presumably the originals are still hidden somewhere." He handed me the file folder. "These are copies of documents we found hidden under the mattress. The originals are in the evidence lockup. You'll find them very interesting."

Inside the folder was a two-page affidavit signed by Gerry Steadman. It stated that Steadman had given Ernhardt two million dollars, but only one million had made it to the Committee. It further stated that he, Steadman, would keep quiet about the discrepancy if Ernhardt paid him two hundred and fifty thousand dollars. Wow! That was definitely food for thought. It explained why the cops had focused on Ernhardt as a prime suspect. They had no way of knowing that the affidavit was bullshit. Steadman, AKA Dougie Tarkenen, had never had two million dollars. Dougie had obviously been trying to set Ernhardt up. But for what? Dougie couldn't have known that murder was in the offing.

"If you take that at face value," Stala said, "your friend gave Ernhardt two million dollars. That's a lot of money to save up on a reporter's salary."

"It's ridiculous. Dougie never had two million dollars." I omitted the fact that he'd had a hell of a lot more than the average newspaper reporter.

I thought out loud. "Dougie was running some kind of game. I don't know exactly what kind of a game, but it certainly gives Ernhardt a motive for murder. And that tape—it's probably the most incriminating of them all. You've heard it. There's someone talking about rigging bureaucratic approval for Chinese access to Canadian oil. And there's a reference to using Chinese muscle to get rid of opposition. And that gives whoever is speaking on the tape a good motive for murder as well as Ernhardt."

Stala nodded. "It does that. But we need hard evidence."

"What have you got so far?"

"Ernhardt had powder residue on his hand, but that's explained by the fact that he had been target shooting. The only prints on the gun are on the barrel, but they're your friend's, like he'd grabbed the gun to deflect it. The stock had been wiped clean. The gun is unregistered. We know Ernhardt was there that night, but he says he left around eight thirty. But someone was in the room at nine, because the waiter heard the sounds of an argument when he delivered a bottle of wine."

A question occurred to me. "How do you know Ernhardt was there that night? Did he voluntarily come forward?"

"No. A reporter from the *Ottawa Times*, Alex Porter, was there that night interviewing someone, and he saw Ernhardt walk through the lobby."

"Alex didn't tell me he was the one who fingered Ernhardt. I didn't know he was there that night."

Stala frowned. "Probably because I asked him to keep quiet about it. I don't like leaks."

"I've noticed that," I said. "You should have been a shipwright."

Stala ignored me. "Anyway, that's not enough to get us an indictment. The Crown attorney wants more. Connect Ernhardt to the gun, a witness who puts him at the hotel after nine, or—fantasy time—a confession." Stala gave a what-are-ya-gonna-do kind of shrug. "By the way, we found Tarkenen's dentist. His records match the victim."

That jolted me a bit. Dougie? Victim? The two words didn't

seem to belong together. Neither did my knowledge of Dougie and the emerging image of someone running some kind of convoluted con. What the hell had Dougie been up to?

Stala continued, "In light of the new ID, we went back and looked at Steadman's identification papers, driver's license, credit cards. Fakes, very good and expensive fakes, but fakes nevertheless. Your friend must have spent maybe ten grand on them."

"Well, Dougie earned a good salary and he didn't spend much."

I needed to go someplace where I could think. "I'm going to keep plowing through the story material that Dougie put together. Something might strike me. Also, I'm meeting Ernhardt and the Committee tonight. That'll give us some more names to work with."

"Give me a call tomorrow morning," Stala said. "I'll be here for a couple of hours at least."

I found a post office and mailed one of the copied memory sticks to Danny. I was going to send the other one to Oshie but thought better of it. It would look too much like an insurance policy, which it was, and I didn't want Oshie thinking I needed insurance. So I sent it to my dad, with a note asking him to hold on to it for me.

My meeting with the Committee wasn't until that evening, so I had a lot of time to kill and no sophisticated weapons to do it with. Outnumbered by the threatening hours, I began a war of attrition with a slow walk around Parliament Hill. Two down. A prolonged window-shop did in a few more, and then supper hour took care of another one. The last of them was dealt with by a slow read of the *Globe and Mail*, and then it was time to take a cab to Ernhardt's house in the suburbs.

The Ernhardt abode was set well back on a spacious lot. Through still-bare maple trees, roadside viewers would catch appealing glimpses of a red brick structure that many, but not I, would have called a mansion. I was damned if I was going to dignify Ernhardt's weasel hole by calling it a mansion. It was, nevertheless, an imposing weasel hole. An attractive brown-skinned woman, a real-life maid, answered the door. Upon hearing my name, she granted me entrance.

The Committee was loosely gathered in what they wouldn't have referred to as the living room. It took up most of the rear of the house, with a back wall entirely of glass. It might have afforded a scenic view, but now it offered only reflections, lamentably unscenic.

There were three or four clumps of important-looking men engaged in earnest conversation. My entrance had in no way changed the racial or gender purity of the room. When Ernhardt saw me, he detached himself from one of the groups, launched a smile in my direction and followed it with a cringe-worthy unctuousness. "Mr. Johnson, thanks for coming by. Great to see you. Can I get you a drink?"

"Thanks, Cliff. Would you happen to have a few drops of the Macallan?"

He chuckled. "We certainly do. There's a few people here who appreciate"—and here he affected a Scottish accent—"a wee dram of the golden nectar." He led me to the bar and poured me a shot from the appropriate bottle. I resisted the urge to ask for Coke in it. "Let me introduce you to some of our people." He placed his hand lightly on my elbow and guided me to a group of four men who were in various stages of unwinding. All of them had loosened their ties, and one rebel had removed his suit jacket.

"Gentlemen, let me introduce Jimmie Johnson. As I mentioned earlier, he's an old friend and colleague of Gerry Steadman, and, if I'm not mistaken, he has an eye toward taking over some of Gerry's files. Am I right, Jimmie?"

"Well, Cliff, I'm still in a bit of shock at losing Gerry. We go way back together. But if you think it might be useful to try to rebuild the network that Gerry put together, I think I could do it." What utter bullshit! But it came out so easily.

One of the men, almost my height but considerably heavier, reached out and shook my hand. "Mr. Johnson, Colin Peterson. We all miss Gerry, but sometimes a man's work is more important than the man. In spite of his tragic death, his work must go on. If you could reconnect us with his backers, it would forward the agenda immensely."

I nodded and looked contemplative. The man in shirtsleeves waved his drink in my direction. "Glad you dropped in, Mr. Johnson. I'm Arnold Moody, Dr. Moody to these guys. What's your take on the shooting? I gather the police aren't making much headway."

"It doesn't make much sense. Gerry was such a sweetheart of a guy, no enemies at all. I can only guess the motive was robbery. Gerry did occasionally deal in large amounts of cash." There was a reverent pause, presumably at the mention of money. The other two introduced themselves, and I unfortunately forgot their names, remembering only that one was "in communications" and one "in manufacturing."

Ernhardt led me over to another group and we did another round of introductions. One guy announced himself as Tap Dickens of Crude Operations Inc. and gave me a coolly appraising look from behind steel-rimmed spectacles. Broad-shouldered, he was younger and fitter-looking than any of the others. As we went through the standard small talk, Dickens continued to look me up and down. At the first pause in the choreographed inanities, he took half a step toward me and said, "Mr. Johnson, I'm afraid I'm not as impressed by your friend Mr. Steadman as these gentlemen are. Not to speak ill of the dead, but I think he might have oversold himself. My contacts in Beijing have never heard of him."

"I'm not surprised," I said. "China is a big country, and there are numerous different factions, none of them fully aware of what the others are up to. There are three different factions in the central committee, there's the politburo, and the army is also a major economic player. And on top of that there's the rise of regional semiprivate industrial concerns." Where the hell did I get all this stuff? It just flowed out of me.

Dickens frowned at me. "You seem remarkably up-to-date on Chinese affairs. Where do you get your information?"

"I've always been interested in China. My great-uncle was a friend of Norman Bethune. Black sheep of the family, of course, but any connection is a good connection, eh?" It was almost as if I was possessed, my mind hijacked by a glib, smooth-talking *operator*.

Ernhardt certainly liked my act. He put his arm around me and said, "I think we're really lucky you contacted us, Jimmie. It's important that we reestablish the link with Gerry's Chinese clients, and I think you can do it."

I nodded humbly and glanced at Dickens. He wasn't buying it. *Oh well, you can't impress everybody.* During the course of the next half hour, I was introduced to and schmoozed with all of the members of the Committee. There were the other "collectors," each of them displaying the same wide smiles and narrow eyes, and the assorted businessmen who bent my ear about the immorality of "entitlements" while promoting the "rights of capital."

And then there was the other economist, a columnist for the *National Post*. He went on for an excruciatingly long time about how all the problems of First Nations communities could be solved by giving individuals the right to own land on their reserves. I couldn't help but think, or maybe it was Dougie thinking with my brain, that First Nations people needed a hell of a lot more than ownership of their meager allotment of reserve land. What they really needed was ownership of some of the resources in their territories. I shook my head to get Dougie out of my brain and flashed a generic smile all around. "Damn right. Economic policy shouldn't be racially based." But Dougie again (*damn it, man, get out of my head—I'm trying to concentrate*) insisted on the last word. "But economic policy was racially based for years. First Nations weren't allowed to commercially fish or vote or consult lawyers." *Dougie! Get out of my head. I'm doing a high-wire balancing act here and I don't need anyone jiggling the wire.*

I almost felt him give me the familiar punch on the shoulder, and then I was left alone with a bunch of people I didn't really want to be with. But I smiled and I nodded and I agreed and I acquiesced, and, having passed through the valley of the shadows of falsehood, I was eventually presented to the Chairman.

He was sitting in a chair by the window. Two acolytes attended to him, leaning over as if trying to inhale the man's essence, the pheromone of power. He had obviously transcended the need for the standard suit of business blue and was dressed in beige slacks, brown tweed sports jacket, and—I swear this is true—a maroon ascot. He must have been over seventy, but he was militarily upright in the chair and regarded the room with the unblinking calm of a tortoise king.

Ernhardt introduced me, and when the Chairman spoke, I felt a chill as I recognized his voice. It was the unknown voice from Dougie's tapes, the voice I'd heard pontificating about introducing genetically engineered salmon to the West Coast and also about guaranteeing bureaucratic endorsement for Chinese access to Canadian oil. And, I uncomfortably recalled, the need to eliminate opposition to the Committee's interests.

The Chairman was staring at me, and I realized I hadn't heard a word he'd said. However, I'd had enough drunken bar conversations with spacey girls dancing to loud music to realize that conversation doesn't necessarily need to be coherent. I summoned up a knowledgeable smile and threw out a word at random: "Absolutely."

That seemed to do the trick, for the Chairman continued in his quietly forceful voice. "I was shocked, as we all were, by the death of Mr. Steadman. I want—we all want—his killer caught." His gaze never wavered from my face, and I was afraid he was reading me like a laser beam reads a DVD. He continued, "It is my sincere hope, our sincere hope, that his death was in no way, in absolutely no way, connected with the project that we were engaged in." He continued to rake me with his eyes. "The fact that you shared so much history with Mr. Steadman gives us a degree of solace, if I may use that word, on two counts. Firstly, you may be able to shed some light on the circumstances that led to his death, and that would relieve the totally unwarranted but nevertheless distracting attention that is being focused on Mr. Ernhardt." He was momentarily diverted by a slight cough and, clearly annoyed at this hint of weakness, covered his mouth with the back of one hand. One of the acolytes offered him something in a glass, and he indulged in the smallest of sips before relocking his eyes on my face. "And secondly, if Mr. Steadman confided at all in you, you may be able, to some degree, to resume his role, or should I say his responsibilities, in respect to the project we were engaged in. Do you think you could do that, Mr. Johnson?"

I put both hands in my pockets and gazed at the ceiling. After a suitably deliberative pause, I nodded slowly. "Gerry confided in me to the extent of revealing some of his contacts. Hell, it was the least he could do after what we'd been through together. Given time and the necessary resources"—here I paused and looked the

Chairman in the eye—"I believe I could pull something together."

The Chairman looked at me for a long time. "Mr. Johnson, you need to know three things. My name outside of this room is Paul Salinger, the business that we are engaged in is of the absolute utmost importance, and we can tolerate absolutely no interference."

I resisted the urge to grovel and placed my feet a little farther apart. Bending over slightly, I stared back at the Chairman with what I hoped was an equally intimidating stare. "My friend is dead. Your project may be dead unless I can reconcile certain people's reluctance with other people's ambitions. Let me see what I can put together."

The Chairman may have nodded. I'm fairly certain that I felt relief flood my body. But there was no doubt about Ernhardt's gentle pressure on my arm as he led me back to the bar. My glass was empty, and, in the only thing I will ever say to Ernhardt's credit, he refilled it. "You made an impression on the old man. I can tell he liked you."

"It was good to finally meet him. Gerry and I came up through the minors together. He made the majors before I did, but I'm a first-line player too. A smart GM and a smart player can help each other's careers, know what I mean?"

Ernhardt smarmed a grin at me. "The Chairman and the other guys totally support you. The only dissenter is Tap Dickens, who's being a hard-ass because, I don't know, maybe because he feels left out or something. Why don't the three of us get together for a coffee tomorrow and try to get comfortable with each other?"

"I've got a 2:00 PM flight, but sure, I wouldn't mind talking to Dickens. We all need to be working out of the same playbook. Let's say nine thirty, in the coffee shop at my hotel. And now, Cliff, if you wouldn't mind calling me a cab, I should start making calls to Beijing."

"No need for a cab. There's lots of drivers outside. Let me get you set up."

Which he did, in a Mercedes something or other driven by a pleasant gentleman who seemed not at all unhappy with my tense silence and who delivered me in the most efficient manner possible to the Hotel Chateauvert.

I had a hard time getting to sleep because I was excited about flying home the next day. I'd never been away from Oshie and the kids for this long, and I could feel myself diminishing. Maybe that's why the character of Jimmie Johnson had been able to overtake me so completely.

Morning found me in the coffee shop waiting for Cliff Ernhardt and Tap Dickens. When they arrived I could see that Dickens's mood hadn't improved since the previous evening. He was still suspicious and hostile, and his attitude was clearly worrying Ernhardt, who babbled nervously about upcoming tax legislation while I tried to look interested. Dickens sat across from me and said nothing. Even when the waitress took our orders, he just shook his head silently. Finally I decided that Jimmie Johnson should be irritated.

"Dickens, what's your problem? I'm doing my best to help you guys out and all I get from you is static."

Dickens looked at me for the first time. "I don't think you're trying to help us as much as you're trying to help yourself. I never met your friend Gerry Steadman, and no one I know has heard of him. I think he was a small-timer playing over his head. The problem is, Mr. Johnson, that this is the big leagues. We can't afford minor leaguers. I've got a lot riding on this project, a hell of a lot, and I can't afford anyone dropping the ball."

I appealed to Ernhardt. "Cliff, was Gerry's money minor league?"

"Oh no, Jimmie, the money was major league. No doubt about that."

This placated Dickens somewhat and his intensity diminished by a couple of decimal points. "All right, I'm going to assume that we're all on the same team. But I want to be absolutely crystal-fucking-clear that if anyone screws this deal up, I will be very angry. And so will my Chinese contacts. They want this pipeline. Hell, they need it. And they're not as namby-pamby as we are. I feel sorry for anyone who gets in their way."

I was saved from having to make an immediate reply when the waitress arrived with my corned beef hash and a poached egg for Ernhardt. Only after I'd swallowed a healthy forkful did I respond to Dickens. Waving my fork vaguely in his direction, I said, "Tap, I may have been born in the country, but I've been downtown ever since. And I've been around the block ninety-nine times with no plans to make it a hundred. Know what I mean?"

I wasn't sure what I meant, but I congratulated myself for sounding impressively tough without actually making any threats. I returned to my corned beef hash. Ernhardt ignored his poached egg while chattering on about the need for teamwork and "parking our egos at the door." Dickens listened in silence and had the decency to refrain from glowering. I quickly disposed of my breakfast, and as we stood to leave, disaster struck.

I was standing at the till when I saw Alex Porter, the reporter with the *Ottawa Times*, walk in. He saw me and, probably because I was standing a little apart from Ernhardt and Dickens, didn't realize that I was with them. He approached with a grin. "Ollie, I haven't seen you for a few days. Any luck finding that story that Dougie was working on?"

Ernhardt's eyes widened and Dickens's narrowed. They stared at me for just a moment before deciding to put as much distance between us as possible. I was left alone with Alex, who seemed to realize that something had just happened, even if he didn't know exactly what. He gave me a blank look and spread his hands. "What?"

Mentally cursing, I forced myself to smile and say something pleasant. "Hi, Alex. I've been busy. Gotta go." And I went. Back in my hotel room, I started a damage assessment. Jimmie Johnson was obviously dead, but that was okay. Jimmie was expendable. I'd used him to get close to Ernhardt, and I'd learned some valuable things. One: Dougie had been posing as a player named Gerry Steadman, and his act had gained credibility from the fact that he'd been able to splash around a million dollars in "access fees" or "consulting fees" or whatever was the current terminology for bribery. Two: He'd gained access to Cliff Ernhardt and the Committee and the Chairman, and had insinuated himself into the political machinations around Chinese access to Canadian oil. Three: For some unfathomable reason, Dougie had been trying to set up Cliff Ernhardt for some kind of a fall, which had turned out to be, obviously unintended, Dougie's, AKA Steadman's, murder.

So what was my next move? Should I go ahead and fly home, or did my blown cover mean I should stay in Ottawa to deal with whatever consequences came howling out of the darkness? It occurred to me that I should probably report to Staff Sergeant Stala. He was in his office when I phoned. "I met a bunch of interesting people last night. Every one of them is a moral black hole capable of worse things than murder. First of all, there's the fourteen members of the Committee, which includes Ernhardt. Then there's the Chairman, Paul Salinger. That's his voice on tape number ten, asking in a very circumspect, roundabout way if Gerry Steadman, through his Chinese connections, could provide killers to remove opposition. There's one other player, Tap Dickens, a hard-ass from Alberta who owns Crude Operations, the pipeline company. He was with me and Ernhardt when my cover got blown, and he was none too happy about it."

"Your cover was blown? Now you tell me. What happened?"

I explained the unfortunate incident. "I can see Ernhardt and his gang going to your boss with a complaint that Jimmie Johnson was vetted by you."

"I can take care of myself. But what about you? You've pissed off some pretty heavy hitters. What if they come after you?" He paused for thought. "I'm going to have to let my boss talk to you. If you need protection, he'll have to authorize it. I'll set up a meeting, but we'll never get him tomorrow. It'll have to wait for Monday. In the meantime, don't leave your hotel room. If there's any attempt at contact from any of these guys, call me immediately. I'll leave my cell on all weekend. All right?"

"All right." I hung up and morosely considered how I was going to tell Oshie that I wouldn't be home today. She took it really well and managed to dissipate most of my guilty feelings, but then I talked to Daiki and Ren and the guilt came back with reinforcements. I spent a miserable evening with sleep denying me her comforting ministrations.

And the evening sky imagined our fate.

Fifteen

I got the phone call Sunday evening. It was Phil Trimmer. He was trying to sound angry but couldn't hide the fear. "Swanson, you asshole!"

My stomach churned uncomfortably. "What's the problem?"

"Ernhardt and some of his friends want to know why, when they sent me to follow Jimmie Johnson, I neglected to tell them that Jimmie Johnson was actually Ollie Swanson, best friend of that fucking reporter, Dougie Tarkenen, who was working on a story that could be extremely embarrassing to Ernhardt and his friends."

"Which friends?"

"You wouldn't know them. They're from a long way away."

"China?"

"You're a smart guy, Swanson. Anyway, I need you to get over here and help dig me out of the shithole you've got me into."

"Are they with you now?"

There was the slightest pause. "No. They want the two of us to go meet them."

"Where?"

"Don't know. I'm supposed to phone them when you get here."

"What number did they give you?"

"Christ, Swanson! I'm in enough trouble already because of you. Just get the fuck over here."

He hung up before I could ask more questions. I immediately dialed Stala's cell. It was shut off. Shit! He had promised to keep it on. What the hell was I supposed to do now? I could always try

Stala's number later. I grabbed my jacket along with the keys to Dougie's dirt bike and left.

I rode the elevator down to the parking garage, found the bike where I'd left it and took off for 721 Belmont Street. I followed the same route to Phil's house as before, but this time I didn't stop to buy a baseball bat. I didn't think the Chinese would want to play ball.

Just like the last time I'd visited Phil, I parked the bike half a block away, but now I approached the house from the back alley. Within two minutes I was standing behind a black minivan, staring at Phil's backyard patio. I made another attempt to phone Stala, but his goddamn phone was still off. I went back to staring at the rear of Phil's house. The inside lights were on, but the back porch light was off. I watched for maybe five minutes, which seemed like an hour, and there was no movement or sound. I took a deep breath and ran crouched over to the back window. I risked a quick peek inside and saw nothing. I forced myself to stand up and take a longer look, and I wished I hadn't.

Phil Trimmer was lying on his back in the middle of his kitchen floor. He was covered in blood. I scanned the room but saw no sign of anyone else. I looked behind me and saw no one. Finally I approached the back door and tried the knob. It was unlocked, so I opened the door and forced myself to enter the house. Phil hadn't moved, and as I crouched down to feel his pulse I could see that he had been badly beaten.

I had my fingertips pressed to what I thought was his carotid artery and my face close to his chest, trying to detect signs of breathing, when something shrilled in my ear. I leapt like a startled deer, adrenaline pumping through my veins. Landing in a defensive crouch, my intentions oscillated wildly from fight to flight to fainting with fear. After interminable milliseconds my rational human brain wrested control from my gibbering animal brain, and I realized that the sound was Phil's cell phone. Following a pause for reset and recovery, I bent down and gingerly extracted it from his pocket. I flipped it open and said, "Hello."

"You could be next, Swanson. Or your family. You better get back to the wife and kids and stop trying to play with the big boys." Whoever it was hung up.

I felt like I was underwater. There were no sounds, and everything was slightly blurry. And my motions were slow and clumsy, as if I were trying to escape from the monster in a nightmare. The sound of a siren brought me to my senses. It was close. I stuffed Phil's phone in my pocket and ran out the back door.

As I ran down the alley, a police cruiser screeched to a stop at Phil's front door. In a minute I was on the bike and going quickly away from that place. When I'd first come to Ottawa, I'd followed an instinct that told me events might lead to me having to hide out somewhere, and I'd established a hidey-hole in the Little Italy district. This seemed to be an appropriate time to use it.

In fifteen minutes I arrived at 953 Adele Avenue. I approached by the back alley, parked the bike in the yard and let myself into the basement suite I'd rented almost two weeks before. I couldn't remember where the light switch was and I fumbled around in the dark for maybe five minutes before I managed to find it. I switched the light on and stood with my head back, trying to think. I always thought with my head tilted back, and I needed the lights on because I couldn't think properly in the dark.

Unfortunately, my brain was locked into the sort of endless feedback loop that never goes anywhere, so I checked my watch. It was nine. I realized I needed to phone Stala. This time he answered, and I barely stopped myself from screaming at him. "Where the hell have you been? I've been trying to get you!"

"Sorry. My phone went dead. I had to charge it."

"I had a call from Phil Trimmer. He's the private dick that stole those tapes from me. In the last week or so we came to sort of an arrangement, and he switched sides, from Ernhardt's to mine. When my cover got blown, it also blew Phil's, because he didn't tell Ernhardt that Jimmie Johnson was really Ollie Swanson. So they leaned on him. He told me I had to go over to his place so we could meet these guys and sort things out. I couldn't get a hold of you, so I went. When I got there, Trimmer was dead, I'm pretty sure. Then a call came in on his cell. Somebody said I could be next and they also threatened my family. Then I heard a siren so I took off. Now I'm hiding out."

"Fuck! I totally fucked things up. Where are you? You need protection. And your family."

"I'm safe for now. And my next call is going to be to the Richmond RCMP to watch my house. But I think you should get someone to watch my hotel room. They might try to take a run at me there."

"Okay, I'll do that right now. But I still want to see you tomorrow. I set up a meeting with my boss at nine in the morning. Now we'll have even more stuff on the agenda."

"I'll be there. But right now I'd like to confirm that Trimmer is really dead. And you should brief whoever gets assigned to that case."

"I'll phone you back."

I paced around for ten minutes before Stala called back. "You were right. He's dead, cause of death unknown at this point. The detective who took the call is a friend of mine. Good cop. He'll be at the meeting tomorrow. You're absolutely sure you're okay?"

"I rented a place two weeks ago, phony name. That's where I am now. When I left Phil's place I was riding a dirt bike. No car could have followed me here."

"Sounds good. But don't go anywhere. Stay put until our meeting tomorrow."

"You got it." After I hung up I left for Ernhardt's house. The door was opened by his maid, who appeared to recognize me, and because of that she reluctantly granted me admission.

"Mr. Ernhardt is with someone," she said in slightly accented English. "I'll see if he can see you. Please wait here."

I was still admiring the well-furnished foyer when Ernhardt came striding in. "What the hell are you doing here? Get the hell out! Now! Before I call the police."

I punched him in the mouth just as hard as I possibly could. I felt several of his teeth rip out of his gums as his head snapped back. By the time he landed on his back on the floor, blood was gushing from his upper and lower lips as well as his gums. I stepped forward and kicked him in the groin. His eyes opened wide and he gurgled in pain as he rolled over into a fetal position. I kicked him again, but it didn't have the same effect. That was disappointing. "You mendacious little turd burglar. You threatened my family. This is what happens to people who threaten my family."

He was shaking his head back and forth and moaning, trying to say something, but his mouth was too damaged to form words. I felt I still hadn't expressed myself adequately, so I picked up an expensive-looking lamp from an expensive-looking table and smashed it against the wall. Then I did the same with the table. A graceful-looking antique chair was soon reduced to kindling. The noise must have attracted Ernhardt's guest, because just as I started to destroy a really beautiful armoire, an Asian man appeared at the far end of the foyer. He surveyed the scene with an impressive calm, appearing not the least bit apprehensive, just a bit puzzled.

"Colonial furniture," I said. "I detest colonial furniture." Then I left.

As I rode through the dark streets back to my hideaway, I realized I was displaying an alarming propensity for violence. Why? I guessed I really didn't like people like these. They'd been screwing people like me for too long. The Family Compact of today was less close and even more compact than it had been in the nineteenth century.

As soon as I got back to Adele Avenue, I phoned Danny. "Cousin, the shit has hit the fan. Someone killed Phil Trimmer and then threatened to do the same to me. Here's the bad part. They also threatened Oshie and the kids." I had to pause to let Danny swear violently. I continued, "So do you think Louise could organize regular patrols of the house? I'll have people on the inside if the cops can watch the outside."

Danny's voice was shaking just a little. "Who do these fuckers think they're dealing with? Of course Louise will organize surveillance of the house. It'll be done right. Who are you going to put inside the house?"

"The Barely Brothers."

This brought a laugh from Danny. "Yeah, they'll be good for that. If anyone gets by the cops they'll wish they hadn't. But how about you? Do you need reinforcements?"

"Not right now. The Ottawa cops have got my back. Also I sent a message, via Cliff Ernhardt, that these guys aren't dealing with some cream-puff bureaucrat."

"I'm going to talk to Louise right now. You be careful. And don't worry about Oshie and the kids. They will be well covered. I mean well covered."

He hung up and I placed a call to the leader of the Barely Brothers, who weren't brothers and weren't barely anything. They had originally been the Barley Brothers, but their friends weren't real good spellers and so someone's error became the new reality.

Their leader, Wall to Wall McKee, was a Queensborough guy, as was the rest of the gang, and they all had that unique Queensborough edge. They were modern-day hunter-gatherers, but what they hunted and gathered were items that were mostly not organic and items that were mostly—how shall I say it?—not theirs. They'd all deckhanded for me at various times, and I'd pulled them out of various scrapes. Wally was now running his own carpet-laying business, and Half a Day Ray worked for him but only managed to get to work in the afternoons. That was okay because the business was more or less a cover for other, less mainstream activities. The third member was One-Eyed Wayne, so named, I'd explained to Oshie, because of his shock of bright red hair. This earned me a punch on the shoulder and an epithet that, because the kids were there, was pronounced "artsmay-assay."

The Barely Brothers did what they needed to do to survive but spent much of their time cheerfully boozing and brawling and extricating themselves with amazing ingenuity from the many "difficulties" they got themselves into.

When Wall to Wall answered the phone he was delighted to hear from me. "Ollie, long time, long time. What the hell are you doing in Ottawa? I didn't know you'd gone into politics. Don't tell your mother. It would break her heart."

"Wally, I can't go into details, but some sleazebags have threatened Oshie and the kids. I can't be there right now, so I was hoping you and Half a Day and One-Eyed Wayne could move into the basement suite and pretend to be doing renovations, or do some renovations, but mainly keep an eye on everyone."

Wall to Wall was suddenly less genial. "Ollie, who are these guys? Do they know who they're dealing with? I assume they didn't deliver the threat in person."

"No. It was over the phone. But I did manage to catch up to

one of them. He was slightly off-key, so I tuned him up a little."

I was treated to the familiar hoarse chuckle. "Okay, pal. Don't worry about a thing. I'll collect the boys and we'll head over there right now."

Next, I had to warn Oshie that the brothers were on their way over and would be staying for a while. And I had to explain why. I downplayed everything as much as I could: I'd upset some people, they'd made the standard generic threat, so I was just taking some precautions. And—bonus!—we could actually get the new carpet we'd been talking about. She pretended to buy all this and finished up with, "Ollie, I know you're doing what you need to do. But the kids need things too. And one of them is you."

"I know, honey. I can see the end of this. I think it's almost to the point where the police can take over and nail the bad guys and I can come home." I hung up and felt miserable until sleep knitted up my raveled vest of guilt.

There was no food in the hideout, so I had to go hungry in the morning. My stomach was growling rebelliously when I left for my meeting with Stala and his boss and the detective who was working the Phil Trimmer murder. Fortunately, I found them still in the coffee-and-muffin phase of their morning and I was able to participate.

Stala introduced his boss, Inspector Robert Mattingly. He gazed at me with sad eyes set deeply in a lined and saggy face. Detective Ray Flowers, compact and competent-looking in blue blazer and gray slacks, didn't wait to be introduced but stood up and shook my hand and gave me a brisk nod. Inspector Mattingly began the proceedings. "Staff Sergeant Stala has filled me in on all of the details of this case, including your own, uh, unorthodox involvement, and I have chosen not to know a lot of it. Having said that, we're a results-oriented group and we appreciate your contributions to the case. But they have to stop. We can't afford to have a civilian get hurt, much less have a civilian running around ignoring proper procedures."

"I'd love to bow out and get back to my family. My only interest is finding the murderer of my friend . . . and Phil Trimmer. I assume they're the same person, or at least masterminded by the same person. By the way"—I fumbled in my pocket—"here's Trimmer's phone. I haven't tried the last-call button yet."

Detective Flowers used a hankie to pick up the phone. "I'll need your fingerprints so we can eliminate them from any others that might be on here." He pressed one of the buttons. "The last call to you came from a payphone. But we'll check the call history and maybe come up with something."

"A police car pulled up just as I was leaving his house. Who phoned in the report?" I asked.

"Anonymous call. We've got the 9-1-1 tape, but it doesn't give us much."

"Phil hinted to me that the guys who were leaning on him were Chinese," I said. "I heard that there was a Chinese guy visiting Ernhardt last night. The maid might know who he was."

Stala gave me a hard look. "You heard there was a Chinese guy visiting Ernhardt? And who'd you hear that from? You were stashed away in your safe house."

I tried not to look uncomfortable. "Informed sources."

Inspector Mattingly sighed deeply. "Mr. Swanson, this is not some American detective potboiler. This is Canada in the twenty-first century, and all police investigations have to follow strict procedures. Otherwise, things get fucked up. We don't want to fuck this up, do we, Mr. Swanson?"

I spread my hands and looked innocent. "It's all good so far." There was a bit of a pause while looks were exchanged. I continued, "Have you established the cause of death? Was it the beating?"

Detective Flowers answered. "Apparently not. The heart stopped. Toxicology is looking at it, but those guys take forever."

"That doesn't sound right," I said. "He was, I dunno, mid-thirties, and he seemed reasonably healthy."

Flowers agreed. "I'm with you on that. But we won't know anything more until toxicology does their thing." He looked at Mattingly.

Mattingly seemed deeply saddened by this. "All right, I'll get after them. Speed things up as much as I can."

Flowers said, "There's one other thing. There were two blood types at the scene: the victim's and a person unknown. Trimmer maybe went down fighting, maybe nailed the killer in the nose. There was a lot of the unknown blood."

"That's good to know." Then I asked, "Did anyone try to get into my room at the hotel?"

Stala answered this one. "No. I had a guy in your room half an hour after I talked to you."

We all thought things over for a minute. Finally I said, "Have you talked to any of the Committee or Tap Dickens? They're all suspects in my mind, at least as far as organizing the murders."

Stala replied, "We're making appointments to talk to them, but they're playing hard to get. We'll keep after it."

There didn't seem to be anything else to discuss, so I said, "I'd like to get my stuff from the hotel room and check out. Does one of you want to escort me over there?"

Stala said, "I'll do it. But first, we'll get your prints."

On the way over to the hotel, Stala asked me, "When you first came to Ottawa, you were looking for your friend, who had supposedly disappeared on Canoe Lake. You found his Jeep out there. But he was alive up to July 3, when he was shot at the Château Laurier. Why the fake disappearing act? Any ideas on that?"

"It's weird, I know. Maybe the killer was trying to maintain the fiction that Gerry Steadman was a real person, so he had to make Dougie disappear. We probably won't know until we find the killer and ask him."

When we got to my room, we were greeted by a very bored-looking cop who told us there was nothing to report, and Stala sent him on his way. I packed up all my stuff and we went down to the lobby so I could check out of both my room and the one I'd rented for the late and somewhat lamented Jimmie Johnson. Stala drove me to my hideout, taking suitably evasive action in case the bad guys were watching, and after I'd dropped off my stuff, he drove me back to the police station so I could pick up Dougie's bike.

Stala said he'd phone me with any new developments. "And Swanson, don't on any occasion leave your hideout. If you get bored, call me and I'll send someone to entertain you. But I don't want you running around loose. Deal?"

I mumbled what could be construed as an agreement and climbed onto the dirt bike for the run back to my basement hideaway. When I got in, I set about unpacking my stuff and making the place comfortable. And while I was doing that I thought things over. Stala had a point. Somebody had arranged Dougie's fake disappearance on Canoe Lake, weeks before he was actually shot at the Château Laurier. Had Dougie done that, or the killer, or persons unknown? And why? And the documents the cops had found in Dougie's hotel room appeared to indicate that my old friend was setting Ernhardt up for something. But what and why? Was that just a way of getting leverage on Ernhardt? If so, what was Dougie's endgame? My success at formulating questions was not matched by success in answering them.

Just before noon I phoned Stala. "Did you find anything useful on Trimmer's phone?"

"Not yet. We're running down the stored phone numbers, but they're mostly his bookies, women friends, and cab companies. He made a few calls to Ernhardt, and we'll ask him about that this afternoon."

"Who was the Asian guy visiting Ernhardt on the night that Trimmer got killed?"

"We sent around a uniform to talk to the maid. It was a Mr. Chen. She has no idea where he's from. We'll ask Ernhardt. The maid also told us that the house was visited by a large man who punched Ernhardt and smashed up some valuable colonial furniture. You're Swedish. You a big IKEA fan?"

"That's an ethnic slur." I tried to sound indignant. "But I'll ignore it if you lend me a laptop. I need to read more of Dougie's story. Also, there's no food in this place. You want to take me shopping?"

"I'll send someone over." He hung up. Half an hour later a uniformed constable knocked on my door. She handed me a laptop and said, "Stala wants this back. There's a supermarket three blocks over on Landsing Road. You want to walk over or ride?"

I didn't want to walk back to my place carrying multiple grocery bags, so we went in the patrol car. Walking up and down the aisles of the supermarket, picking out cans of this and that, various unhealthy snacks, and lots of bacon and eggs, I forgot about politics and people killing other people, and I felt almost normal. The policewoman, Karen, helped me carry in the groceries, and then I was alone again. I made two bacon-and-egg sandwiches and turned on the TV. There was a lacrosse game on, and I munched away happily while I watched the most underrated sport in the world and the only one in which Toronto has a decent team. The Toronto Rock played as if they cared and were rewarded with a 22–18 victory over the Buffalo Bandits.

After all that excitement I needed a nap, so I reclined on the couch while three sports commentators nattered excitedly about something that I couldn't quite grasp. When I woke up I had a stiff neck and drool on my cheek, and the same three guys were still nattering. After wiping my face with a clean dishcloth, I stood in the living room and stared at the wall. The wall was unimpressed. At 4:00 PM I phoned Stala again. "You talk to Ernhardt yet?"

"Yeah, he graced us with his presence for thirty-five minutes, all lawyered up with the first Dyck of Dyck, Dyck, Dyck and Dungwall. Admits he knew Trimmer, occasionally employed him for security work, but that was all. He had a bit of difficulty talking because, apparently, he was attacked at his house last night by a deranged man."

"That's awful," I said. "Is no one safe?"

"Evidently, no one with colonial furniture."

I said, "I think you need to talk to the Chairman, Paul Salinger. But you're probably not going to get much if you don't have some way of pressuring him. Don't forget, we've got him on tape number ten hinting about using Chinese muscle to eliminate opposition. Isn't that what just happened with Phil Trimmer?"

"It's suggestive but not conclusive. But we're getting our forensic accounting guys to try to follow the money trail, which may give us something useful. However, that takes time."

"Any more info on Mr. Chen?"

"Ernhardt admitted he knew him. Chinese national. Businessman. Ernhardt claims he has consular sponsorship."

"This is depressing," I said. "All these vermin seem to be protected. I'd like to talk to them away from their lawyers and consular liaisons and deputy assistants. I'll bet I could get some answers out of them."

"I thought all you West-Coast guys were touchy-feely liberals. You're talking like Dirty Harry."

My voice hardened a little. "I just want to help these people explore their feelings. Feelings of pain."

"Our way works better in the long run."

"Stala, what if we don't have a long run?"

"I know how you feel, but you've signed up to play nice. And just so you know, I'll be sending someone by your hideout tonight for a bed check. You better be there."

"Tell them to bring their own pajamas." But I wasn't quick enough. Stala had already hung up. Damn! Wasted a good line.

I decided to do something useful, so I found the memory stick that had Dougie's story on it and inserted it into the laptop. I'd read to the end of the first installment in what was evidently a protracted series. I picked up where I'd left off.

The first part had laid out the history of corruption in Ottawa, listing some of the biggest scandals. The next installments laid out the web of finances that tied together the propaganda machine run by Cliff Ernhardt, the wealthy donors with a political agenda, and the politicians and bureaucrats who would implement that agenda. It was sort of what most Canadians had always suspected, but Dougie had confirmed those suspicions in ten-foot-high scarlet letters.

The last two installments laid out "Betrayal Three," the acquisition of Canadian oil by Chinese interests and the transport of that oil through a pipeline to the West Coast. This was the part of the story that was still playing out, and Dougie laid out the plans to co-opt the politicians and bureaucrats who would have to approve the project.

I knew that this part of the story presented a real danger to the Committee. Old scandals were old scandals. Some mid-level bureaucrat might take the rap. But this was a deal in progress and there were billions of dollars at stake. The last few paragraphs of the story talked about the environmental review of the pipeline to the West Coast and raised questions about the willingness of various bureaucrats to be honest about the environmental risks.

Ernhardt and the Committee knew almost nothing about the story, but they had vague fears. Ernhardt thought Dougie and Gerry Steadman were two different people, and that Gerry was leaking info to Dougie. That's why they'd gone to so much trouble to get the tapes back. And now that the pesky reporter had somehow disappeared, one way or another, they thought they were in the clear. I realized the story was more than just a story, a tale to edify and entertain Canadians. It was a potential weapon, a weapon of mass instruction that could destroy the Committee and everything it was trying to accomplish. I just had to decide how to use it.

Thinking burns a lot of calories, so I set about organizing a stir-fry for supper. The meats defeated the vegetables in a romp, and my appetite got a game misconduct. Then I phoned home and was surprised when the phone was answered by Wall to Wall McKee. "Wally," I said. "How's it going?"

"Oh, hi, Ollie. It's going good from the standpoint of a lack of bad guys. But there have been difficulties in terms of the redecorating project."

"Oh yeah? What?"

"Ollie, your dear wife—and you know I do love her dearly—is insisting on area rugs in the rec room."

"What's wrong with that?"

"Nomenclature, Ollie, nomenclature. Because all rugs cover area, there can be no separate class of rugs designated as area rugs. You see my point?"

"Okay, Wally, let me speak to her."

Oshie came on, laughing, and I wanted to be there with her.

"Ollie, you have the most interesting friends. I'm learning so much about rugs and carpets and all kinds of things."

"It's going well?"

"Oh yes. I just like to tease Wally. But they're all a lot of fun. The kids love them. One-Eyed Wayne walked them to school today and Half a Day Ray picked them up. Their friends are all jealous."

"That's great. I didn't want this to disrupt their lives." A decision suddenly announced itself to my brain. I would fly home the next day. Rationale? Stala had said we needed to wait for toxicology to come up with the cause of death, we had to wait for interviews with all the members of the Committee, and we had to wait for the results of the forensic audit. If I had to do all that waiting, I preferred to do it at home with my wife and kids. When I told Oshie that, she was overjoyed.

"Tell me what time your flight gets in. We'll pick you up."

I hung up feeling happier than I had in days.

Sixteen

I phoned Stala in the morning to tell him I was going home, and he was okay with that. "You've given us some valuable leads, Ollie. But from here on in it's going to take patience and a lot of old-fashioned police work."

"Well, keep me posted. And if you've got any questions, give me a call."

I took a cab to the airport, leaving Dougie's dirt bike in the kitchen of my hideaway. You never knew when a hideaway and a dirt bike might come in handy again. The flight was interminable. I fidgeted and stared out the window at nothing but cloud and fidgeted some more and ate seven bags of what the stewardess claimed were salted peanuts. Finally I felt the nose of the plane tilt slightly down and we began our descent into my real life.

I only had carry-on luggage, so I made it fairly quickly into the domestic arrivals area. Almost immediately I spotted Ren and Daiki running toward me, with Oshie not too far behind. And roughly triangulated around them, at a distance sufficient so as not to seem attached but close enough to pose a threat to anyone in the triangle, I saw three rough-looking men who were casually observing the scene around us.

Ren and Daiki were soon on top of me, and I dropped my bags and scooped them up. And then Oshie was there, and we kissed as best we could. The three rough-looking men were drawing slowly closer, and finally I put the boys down and accosted the closest thug, the widest one with the most scar tissue on his face. "Wall to Wall, how are you, man?"

He grabbed my hand and tried to squeeze me into submission. "Ollie, welcome home. We've enjoyed hanging out with your family."

Half a Day Ray took the toothpick out of his mouth with his left hand and high-fived me with his right. Never one for words, he gave me a nod and a wink and ruffled Daiki's hair.

One-Eyed Wayne, his scrawny frame bulked up by the black leather jacket he always wore, gave me a wise look and a half salute. "Ollie, how was the fishing in Ottawa?"

I laughed. "It was different, Wayne. You're never sure who is playing whom."

Wall to Wall gave me a pat on the back. "We'll say goodbye now, Ollie. But we'll see you in the morning. We've still got to finish that carpet."

They wandered off and the boys picked up my two bags and Oshie led me to the car. When we walked into the kitchen of my house, I immediately collapsed into a chair and just sort of absorbed everything. Ren and Daiki were both talking at once and I listened to them while looking around the kitchen and holding Oshie's hand. We let the kids stay up a half hour later than usual, and by the time they went to bed I felt part of it all again.

Oshie took a bottle of Riesling out of the fridge, and while she sipped and I drank, I filled her in on most of the details of what had transpired in Ottawa. She insisted on asking awkward questions. "So how did you persuade Phil Trimmer to give you the tapes?"

I squirmed a bit. "You may not realize this, sweetie, but I have a forceful personality."

She squeezed my hand. "How forceful?"

"Well, I was a little rough with him."

She let go of my hand. "Was he the only one you were rough with?"

I took a deep breath and told her as much of the truth as I dared. "Right after they threatened you and the kids, I went over to Cliff Ernhardt's house and punched him in the mouth. And broke some of his furniture."

"What kind of furniture?"

"I think it was colonial."

She took my hand again. "Ollie, I don't like to even think of you beating people up, but I admire you for standing up for all that's good and decent in home furnishings. Let's go to bed."

That night Oshie made love to the new in me and I made love to the old in her, and then we made love to the ongoing us. Afterward she lay with her head on my chest and I watched out the window as clouds opened and closed like stage curtains, revealing and then concealing an almost full moon. I fell asleep.

In the morning we had the usual school-day breakfast, pleasantly hectic, with lots of chatter and plans for later. After the boys had finished their cereal and gathered up all their school paraphernalia, I walked them to school and told them I'd pick them up afterward. As much as I didn't like to admit it, nothing had been resolved, and the threat to Oshie and the kids had not been withdrawn. I went back to the house for a final cup of coffee and was glad to see Wall to Wall's van in the driveway.

When I walked into the kitchen, the Barely Brothers were seated around the table and Oshie was arguing with Wally. "Why do you say 'carpeting' to refer to carpets? You don't say you're sitting on a *chairing*. It's just a chair."

Wall to Wall was not deterred. "This house has flooring, roofing, and siding. And I'm installing carpeting. I won't charge extra for the 'ing.'"

I said, "If I can interrupt this scintillating discussion for just a moment, I'm going down to check on the boat. I'll pick the kids up after school." I spent most of the day puttering on the boat. Then I picked up the kids and, when I got home, asked if Staff Sergeant Stala had called. He hadn't, and he didn't for a whole week.

When he did call, he had some interesting information. "We finally got the toxicology report on Phil Trimmer. His heart stopped because he had been injected with aconite. Know what that is?" He didn't even wait for a reply. "It's a plant-based poison used by some of the hill tribes in China. They use it on poison arrows."

"Another Chinese connection," I said.

"Yeah, well, here's another one. Our financial guys have discovered that Crude Operations is 49 percent Chinese owned. Also, it has two Chinese nationals on its board of directors."

"These directors. Where do they live?" I asked.

"Calgary."

"Do they have household staff? Butlers, chauffeurs, anything like that?"

"I can see where you're going with this," Stala said. "We'll check it out."

I pressed on. "Have you talked to the Chairman, Paul Salinger?"

"He politely told us to fuck off. Not in those words, of course. When I pressed him on his comments about using Chinese muscle, he just laughed and said we'd misunderstood his words."

"I doubt that." I snorted. "All those guys, especially him and Ernhardt, can make the English language sit up, beg, and then blow bubbles through the orifice of your choice. And they can also make it say something without really saying it." I paused to calm down a bit. "I'm positive that whoever killed Trimmer was linked to Tap Dickens, in which case there could be connections to one of those Chinese directors in Calgary. I think that's where we should focus our efforts."

"I'm looking through my contacts to see who I know with the Calgary police. At the very least they'll be able to get us a list of the household employees. It'll take a couple of days. I'll be in touch."

After Stala hung up I continued to think over this new information. Tap Dickens was tightly linked to the Chinese. Ernhardt met with a Mr. Chen on the night of Trimmer's murder. Ernhardt claimed Chen had consular backing. True or false? The guy who could probably answer that was Paul Salinger. Should I approach him? And if I did, should I get approval from Stala?

I pondered this over the next few days while I continued to get my boat ready for the shrimp season and, coordinating with the Barely Brothers, continued to keep a watch on my family. One afternoon Louise, Danny's RCMP-officer wife, came by to take Oshie and the kids shopping, so I took the opportunity to take the Barely Brothers out for lunch. We went to the Steveston Hotel. When we were settled at a table, pints in our hands and fish and chips on the way (life can be so bountiful), I said to the guys, "Look, I just want you to know I really appreciate what you're doing. I hope this situation is over soon, because we're running out of rooms for you to carpet."

Half a Day Ray responded, "Don't worry about it, Ollie. We owe you a few favors. And once the carpets are done you can take advantage of my new business, Good Enough Repairs. Our motto: If it ain't broke, give us a call."

"Jeez, Ray, that doesn't really inspire a lot of confidence."

"Ollie, we don't want to be overwhelmed with work. We've got lives, you know."

"Good point," I acknowledged.

One-Eyed Wayne leaned forward and confided, "He wanted to get me to paint the sign on the van, but I couldn't because I've got dylsexia."

It took me a moment to clue in. "You mean dyslexia."

Wayne looked hurt. "Ollie, if I could say it, I wouldn't have it." The others all nodded their heads.

From there the conversation grew increasingly surreal, as it usually did when we spent time together. Wall to Wall launched into a story about the time he'd taken a Club Med vacation. "Cheap cocaine was flowing like, well, cheap cocaine. I came home with cracked sinuses and a serious addiction to talcum powder. To this day, I can't change my sister's kid's diapers without violating my probation agreement."

When the waitress had retreated after bringing the fourth round, One-Eyed Wayne said, "Tell Ollie about that holiday we took in the ambulance."

Wall to Wall chuckled. "Yeah, that was a good one. The last year the Grey Cup was in Toronto, we decided to drive back there in an old ambulance."

I interrupted. "Why an ambulance?"

"We got a really good deal on it." He paused in thought. "A really good deal. Plus, it's always nice to drive something with flashing lights and a siren. It's a feature, you know? So anyway, the trip is fun, we're making good time, and then, on the highway just outside—where the hell was it?"

One-Eyed Wayne and Half a Day Ray intoned in unison, "Eyebrow, Saskatchewan."

Wall to Wall nodded. "Eyebrow, Saskatchewan. There's this long hill going down into town, and at the top of the hill there'd been an accident. A cop pulls us over and tells us there's two victims and we've got to take them to the hospital. I says sure. Turns out the two victims are drivers of the opposing vehicles and their only injuries seem to be severe lacerations to their decency, resulting in aggravated subdural assholeness. They're ragging on each other about whose fault it was, bitching to the police officers about allowing too many accidents, and when they see us they start ragging on us. Like, 'where's your uniforms' and 'you don't look like paramedics' and like that."

"They were *such* assholes," Half a Day Ray chipped in, "they could have made a living at it, crapping for celebrities who're too busy adopting children and stuff."

"So anyway," Wall to Wall continued, "I says we're off duty but if you want you can come with us or wait for an hour. So they get in the back of the ambulance with Ray and Wayne, and we're off."

One-Eyed Wayne took up the story. "The first step in reducing their whataya call it, their terminal assholeness, was to get their clothes off. Naked assholes are very rare. Now, you might think that would be difficult, but Ray had put on a stethoscope, and when a guy wearing a stethoscope says, 'I want to examine you, take off your shirt,' you do it. And then taking off your pants seems logical. Then we made the guys lie on the stretchers, and I took the blood-pressure thingie and wrapped it around one guy's head and started pumping it up while Ray applied the stethoscope to the other guy's forehead. His eyes got all round, and he's like, 'What the hell are you doing?' So I says, 'We're alternative paramedical practitioners and we believe that monitoring the mind is the key to true healing. You do want to heal, don't you?'"

Giggling, Half a Day Ray took up the story. "So both of them are saying they're not really hurt and they'll be fine and they don't really need treatment and I'm staring at them and I say, 'Denial is a disease. We all need treatment.' Meanwhile Wayne has found a box of long pins, and he starts laying them out on the stretcher beside the chubby asshole. He's real panicky now, and he says, 'What are those for?' I say, 'We believe in preventive acupuncture. Twenty or thirty needles will change your life.' So he screams, 'I don't want to change my life.' At this point Wally stops the ambulance, comes around the back and says if the clients don't want to be treated, our code of ethics says we've gotta leave 'em alone. So we go back to the cab with Wally, making sure we've got their clothes in a garbage bag, and we're off again."

Wall to Wall chuckled reminiscently. "The ambulance had an intercom, so I turned it on so the assholes could hear our conversation, and then I started on, 'Do you know how much organs are worth these days? A good heart can net you fifty thousand dollars.' And Wayne picks up on it. 'Yeah, eyes, you know eyes are in huge demand.' And Ray says, 'So what have we got in the back there. Two hearts, four lungs, four eyes, four spleens.' And I says, 'Two spleens, only two spleens, Ray. But still, there's a fortune in spare body parts in the back of this ambulance. Do you think we should take them to that *special* hospital?' And then I go, 'Oops, I didn't know this thing was on.' And then I shut off the intercom. Half an hour later we hadn't heard a thing from the back. Complete silence. So we pull up at the hospital and I go into emergency and tell an orderly that I've got these two guys who are acting sort of strange, very paranoid, does he want to come and take a look. I take him to the ambulance, pop open the back door and say, 'How much'll you give me for these two?' And they came out of that ambulance like screaming banshees from asshole hell. They took off down the street with people leaping out of the way as if naked craziness was contagious, and the orderly right behind them, yelling, 'You're number thirty-two. It won't be a long wait.' So we left. Mission accomplished."

I couldn't help but ask, "And what exactly was your mission?"

Wall to Wall looked disappointed. "Asshole suppression, Ollie. It's what we do."

Half a Day Ray and One-Eyed Wayne lowered their eyes and

looked modestly virtuous, like men with a calling. And soon they were: calling for more beer.

In the interests of keeping up my end of the conversation, I confessed to them my Ottawa sins—specifically, my rampage against colonial furniture. "I surprised myself, you know? I didn't know I had that much violence in me, brutalizing a defenseless armoire."

They all made consoling noises, and about then the dreaded five-beer nostalgia set in. One-Eyed Wayne started it. "Wow, you know what? How long we known each other? And really, you know, we haven't changed that much. Still the same classy, tight-knit bunch we always was."

Wall to Wall continued, "Damn it, you're right. We're a little older, but we've still got all of our fingers and toes, most of our hair, some of our teeth, a few of our brain cells, and all but one of our eyes. That's fuckin' amazing, you know?"

One-Eyed Wayne raised his glass. "Four good-lookin', good-timin' guys. Here's to us."

I was just drunk enough to relinquish the standard male code of reticence and enter the dreaded shared-intimacy zone. "I dunno, maybe you guys are good-looking. Standards have changed. But I've never considered myself good-looking."

Half a Day Ray got all solicitous. "Ollie, what makes you say a thing like that?"

"Well, when you're young and good-looking, you get laid a lot. I was definitely young once, but I never got laid a lot. Ergo, I can't be good-looking."

Wall to Wall laid a paw on my shoulder. "Flawed logic, Ollie. You didn't define 'a lot.' And sometimes geeky young guys grow into distinguished-looking old guys. Ergo, it's within the realm of possibility that you are good-looking."

Half a Day Ray had become a little agitated. "Ergo? Ergo? What the hell we talkin' about the Ergoes for? They ain't even in the eastern final this year."

I took the easy way out and let that pass. "Thanks, Wally. So now I'm old?" I looked at my watch. It was three thirty. "Jesus, it's only the middle of the afternoon and I'm half pissed."

"Well, you know what they say." Half a Day Ray raised his glass. "You can't drink all day if you don't start in the morning."

I stood up. "Well, Wally pointed out that I'm old now, so that gives me an excuse to bail. I'll see you in the morning. Better make that the afternoon."

I left my truck in the parking lot and took a cab home, reflecting on how the Barely Brothers seemed to exist in a different dimension than the rest of us, sort of a twilight zone outside the constraints of normal life. Although sometimes normal life seemed like kind of a twilight zone to me. My thoughts tended to get deeply self-referential after drinking at midday.

Oshie and Louise and the kids weren't back yet, so I wandered aimlessly around the house. It occurred to me to do a little research on the two Chinese directors of Crude Operations. I turned on the computer, Googled the company, went to their homepage, clicked on the board of directors, and voilà, there they were: a Mr. Chen and a Mr. Lee. Mr. Chen was the gentleman I'd seen briefly at Ernhardt's place, the night of the great furniture massacre.

The phone rang. It was Staff Sergeant Stala. "Swanson, I just wanted to update you on the private staff of those two Chinese directors."

"What a coincidence. I was just checking them out on the Internet. The one called Chen is the same guy who was at Ernhardt's place the night Phil Trimmer got whacked."

"That's encouraging," Stala replied. "Chen and the other guy, between the two of them, have seven household staff: two cooks, two nannies, two maids, and a driver. The Calgary police are a little interested in the driver. Seems he's got heavy connections in Vancouver and he's been fingered as a major snakehead—a people smuggler."

"So he's a bad guy. What's his name?"

"Sun Li 'Sonny' Feng. Swanson, he's a bad guy who's connected to other bad guys. Bad guys in your area."

"I hear you, Stala. I'll let my RCMP friends know that. Anything else?"

"No. We're still pounding away at Ernhardt and the other committee members, but it's tough sledding. I want to spend a little more time on this Chinese angle. I'll talk to you later."

Not too much later I heard a car door slam, then the front door opened, and then there was pandemonium. The kids had got haircuts, which, they informed me, made their heads feel really funny. They also had new runners, so they obviously needed to show me how fast they could run now. In the background, Oshie and Louise settled down on the couch and looked amused. When the whirlwind had escaped outside, I turned my attention to the two women. "You guys had a good time?"

Oshie laughed. "Do you remember how much fun it can be to go down an up escalator?"

"In Sointula, the stairs don't move. By the time I saw an escalator, I was too grown up to fool around on them."

Oshie raised her eyebrows. "Too grown up? Ollie, who started the pillow fight last night and knocked over the hamster cage?"

"But I never pillow-fight on an escalator." And so we bantered for a while and when Louise left, I followed her out to her car. She looked at me expectantly. "Louise, the Calgary cops think one of our bad guys could be named Sun Li Feng. Nickname Sonny. He's got gang connections in Vancouver, possible snakehead. Can you see if you've got any info on him?"

"No problem, Ollie."

"And Louise, I gave the Barely Brothers the night off."

"Okay, I'll put an unmarked car in the area as well as the uniformed patrols."

"Thanks, Louise." When I went back inside, Oshie gave me a look but didn't say anything.

The next day was Wednesday. Louise phoned to say that Feng was definitely on their radar. He had been tied to a ring that was importing young girls and forcing them into prostitution. They hadn't nailed him on the human trafficking charge, but they'd got him for aggravated assault for beating up a witness. The girl had almost died, but had had the nerve to testify. I admired her guts.

"Louise, can you send his prints to Staff Sergeant Stala for possible matches with the two murder scenes? And I'd really like to see a photo of Sonny Feng, just so I know who I'm dealing with."

"I'll see what I can do."

The Barely Brothers were back on the job, so I took the opportunity to go down to the boat to putter and think. Usually when I was on the boat, I found a sort of spiritual peace. That was partly because the boat always made me think of its builder, Oshie's dad, Otokichi Tanaka. And partly it was because being on the boat was sort of like being in a cathedral; the way certain lines and boundaries enclosed spaces made them special and restful. But now I felt only a restless anxiety. I realized that graceful lines, sublime proportion, attention to detail, and exquisite craftsmanship were not sufficient to insulate one from evil.

Thoughts ran through my brain like cars on a freeway, appearing suddenly and just as suddenly gone. Then one of them honked loudly and parked in front of me. Friday was the day for the evening get together of the Committee. It would be a good opportunity to confront Ernhardt and the Chairman, and maybe Tap Dickens. I knew I was being impatient, but I was sure that if I pressured them they'd make a mistake. But was I sure I could get away with entering the lion's den? Well, yes. Did I want to tell Stala? Well, no. Did I want to take Danny as backup? Yes and no. Yes, because these were dangerous people who I'd really pissed off. No, because Danny was married to an RCMP officer, and when I was in Ottawa, illegal events often occurred in my vicinity. So I'd do it alone: go in with no warning and get out fast. It was a plan that had never failed in the past.

Oshie was not really pleased with the idea, but I assured her I'd only be gone for three days. On Thursday I flew to Ottawa and took a cab to my hideout. All day Friday I fidgeted and watched TV and wished I dared go for a walk. At eight that evening I pushed Dougie's dirt bike out onto the back driveway and took off for Ernhardt's place. His house didn't look quite so attractive as I approached it this time. It seemed tarnished, and somehow less substantial. But the same maid answered the door and sensibly didn't try to stop me as I brushed past her and made for the living room.

The same important-looking men were arranged impressively around the room, but I received a much different reception as Ollie Swanson than I had as Jimmie Johnson. The room fell silent and I became the focus of attention, sort of like a cadaver at an autopsy.

"Hi, everyone." I grinned and waved. "Staff Sergeant Stala sent me over to talk to a few of you. Thought you might feel more comfortable with no police in the room." God, the lies came so easily whenever I was in Ottawa. Must be something in the air.

Most of the assembled power brokers started divesting themselves of drinks, picking up their coats and moving toward the door. "Actually"—I tried to make my voice more authoritative—"it's only necessary that I talk to you and you and you." I pointed at Cliff Ernhardt, the Chairman, AKA Paul Salinger, and Tap Dickens.

When the others had gone I walked to the bar, poured myself a scotch and water and perched on one of the barstools. The others hadn't moved, their eyes fixed on me like, well, like a cadaver on a morgue table. I tried not to feel intimidated.

"So here's how we see it, Stala and me. There're a couple of different agendas at play here. There've been two killings. We want to solve those killings. You gentlemen, on the other hand, only want to pursue your various projects, of which the most important right now is getting oil to China. Now, there may appear to be a conflict between those two agendas, but there doesn't need to be. But there sure as hell could be if we don't start getting some cooperation."

The Chairman spoke. "I understand your real name is Ollie Swanson. Swedish, I suppose. My family had a Swedish handyman once. Dedicated chap, but not very bright. Couldn't take instruction at all."

I refused to take the bait. "I don't take instruction well either. Maybe it's a national trait."

Tap Dickens eyed me suspiciously. "Swanson, you mind if we check you for a wire?"

I put my drink on the bar and began disrobing. "Don't get excited, guys. You can look, but don't touch." With my jacket and shirt off, I dropped my pants to my knees and slowly turned in a full circle. I didn't hear any whistles, although I knew they wanted to. When I was all rebuttoned, the Chairman spoke again. "Mr. Swanson, we have absolutely no idea who killed Gerry

Steadman. I know the police, for reasons unknown to us, think that Mr. Ernhardt was involved, but I can assure you that he wasn't."

"Mr. Salinger, I've heard you on a tape, appealing to Gerry Steadman for Chinese muscle to help, in your words, to 'eliminate opposition.' One of Dickens's Chinese board members was visiting Cliff Ernhardt the same night that Ernhardt's employee, Phil Trimmer, was 'eliminated.' You telling me that was just a coincidence? We know that Mr. Chen's driver is a gangster. We know that both he and Chen were in Ottawa the night Phil was tortured and killed. And we know that Phil died from being injected with a Chinese poison. Are you mugs going to keep stonewalling me on this?"

The three of them exchanged looks and there was a long pause. I could swear that the possibility of negotiations was in the air. Then Dickens broke in angrily. "Fuck you, Swanson. You're an insect, and all you can do is annoy us. Well, I'm annoyed. If I see you again, I'll swat you like a fucking fly."

I looked at Ernhardt and the Chairman. Their faces were professionally impassive. I gave them some time to open the door just a crack. Nothing. I made one last try. "Ernhardt, if you help us prove that Dickens's boys were in town the night of Steadman's murder, it might let you off the hook."

"Goddamn you, Swanson!" Dickens took a step toward me. But only one step.

I looked back at Ernhardt and the Chairman. They were both looking at Dickens. I gave them lots of time to say something. Anything. They didn't. So I did. "Well, gentlemen, I came in the spirit of reconciliation. There has been a failure to reciprocate. Let the hostilities resume."

I left by the front door, and as I was walking down the driveway to where I'd left the bike, a black SUV appeared from behind the house. I mounted the bike and turned left out of the driveway. The SUV followed. I realized, with a sense of apprehension verging on panic, that my bike was not only considerably outweighed by the SUV, it was considerably slower.

I turned off Ernhardt's street onto a less residential feeder road, and the SUV drew closer. Just as I was considering ditching the bike and taking off on foot, I came abreast of a mall. Wheeling into the parking lot, I searched for some sort of terrain where my bike might have an advantage. There were no dirt hills or ravines, but there was a set of stairs leading up to the mall's second level. I gunned the bike up the stairs, earning a thumbs-up from a couple of teenagers, and exited the mall on the opposite side. The SUV was nowhere in sight, but just to be safe, on the way back to my hideout I detoured through two parks and a schoolyard.

I spent a restless night at the hideout and in the morning was faced with a decision. My flight home wasn't until three in the afternoon, so I had plenty of time to see Stala if I wanted to. But did I want to? I hadn't really learned much, and he'd probably be upset at my meeting with the Committee. In the end, I decided that I owed Stala an update and he couldn't arrest me for meeting with Ottawa's most upstanding citizens.

At one that afternoon I phoned for a cab to police headquarters. Stala received me with a sort of resigned surprise. When I told him about the meeting, he rolled his eyes. "If you keep doing that," I said, "your eyes will stay that way and then you'll have to wear dark glasses and learn to play the guitar."

Stala ignored my warning. "So, did you get any of those characters to confess?"

"Not exactly. But there's a potential split there between Dickens and the other two. I just didn't have the tools to exploit it."

"Well, at least you tried," Stala said. "And you never know:

you might have planted the seeds of something. By the way, the prints that the Richmond RCMP sent of Sun Li Feng didn't match anything from either of the murder scenes."

We sat and cogitated for a while and then I said I needed a police escort to the airport. Stala almost rolled his eyes, but just sighed and got up and put on his jacket. Just before I entered the secure area, he said, "Who's going to watch you on the other end?"

I hadn't thought of that. It hadn't quite sunk in that Ollie Swanson could be personally threatened on his home turf. "I'll make a call," I said as I waved goodbye. In the waiting room I phoned Danny, thinking no one would dare tackle two Swansons. He said he'd meet me when I got in. Which, five hours later, I did and he did.

There was a bit of a traffic jam leaving the airport, and as we sat in Danny's truck, he said, "Okay, threat assessment. It looks like these guys have killed two people, they've threatened you and your family, and Louise informs me that they've got ties to gangs in this area. How seriously do we have to take this? Should we send Oshie and the kids up to Sointula?"

The question made me uncomfortable. Up to now, the threat had always seemed sort of hypothetical, and my safety precautions had been in the spirit of better safe than sorry. But now the threat loomed closer out of the fog of uncertainty, and I felt increasingly nervous. I didn't want to pull the kids out of school, and, most of all, I didn't want to admit to Oshie that I'd been downplaying the risks. I dithered. "Let me think about it. I'll call you in the morning."

After supper, I sat on the back patio and mulled things over. From mulling to mindlessness was not far to go. It wasn't long before all my thoughts fled like seagulls, and I was staring at them as they soared and glided across the horizon. They refused to return to roost in my brain. The evening sky imagined our fate.

Seventeen

In the morning I took the kids to school and then went back to the house to drink coffee and try to convince myself that everything would be okay. I could hear the Barely Brothers banging away in the basement, but I knew I couldn't keep them hanging around forever. Oshie could tell something was bothering me, but she always gave me the space to work things out. She sat opposite me at the kitchen table, paying bills and sorting through the mail. Occasionally she would smile and tap the back of my hand with her pencil. Just when I was about to decide to think seriously about making a decision, there was a knock on the door followed by a loud "Anybody home?" and Danny and Louise walked into the kitchen.

I knew this was probably not good, but Oshie was nothing but happy to see them. When we were all seated at the table, gripping fresh cups of coffee, Louise came straight to the point. "We have to talk about security. I've been advised that last night there were a couple of probes."

Oshie looked puzzled. "Probes? What kind of probes?"

Louise placed her hand on top of Oshie's. "There were two attempts to get close to the house. They didn't seem to be serious attempts—more like they were just testing the defenses. The first came at 0130. Our patrol car stopped a new Toyota Camry a block away on River Road. Two male occupants, both known to us as members of the DTK Crew. Said they were out for a drive. The second was at 0400. We had surveillance on a vehicle in connection with another case. It drove out here, circled the block and then drove away. If it had stopped, our guys would have acted, but as it was they didn't have to blow the op."

My curiosity was piqued. "Louise, I've never heard of the DTK Crew. They new?"

"They showed up on our radar three years ago. DTK is the first half of a graffiti tag common in the Watts ghetto in the '70s. It stands for 'down to kill.' The second half of the tag was LAMF—'like a mother fucker.' It's interesting how cultural phenomena spread and mutate. Great PhD thesis for some bright young thing."

Danny leaned forward and took Oshie's other hand. "Osh, Ollie doesn't want to worry you, but all of us think you should take the kids up to Sointula for a while."

Oshie's face brightened. "But that would be great. I know Ollie's parents would love to see the kids, and I would love to get out of this Steveston rat race for a while. I'll go to the school this afternoon and get enough homework for two weeks, and we can leave tomorrow. This will be so much fun."

Danny looked at me as if to say, "See?" and I looked back as if to say, "That's my girl."

Louise kept us focused on business. "Presumably they can fly up tomorrow. Ollie, can you arrange for someone to meet them in Port Hardy?"

"I can arrange for half of Sointula to meet them. And once they're on Malcolm Island, it'll be like being on an aircraft carrier; no unauthorized personnel will have access."

Louise spread three photos on the table, all of the same stocky, mustachioed Asian gentleman. "This is Sun Li 'Sonny' Feng. Oshie, you take one photo with you and post it on the Co-op wall. Ollie, you can have one, and give one to the Barely Brothers. Now we all know who to watch out for."

The next day I drove my family to the South Terminal and off they went in a twin-engine aluminum tube. When I got back to the house, Danny was making lunch for the brothers. "Gentlemen," I said, "if the bad guys want access to this house, I don't see why we should stand in their way. Danny, why don't you ask Louise to pull the patrols for tonight?"

"I can get her to pull them back a ways, and be ready to respond to an alarm."

And so the trap was set. None of us had handguns, but we all had deer rifles. Louise supplied us with three wireless alarms, just in case things got out of control. I put one in my pocket, Danny had one, and Wall to Wall had the other. We just puttered around for the rest of the day, knowing that if there was a strike, it wouldn't come until after dark.

At nine that night we took up our positions. I was in the living room to watch the front door, Danny was in the kitchen, watching the back door, and Wall to Wall was in the basement, which had a door opening into the garage. Half a Day Ray was across the street in our neighbor's garage, where he could see the whole front of the house. One-Eyed Wayne was in the woodshed in the backyard. We all had handheld programmable scrambled VHF radios, better than anything the cops had. We would be able to communicate without worrying about our messages being intercepted by bad guys. The house was in darkness, but a half-moon shone in the clear night sky, so there was reasonable visibility outside.

At two a black SUV cruised by the front of the house. Half a Day Ray saw it too. Five minutes later it went by again. Nothing happened for twenty minutes. Then a dark sedan cruised slowly by with its lights off and parked two houses down. I pressed the Send button on my VHF. "Game on."

I tried to control my nerves with deep breathing, but it started to make me dizzy. Five minutes crept by like the entire first ice age. It became absolutely imperative for me to move, but I was afraid my knees would crack and give us away. When I heard Wall to Wall yell, my heart almost stopped. "Freeze, assholes!"

Rifle in one hand and flashlight in the other, I ran down the stairs but stopped at the bottom of the stairwell. Cautiously, I poked my head out of the stairwell and looked in the direction of the door to the garage. I couldn't see a thing. "Wally, where are you?"

"Right here. There's two guys in front of me and to my left."

I pointed my flashlight in that direction and turned it on. I saw two black-clad figures in half crouches. They each held a handgun. I switched the flashlight off just as Danny came down the stairs and passed behind me and out into the basement. Five seconds later his voice came from the other side of the basement. "We've got you covered on three sides now. Drop your weapons." I turned on the flashlight again. The two thugs, blinded and surrounded, had no choice but to drop their guns. I felt along the wall for the light switch and turned it on.

Wall to Wall came up on the two thugs from behind, gave each an authoritative tap with the barrel of his rifle and yelled, "On the floor, assholes." When they were lying on their bellies with Wall to Wall and Danny standing over them, rifles aimed, I put my rifle down and went up to the two and searched them. They both had additional pistols in ankle holsters and serious-looking knives in belt sheaths.

I told them to roll over, and when they did I recognized one of them as Sonny Feng. The other was a white guy with a shaved head and tattoos gone wild. His nose looked swollen and bruised. Neither of them carried wallets, so I asked the white guy his name. He didn't answer. Wall to Wall came up to the guy, poked the barrel of his gun into the guy's eye and leaned on it. The guy screamed in a high-pitched voice, "Novi, Novi Beravitch."

"Novi," I said. "I hope that's your real name." Wall to Wall leaned a little on his rifle, and Novi screeched his affirmation. "Good. Well, listen, Novi, we need a few answers. Have you ever heard of Gerry Steadman or Phil Trimmer?" He shook his head. "Cliff Ernhardt? Tap Dickens?" He shook his head. I decided to test Sonny Feng. "Okay, you. What's your name?" Feng answered in a burst of what I took to be Mandarin or Cantonese. Back to Novi Beravitch. "Novi, why did you guys sneak into my house tonight?"

"Robbing. We're just trying to make a living." He spoke for the first time in his normal voice, and I felt a shudder of recognition. It was the voice I'd heard on Phil Trimmer's cell phone the night he'd been killed, the voice that had threatened to kill me and my family.

I gave way to a sudden burst of anger. "You're pretty heavily armed for a couple of B and E guys, don't you think?" I kicked him gently in the ribs. He gasped. Okay, it wasn't that gentle of a kick. "I think you and your fellow thug came here to kill me and my family." I kicked him again and he groaned.

"No, no. Robbing. Thieving. That's all we was up to."

He was almost crying and snot was coming out of his nose. It's disgusting what passes for tough guys these days. I ripped a piece of paper towel from the roll on the wall and tossed it to him. "Blow your nose." He honked mightily and threw the crumpled paper towel against the wall.

Half a Day Ray and One-Eyed Wayne had joined the scene. We all looked at each other, and I shrugged. "I don't think we're going to get anything out of these assholes." *At least while they're together*, I thought.

Danny pulled out his cell and called Louise. "We've got two guys here. They snuck in and they were both heavily armed. Why don't you send the waste-disposal unit?"

When the thugs had been taken away, we all carefully unloaded our rifles, and I locked them in a closet. I went to a cupboard by the washer and took a plastic baggie from a box. I walked over to the paper towel Novi had discarded and gingerly picked it up.

"You all saw where this came from?" They all nodded, and I placed the paper towel in the baggie and then got everyone to sign it. "This may be important DNA evidence." Then we went upstairs, where I distributed beers and Wall to Wall told his story.

"I was standing against the wall, beside the door to the garage. I heard the door handle turn and the door squeaked just a little when they opened it. There was just enough light from outside that I could make out two guys, even though they were darkly dressed. If I'd let them get too far into the basement, I would have lost them, so I yelled. The rest of you responded like a well-oiled machine." He raised his beer bottle. "May we always be well-oiled."

We all raised our bottles. "Well-oiled!" And two hours later, we were.

It was almost noon when I got up. Danny was still asleep on the couch. I phoned Louise. "I've got your husband, and if you don't follow my instructions to the letter, I'll send him home."

"You fiend. What do you want?"

"Information on those two thugs we gave you last night."

She laughed. "That wasn't a gift. More of an off-loading. Anyway, you know about Sonny Feng. The other guy, Novi, is another member of the DTK Crew, with an even longer rap sheet than Feng. Several assaults, assault with a deadly weapon, possession with intent, etc., etc. So what we've hung on them so far is B and E and possession of restricted weapons. With their rap sheets, we should be able to hold them until the trial. Also, we sent Beravitch's prints back east to Stala. And we're going over their vehicle with a fine-tooth comb."

"Louise, you've got to hold on to those guys. I'm positive we can tie them to the murder of Phil Trimmer. I recognized Novi's voice. He's the guy who phoned on Phil's cell and threatened me and the family. Also, he might have left blood at the Trimmer murder scene, and I collected a DNA sample last night. I'll give it to Danny to give to you."

Louise sounded impressed. "Sounds like you're starting to get somewhere. One way or another, I'll hang on to those two until Stala says yay or nay. Any chance of speaking to my husband?"

I shook Danny awake, handed him the phone and went to make coffee. As I ground some fresh beans, I analyzed the state of play. The bad guys had killed two people, one of whom was my best friend. The bad guys had threatened me and my family. The bad guys had attempted to follow through on their threat to me and my family. The bad guys were making me very angry.

My anger was a physical sensation. It churned my stomach and tensed my neck muscles and jutted my jaw. It was not a pleasant feeling, and it pretty much limited my thinking to fantasies of hurting someone—anyone. It was several moments before I could suppress the anger enough to think properly.

An old sports cliché popped into my brain: the best defense is a good offense. Maybe, I thought, it was time to transition from defense to offense. How could I do that? What plowshares did I have that could be beaten into swords? Well, I had some pretty hard-nosed friends, and . . . I had a lot of money.

Danny wandered into the kitchen a couple of minutes later and helped me wait for the coffee to perk. He yawned and said Louise was impressed with our efforts. What, he wondered, would be our next move?

I poured us both a cup of coffee. "Danny," I said, "I'm tired of letting these guys threaten us, and us just sitting around waiting for them to come after us. I want to take the fight to them. I want to kick the shit out of them on their own turf."

Danny considered this. "You mean, go to Ottawa to do battle?"

"Not yet. I think right now the target is Tap Dickens. I think he's the one who sent those thugs after us. He and the mysterious Mr. Chen, who's on the board of Dickens's pipeline company. They need to realize that they can't come after my family without paying a price."

"So you want to go and fight a war in Alberta. You'll need an army for that."

"What's the use of having almost a million dollars if you can't buy an army?"

Danny looked intrigued. "You could definitely pull a few guys together with that kind of money. So what's the target?"

"Dickens's business. Shut down his pipelines. We could cost him millions of dollars. And with that sort of leverage, we might be able to get him to give us Cliff Ernhardt."

"Jesus, Ollie. No one can accuse you of thinking small. How many guys you figure we'll need?"

"Fifty, sixty guys. No bikers or psycho killers. Just good West-Coast ruffians who don't mind getting their knuckles bruised. Pay them two hundred a day, including jail time, if any. Plus expenses. I've got nothing else to spend my money on. Nothing this important, anyway. Danny, we could put together a force to be reckoned with."

The Barely Brothers walked into the kitchen. Wall to Wall spoke up. "I heard that. Where, when, and who? This could be more fun than a full line-brawl. And there's no referees."

I said, "Wally, one of the bad guys in this whole mess is an Alberta oil guy named Tap Dickens. I want to hurt him by cutting off his revenue stream, which happens to be pipelines. And if we hurt him bad enough, well, it'll make me feel better for one thing, and maybe he'll give us something to make us stop the hurting."

He feigned thoughtfulness. "But Ollie, is that fair? After all the time and effort and ingenuity our Alberta cousins have spent putting all that oil into the ground, what right do we have to deny them the right to do what they want with it? And I'm sure they must be responsible for putting it into the ground. Otherwise, why would they be so proud of themselves?"

His query was met with a contemplative silence.

And so we began to assemble the troops. Calls went out to Port Simpson, Kitwanga and Kitwancool, Prince Rupert, Masset and Queen Charlotte City, Bella Bella, Bella Coola, Klemtu, Hartley Bay, Rivers Inlet, Port Hardy, Port Alberni, Sointula, Alert Bay, Campbell River, French Creek, Ucluelet, Musqueam, and all the little communities hidden along the Fraser River.

We got crazy Doug Kumara from Ucluelet, the Waddell brothers from Alert Bay, several brooding Yugoslavs from Vancouver, an assortment of beards from Queen Charlotte City, enough Sointula Finns to conquer Russia (five or six—one of them was a carpenter, and I'm not sure if he said "finish" or "Finnish"). There were First Nations guys from Port Simpson to Capilano, and a couple of rugby players that One-Eyed Wayne had gone to high school with. They were mostly fishermen—all gear types, from nets to hooks to traps—a few hand loggers, shake bolt cutters, salal pickers, and a mixed bag of off-the-grid malcontents. A truly sterling crew.

I decided to house them at the Richmond Inn because it gave me a group rate of only seventy-five dollars a night. I figured two guys to a room, four nights max, would run me about nine grand. Airfare, maybe thirty-five. Wages for sixty guys for, at most, a week would run about eighty-four thousand. Grub: two thousand. Oh yeah, I forgot alcohol: four, better make that six thousand. The pleasure of kicking the crap out of a bunch of Alberta oilmen? Priceless! And the best thing was, at those rates I could afford to run nine, maybe ten, campaigns.

So one afternoon I was standing in the lobby, directing incoming troops to their rooms and already registered troops to the bar, when I was snuck up upon by my favorite Port Hardyite, Johnny Hanuse. He approached me in a low, deliberate stalk (his mother's lineage had gained him entrance to the Cougar Clan), and I countered with exaggerated shooing motions (my matrilineal lineage had bequeathed to me the I'm-too-busy-for-this response). He laughed and introduced me to a slender young man who looked just old enough to have gained a skull in the old days and was slightly disappointed that times had changed.

"Ollie, you half-breed Findian, this is my nephew Simon. I wanted him to meet you because he thinks all white guys are really smart." He laughed and gave me a dancing hug. "You asshole, my mother still thinks it was your fault we got thrown in jail for clear-cutting the telephone poles on Halloween night. I will remember to my dying day Dougie Tarkenen with his climbing spurs on, up there cutting the wires so those stupid white-man poles would hit the dirt. Where is that stupid, lovely son of a bitch?"

"He's dead, Johnny. He was working in Ottawa and someone killed him. This whole deal we're doing now? It's all about nailing whoever killed Dougie."

Johnny threw his head back and cursed in a manner that could be characterized as really serious cursing. "You hear that, Simon? Good people never live long enough."

Simon shook my hand and offered condolences about Dougie, but I could sense his excitement. He was fresh-faced and guileless, maybe twenty at the most, but he carried himself with a confidence that stopped just short of cockiness. "Jeez," I said. "I don't want to be contributing to the delinquency of a minor."

"You don't have to contribute," he said. "I'm self-sufficient in the delinquency department."

I laughed as I thought to myself, *This kid's all right. Johnny must really trust him or he wouldn't have brought him.*

My cell phone rang and Johnny and Simon wandered off, yelling greetings to all the people they knew. Coastal BC is actually a pretty small community.

It was Louise on the phone. "The car the two thugs drove to your place was owned indirectly by Sonny Feng, through a holding company. When we searched it we found, hidden in the door panel, a bag of gray powder. We've run a few tests. It's not any drug we recognize. Any ideas?"

I thought a moment and was rewarded with a flash of inspiration. "Test for aconite. It's a Chinese poison. Affects the heart."

"I'll pass that along. It could be one more nail in their coffin."

The next day the warriors continued to gather. The burly brown-skinned men who were the first to inhabit this misty green land and the small brown-skinned men who were the first to seine herring in these waters, blond Finns with shoulders like plow handles, Norwegian halibut fishermen with hands like meat hooks, two second-row forwards with legs like tree trunks, the men of axe and chainsaw, east-coasters who had no love for the interior flatlanders, bearded behemoths of uncertain origin, and a skeletal mute wearing abalone-shell earrings. No one was sure who he was. It was thought that he might be somebody's cousin. But he exuded a commendable fierceness, so he was in.

The Barely Brothers were appointed to the transportation committee, meeting planes and buses and ferry boats and driving people to the Richmond Inn. They appointed themselves to the entertainment committee and exceeded their budget in an astonishingly short time.

While the clans gathered, Danny and I drew up battle plans. Tap Dickens and Crude Operations presented two obvious targets. They had an office tower in downtown Calgary, but I didn't think that terrorizing a bunch of accountants and assistant assistants would accomplish much. The pipelines seemed a more strategic target, and much more vulnerable. There were several of them, but they all converged in one area. If the beast had a heart, this was it: the Dragline Valley, in Suckless County. We would strike there.

On a day that dawned like any other day, but a day upon whose record would be written tales of valor and deeds of destiny, our united clans began their journey to glory. We flew to Calgary and boarded four specially fitted-out tour buses.

As we sped along the highway, the vast emptiness mocked our sense of motion. But eventually the landscape began to change. Grain fields gave way to arid nothingness. Flare stacks belched flames with a constant, numbing roar. What withered shrubs that could be seen were surely dead, killed by the nauseating fumes that crept over the land like evil itself.

We stopped on a low rise overlooking the Dragline Valley, and Danny and I walked ahead to reconnoiter. We stood on the hot, dusty road and looked down into the enemy stronghold. Pipelines snaked all across the valley bottom. They joined with other pipelines, twisting into complexes of smaller pipes and vents that passed into the shelter of metal-roofed buildings before disappearing into the earth again. The air thrummed with a constant rhythmic beat, so low-pitched it might have come from the tortured earth itself. Men entered and left the windowless buildings in a ceaseless scurry.

Three of the buildings bore the imprint of the enemy: Crude Operations Inc. I gripped the shoulder of my lieutenant and said, "We strike there and there and there."

We strode back to the buses and mustered the troops. Dividing our forces into three battalions, I placed Wall to Wall in charge of one, Danny in charge of another, and I took command of the last. "Men," I said, "today we strike at the Dark Lord who has threatened our families, our friends, and our neighbors, all of the gentle people of the coast. We strike at he who threatens us with a black poison that will choke our waterways and kill our fish and pollute our land. We must show him our strength, demonstrate to him that the power of the people of the earth is greater than the power of the people of the money. Let us be fearless and resolute and ever mindful of the effectiveness of a punch in the mouth." That was my internal speech. What I said out loud was, "You all know what to do. Let's do it."

The three battalions filed into three of the buses, leaving the fourth by the side of the road, and with rousing cheers emboldening our spirits, we swept down into the fearsome valley. The three targets were not more than a quarter of a mile apart. My bus stopped in front of the first building and waited until the other two buses were positioned in front of their objectives. We launched our attacks simultaneously.

There were only two workers inside the building when we burst through the door. They looked up in alarm as twenty strangers crowded into the machinery-filled space. The machines were big but less complicated than the engine room of a seine boat. There were pipes, primary and bypass, there were valves, and there were pumps. If I'd wanted to be really nasty, I could have closed the valves without shutting off the pumps and probably burned out the pumps. But being Mr. West Coast Sweetheart, I located the kill switch and shut off the pumps. The two workers protested loudly, but Johnny Hanuse told them to shush so they shushed.

A nerve center somewhere sensed the pressure drop. Alarms sounded, and a number of clipboard-carrying importantistas converged on the scene. When they were refused access, the fight began. Most of my troops had moved outside the engine room and that is where they intercepted workers hurrying to fix the problem, so that is where the battle raged.

Raged is a relative word. The level of violence was somewhere between that of a hockey scrum and a rugby scrum. I saw no ears bitten off, but blows were being struck and blood was being shed, although many of the silver-hatted roughnecks contented themselves with yelling and arm waving and barroom posturing.

Johnny Hanuse, however, was having none of that. He had engaged a much larger Silver Hat and opened his eyebrow with a left hook. The Silver Hat grappled defensively, so Johnny drove his head into the guy's nose. It was brutal and bloody, but oh so effective.

His nephew Simon was in trouble. He'd slipped and gone down and was desperately using his arms to fend off kicks aimed at his head. Before I could get there, Johnny did, and the kicker found himself with a severely restricted airway. I got there in time to save the guy's life by reminding Johnny that you didn't kill slaves— unless, of course, they were terminally disrespectful.

Someone caught me with a blow to the ear. It stung. I turned to face the guy, and he attempted to dazzle me with an array of feints and head fakes. I crouched, took one step forward and exploded upwards with my right forearm. His lower jaw crumpled like papier-mâché, and I realized why the forearm shiver has been expunged from the NFL. Unfortunately for my opponent, this wasn't the NFL, and whatever consciousness he may have possessed was severely depleted.

Amid the melee, the dance of angry men, the mute with the abalone-shell earrings flitted purposefully about like a melody in counterpoint. He touched no one but affected many. Dougie would have appreciated the strange beauty of it.

I quickly turned a full circle, checking for incoming. I was under no immediate threat, so I looked across at the other two targets. I could make out lots of activity but couldn't tell who was who or what was what or even why.

I became aware of a shrill keening, which gradually grew louder, and I fancied that Mother Nature herself was crying out. But it was only the sound of two black-and-white vehicles that bore members of the law-and-order tribe. One of them had a bullhorn, which he used to shout over all the other noise, ordering us to stop fighting, which, after a time, we did. Then began the accusations and counter-accusations, and the law-and-order tribe could make no sense of it. I stayed out of the way, biding my time until Dickens appeared.

In a trice (for some reason I had lapsed back into my interior monologue), the Dark Lord appeared. Borne in a flame-red chariot, he dismounted and strode toward us, his countenance radiant with anger. He stopped and stood before us, terrible in the uniform of the enemy: cowboy boots, tight jeans, cowboy hat, and fluorescent silk shirt. He spoke slowly, in a voice vibrating with malignancy. "What the fuck do you think you're doing here?"

"Hi, Tap. We're inspecting your pipelines."

"You have no right to be here. Get off my property. Now!"

I waved a piece of paper at him that I'd typed up that morning. "Tap, my colleague's company, Good Enough Repairs—motto: If it ain't broke, give us a call—has been awarded the contract to inspect this pipeline."

Dickens was quivering with rage. "Bullshit! Bullshit! Fucking bullshit!"

"Tap," I said, "am I to infer that you believe there's been some kind of mistake? Good gracious. You know what? I'll phone head office. Maybe they'll get back to us by tomorrow."

The minions of law and order, sensing that this was essentially a civil matter, and not really wanting to do the paperwork for over a hundred participants in an oil-field brawl, quietly withdrew.

Tap began to stamp on the ground with one cowboy boot, leaving little dimples in the baked clay. "I'll sue your asses off. I'll get every dime you have or ever will have."

"Actually, Tap, Good Enough Repairs is a limited company with limited assets. But if you forced us out of business, it would be a tragedy. One and a half people would lose their jobs."

Dickens seemed tired now. He spoke in a quiet voice. "Swanson, every day this pipeline is shut down, it costs me three-point-seven million dollars. I know we've had our differences in the past. I can be a bit of a hard-ass, but you've got to get that oil flowing again."

"Differences, Tap? Differences? Aside from you torturing and killing a colleague of mine, and then you trying to kill my wife and family, what differences could we possibly have?" I was suddenly tired of playing games. "Pay attention, you reject from an asshole factory. The two thugs that you and Chen sent to kill me and my family? We picked them off like turkeys frozen in a pond. They're in jail. We've got Novi definitely for the Trimmer killing. He's going to roll over on Sonny Feng, Feng is going to roll over on Mr. Chen, and Mr. Chen is going to roll over on you. That's the way it works in the wonderful world of thuggery. As far as the Ottawa branch of Corruption R Us, I've got enough on them to put most of them in jail and all of them out of business. And see this little army I've raised? I can come back next week with twice as many, and the week after that with twice as many again. So. You want to keep butting heads or what?"

He looked skyward for a long moment but could find nothing that denied his defeat. Or, for that matter, that imagined his fate. "You win. You win. What the hell do you want?"

"I want Chen for organizing the murder of Trimmer. And I want whoever killed Gerry Steadman. If it wasn't you, it was one of the Committee. Who?"

Dickens was defeated and desperate. "I'll give you Chen, but you better move fast or he'll be gone. As for the Steadman killing, I'd never even heard his name before he was killed. And you're not going to like this, but unless the Chairman and those guys are running a con on me, they have no idea who killed him either. But listen, you want one of those guys gone, I'll do it. You want to organize some kind of frame, I'm in. Anything to get you off my back."

This was not what I had expected to hear, and I had to think carefully. "Okay, I need whatever leverage you can give me on the Chairman. Anything. There must be lots of dirt that would hurt him if it ever became public."

Dickens was puppylike in his eagerness. "That's easy. Three years ago, I gave him inside information on a certain oil stock just before the company released a geological report on its latest drilling. When the report came out, the stock went through the roof, but Salinger had got in at thirty-six cents a share. A year later, the company released another report that confirmed the oil was there but in relatively small amounts. The stock went through the floor, but I'd warned Salinger and he got out at the peak."

"And you can document this?"

"Everything. I've got about twenty messages back and forth. I made sure I saved them. Plus I can tell you exactly where to find Salinger's buy/sell records."

I asked, "Where's the computer this stuff is on?"

"It's on my laptop, in my truck."

"Give it to me."

"Swanson, I can't give you my laptop. It's got my contacts, my schedule, my business—my whole life is on there."

I made myself sound impatient. Maybe I actually was. "Tap, you're arguing with me. Do you really think you're in a position to argue with me? I was going to copy the hard drive and send it to you, but now maybe I won't. Just get me the fucking laptop." Which he did. And I was not unaware of the fact that the material he had given me to implicate Salinger would implicate him in the same crime. Knowledge is power, and incriminating knowledge is absolute power, and absolute power is, well, pretty fucking cool.

"Okay," I said. "That's Salinger. How do we nail Chen?"

"Search his house. He's got more of that Chinese poison. And you should be able to trace the ten grand a month that Chen was paying Sonny Feng. That's pretty good wages for a chauffeur. And I'm not worried about him ratting me out. His bosses still need me."

"All right, Tap. Me and my trusty band of misfits will go back to where the air's breathable and people are pleasant. And we'll stay there as long as you're a good boy. You see how easy life is when you cooperate?"

I waved to my guys and we got back on the buses. Or rather, we withdrew from the field of battle, exulting that valor had led to victory and the vanquished were scattered before us like dust before a mighty wind. I called Stala and give him the lowdown on Chen. I hoped Stala's Calgary counterparts were as efficient as he was and would move quickly, before Chen fled to the land of no extradition.

When we got to the Calgary airport, I entrusted Dickens's laptop to Danny, because I would be flying on to Ottawa for what I hoped would be my final meeting with the Chairman, Paul Salinger.

I got to Ottawa at ten that night and thought, *What the hell, the danger's over now. I could get a hotel room like a normal person.* But something, maybe nostalgia, urged me to take a cab to my old hideout.

When I opened the door to the basement suite, the first thing I saw was Dougie's old dirt bike propped up in the kitchen. It was a reminder that so far I had failed in my primary mission, which was to find Dougie's killer. I went to bed but couldn't sleep. Dougie had had a plan, some weird plan that involved faking his disappearance on Canoe Lake, then trying to frame Ernhardt for stealing a million dollars, then asking for a quarter million to keep quiet about it. And all this time he was gathering information that enabled him to write a newspaper story that would have blown Ottawa apart—a story that never got published. I had known Dougie so well that I should have been able to figure out his most devious plan, but I couldn't figure out this one. I fell asleep wishing I could talk to Dougie just like in the old days.

And in my dreams, I did. He was standing with his back to me in the middle of a room. He turned slowly until he was facing me, and I could see his shirt was covered with blood. He stared at me with a fierce intensity, then gestured to a typewriter in front of him. I felt dread rising like a cold winter tide as Dougie began to type furiously. Then he began to talk. I couldn't make him out at first because he was mumbling, but then he began to shriek one word, over and over again. "Betrayal. Betrayal. Betrayal!" He ripped the paper out of the typewriter and held it out to me, but I couldn't reach it. I tried desperately to move forward, to reach out and grasp the paper, but I was bound by a creeping paralysis. Then Dougie began to recede from me. I told him to wait, wait for me, but no sound came out of me. Then he disappeared into the darkness and I was alone and crying.

I jerked awake with dread running through my veins. Jesus Christ! What was that all about? I was too far from home and too alone and too bloody stupid to solve my friend's murder. It was 7:00 AM. I got up and showered and then drank coffee while watching the morning news. At eight I left the place for the last time. I went around to the front and knocked on the landlord's door.

When he came to the door, I handed him the key and told him I'd been transferred out west. "By the way," I said, "I left my old dirt bike in the kitchen. Do what you want with it. I won't need it anymore."

I walked east for a while until I found a breakfast joint. I dawdled over steak and eggs until nine thirty, then called a cab and went to meet the Chairman. Paul Salinger's "consulting company" was so exclusive that the address wasn't listed anywhere. But Stala had given it to me, and the cab dropped me in front of a glossy tower that shone with an aura of money and power and complacent blessedness.

I went up to the fifteenth floor and opened the door of Salinger and Associates just in time to see Alex Porter leaving. "Alex," I said. "Surprised to see you here."

He looked a little guilty and muttered something about covering all the bases. He didn't linger to chat. The receptionist was dressed in a pearl-gray power suit and could have passed for vice-president of a lesser firm. When I told her I wanted to see Salinger, she looked politely doubtful and murmured that he was frightfully busy. "Tell him that Ollie Swanson is here."

He apparently became less busy, because after a short consultation with him, the receptionist led me into his office. It was a corner room, of course, and had a great view of the Ottawa River, if you liked looking at the Ottawa River. The furniture was expensive and the accoutrements were tasteful and the whole place made me feel sick. Salinger regarded me from behind a beautiful desk that had probably been carved from the last old-growth teak tree to be wrenched from the Amazon jungle. "What is it now, Swanson?"

I swept all the papers and pictures and assorted decorations off his desk and then sat in the space I'd cleared. "I just wanted to tell you that I haven't succeeded in pinning Steadman's murder on any of you guys, but I'm not giving up. I'm just putting it on the back burner for a while. But there's another issue. A reporter named Dougie Tarkenen ended up with tapes of all the conversations between you and Gerry Steadman. Tarkenen used the material from the tapes, did a bunch more research, tied a whole lot of pieces together and wrote a story that will put several of your committee members in jail and embarrass the rest of you into retirement. Ernhardt's friend, Lou Bernier, killed the story and then Tarkenen went missing. However, I now have the story, and I'll go public with it unless you agree to kill this oil deal you're working on with Dickens. Stop harassing the bureaucrats, turn loose the politicians you've bought, and tell Ernhardt to can the propaganda campaign. You're going to lose the bet you made with Gerry Steadman, even though he's dead. I don't want Alberta oil flowing through BC."

Salinger almost showed an emotion of some kind. "Swanson, I control every newspaper in this city and most of them in the rest of the country. No one will print your story."

I laughed. "You're showing your age, Salinger. Even if you did control all the newspapers, there's a new communications medium out there. It's called the Internet, and nobody controls it. With one click of a mouse, I can expose this story to more readers than the largest ten papers in Canada put together."

Now he was definitely showing an emotion: irritation, maybe even anger. "All right, Swanson, you can embarrass me and put some of my colleagues in jail. But I'm past retirement age. I've got a beautiful house in the south of France. I'll just move there and enjoy my remaining years free from pests like you."

"Uh, no." I gave him my brightest smile. "Dickens sold you out. I've got all the evidence a court will need of your little stock-kiting scheme. If you fuck around with me, Salinger, you won't be going to the south of France. You'll be going to jail and fucking with different people in a different sense." He bowed his head, and I knew I had him. "Look at me, asshole. You need to ensure that no West-Coast pipeline deal goes ahead, either Dickens's or that of any other greedy pig who prances down the pike. The minute I hear that approval has been given for a new pipeline to carry Alberta oil to the BC coast, you'll be in shit so deep your ears will implode. Agreed?"

He knew he was dead, but his deal-making nerves continued to twitch. "But I will be free to pursue other interests?"

"Salinger, you've got about as much negotiating room as a dead slug. Last chance. Yes or no?"

He hesitated just a second, so I stood up and had started to turn away when he quickly said, "Yes. Yes. All right. Yes."

I looked at him. "I won't need that in writing." Then I walked out the door.

On the way to the airport, I thought, *Well, Dougie would be happy with that. He would have been totally against Alberta oil polluting our coast. So that's a victory. That's one for the good guys.* But I didn't feel like celebrating.

Eighteen

Back in Steveston, Danny had paid off and disbanded the troops, all except for Johnny Hanuse and his nephew Simon. They had waited around because Johnny wanted to have a wake for Dougie. We went to the Steveston Hotel and drank a few beers while I explained most of what I knew about Dougie's death. Johnny regretted the lack of anyone to avenge himself on, so he decided to take it out on his own brain cells. My heart wasn't really in it, but I more or less kept up and took advantage of the opportunity to get to know Simon.

He was an interesting kid, smart, but like many rural kids, absolutely determined not to show it. He read a lot and couldn't completely disguise his academic leanings. He was, in fact, not unlike Dougie. But living in a small First Nations community, he didn't have a road map to where he wanted to be.

So I encouraged him to enrol in university, even offering him a place to stay. He said that one of the things holding him back was that he had no idea what he wanted to do for a career. "Listen," I said, "university is not primarily about job training. It's about learning stuff and having fun. Sometimes what you learn is useful and sometimes it's not. But it's all valuable, because it connects you to the collective human brain, everyone who's ever lived and had a thought that became part of our collective knowledge. You know what I mean?"

He became animated. "I'd like that. I want to explore. There's so much out there—just a treasure chest of ideas and knowledge that could link our cultures together."

. Yeah, I could see Dougie in him, all right. Excitement about ideas. That was Dougie all over. I repeated my offer of a place to stay and told him to phone me if he needed advice on enrollment or anything, and then I regretfully took my leave and went home.

The house felt empty until Oshie and the kids flew home from Sointula, where they'd had many excellent adventures with their many excellent cousins. They were a little disappointed to have to leave life in the fun lane, but were soon comfortably back in their routine of school and playmates.

I got an update from Louise. The DNA from Novi Beravitch matched that of the blood left at the Trimmer murder scene. When they explained to Novi that he was going down for that murder, he decided to cooperate and implicated Sonny Feng. The powder they had found in Feng's car had proved to be aconite. That and the fact that Novi Beravitch had fingered him as the actual killer of Phil Trimmer had persuaded Sonny to plead to second-degree murder in exchange for fingering Chen as the one who had ordered the killing. Chen was declining to cooperate, but all three of them had been transferred to Ottawa for trial.

I phoned Stala for his update. He said the Crown was pretty sure they would convict all three villains. "I'm glad we nailed those bastards anyway," I said. "Even if we're not making any progress on Dougie's murder."

"I can understand your being disappointed with lack of progress on your friend's murder," Stala replied. "But why do you even care that Trimmer got whacked? He was a low-life crook."

"Yeah, Phil was a small-time wannabe wise guy. But he only lied to me when he needed to. And he had a wonderful mother."

"You knew his mother?"

"In a manner of speaking."

And then nothing much happened for a couple of weeks. I spent as much time as I could with Oshie and the kids, enjoying the relaxing experience of not having hired gunmen stalking me and my family. But I brooded. Only a little and only once in a while, but occasionally the feeling would strike me that I had failed Dougie. I resolved not to give up the hunt for his killer, but I could see no way forward. I'd shaken all the trees and rattled all the cages and rocked all the boats that I could think of. But I'd accomplished almost nothing except nailing the killers of a peripheral figure who was killed not because he was connected with Dougie's death, but because it was feared he would queer an oil-pipeline project. And, partly because of the material Dougie had gathered, I'd been able to stop the pipeline. And I'd beat a few people up. It wasn't enough.

One afternoon Ren and Daiki came to me and said, "Look, Dad. We found a gun." And they showed me a weapon that, although I'd never seen one before, I quickly identified as a paintball gun.

"Where did you find this?" They told me they'd been playing in Dougie's old Jeep, which was parked in our backyard. Wanting a tire to make a swing like their buddy's, they'd removed the spare tire from the rear of the Jeep. Under the tire, in the tire well, they'd found the gun. "You guys were right to bring me the gun, although I think it's sort of a toy. But it's better to be safe than sorry."

I puzzled over the gun for a while as I tried to picture Dougie running around in the bushes with a bunch of macho males, "killing" each other with paintballs. I just could not summon up that image.

I sat in my kitchen and turned the gun over in my hands, wondering what the hell Dougie had been doing with the thing. There was a small paint stain on the grip, presumably from one of the paintballs. It was an unusually fluorescent red, and with a shock of recognition, I realized it was exactly the same color as the paint that had stained Dougie's T-shirts, the ones that Dougie's landlord had showed to Alex and me. Dougie had been in a paintball war with someone and lost badly, because he had five or six T-shirts that looked like they had received a multitude of hits, right in the heart area.

I phoned Stala. "I may have stumbled on something related to Dougie's murder. Can you send me photos of the body, photos of the crime scene, maybe even the autopsy report?"

"Why not? You've already made me shred the rule book. What's your e-mail?"

While I was waiting for Stala to gather all that material, I found it necessary to go for a walk. I was excited. I could feel that I was on the edge of a breakthrough. I didn't know exactly what it was, but I knew I was getting closer to the killer. When I got back to the house, I turned on my computer and checked my e-mail. Something was taking a long time to download, and I hoped it was the material Stala had sent. It was.

There were fourteen JPEGs and a PDF of the autopsy report. Taking a deep breath, I clicked on the first JPEG, then immediately closed it without looking at it. I got up and walked around the room, mentally flagellating myself for being such a wilting flower. I was looking out the front window when Oshie drove up with the kids. As soon as she walked into the house and saw me, she knew something was wrong. The kids ran upstairs to their rooms and Oshie put her hands on my shoulders and gave me a searching look. I said, "Stala sent me pictures of the crime scene. I can't look at them."

"Tonight, Ollie. After the kids are in bed, we'll look at them together."

So we did. We sat on two chairs in front of my computer and Oshie held my hand while I clicked on the first picture. When it opened up, she squeezed my hand almost as hard as I squeezed hers. It was a full-frame shot of Dougie, on his back, arms outspread, legs slightly apart, bloody, bloody shirt, and more blood in a pool on the left side of the body. His eyes were open and he was staring intently at the ceiling. I looked at the picture for a long time, and after a while it wasn't Dougie anymore. It was just an image.

I clicked on the next picture. It was the same shot from a different angle, as were the next three. The fifth shot was interesting. It must have been taken from close to the back of the room, facing the door. The body was more or less in the middle of the room, twelve or fifteen feet from the door. Just in front of the door lay the gun. To the right of the door there was some kind of workout apparatus mounted against the wall: racks with free weights, some resistance levers for pulling and pushing, an incline bench, and some rubber tubing with D-shaped handles. "I didn't know Dougie worked out," Oshie said.

"He didn't," I replied. "That stuff probably came with the room." We went through the rest of the pictures but saw nothing else of interest.

I opened up the autopsy report. It was seventeen pages long and written in dense medicalese. But you didn't need to know Latin to understand the cause of death: "Gunshot wound to heart. Massive damage to left atrium and pulmonary aorta."

Going back to the beginning of the report, we read through a description of the overall condition of the body: scar on left thigh (I knew where that had come from), healed fracture of left fibula (I knew about that one too), and a lack of tonsils. There had been a bandage on the right forefinger, but, oddly, no wound of any kind under the bandage.

Oshie put her hand on my shoulder. "Ollie, that's very strange."

"Yeah, it's a little strange." I thought about it. "But sometimes I get a bit of an infected hangnail, which really, really hurts, so I put a bandage on to protect it. But anyone looking at it wouldn't see anything wrong. Maybe that's the explanation."

"Maybe." She sounded unconvinced.

I shut off the computer and went to the fridge for a bottle of Chardonnay. I took it and two glasses back to the living room, where Oshie and I sat and talked of things that had nothing to do with dead bodies until it was time for bed.

I fell asleep quickly, and suddenly I was in Dougie's brain. I was looking out through Dougie's eyes as he chased someone. Dougie was holding a gun, and I knew he wanted to kill the person. The chase went on and on, across water and in the air and through different seasons. I was aware of Dougie's despair, and my mounting despair, and finally despair was the atmosphere through which we moved. Then Dougie cornered the guy in the wheelhouse of a fishboat. Dougie raised the gun to shoot just as the guy turned around, and I recognized him. It was Dougie.

When I woke in the morning, I knew who had killed Dougie and why. I just needed to work out a few details. There was about an hour of frenetic activity while the kids got up, breakfasted and left for school. Then Oshie left to visit her parents.

I lingered over my coffee and thought through the events of the past three months. Then I went to the computer and opened up the material that Stala had sent. I spent a long time looking at a particular picture. It was the one shot from the back of the room, showing Dougie's body in the middle of the room, the front wall of the room with the door, and, next to it, the exercise apparatus. I zoomed in on the exercise apparatus. The racks for the weights extended about three quarters of the way up the wall. Lower down was the inclined bench. And at the very top of the weight racks were the two lengths of surgical tubing with D-shaped handles on their ends. I studied them, estimating the length of each to be almost ten feet. The one on the left was about three feet from the door.

I shut off the computer and mentally ran through various scenarios until I was sure I had it right. I heard the front door open and close, and Oshie came in and put her arms around me from behind. "What are you thinking, sweetie?"

I sighed. "I'm thinking I let Dougie down."

"How, sweetie? You had no way of knowing he was going to be killed."

"He wasn't killed, Oshie. He committed suicide."

"What!" She was incredulous. "Dougie wouldn't do that. Why would he? Are you sure, sweetie?"

I was weighed down by guilt and grief, and I felt almost as if I was slandering my dead friend, but I had to get it all out. "He was seriously depressed, Oshie. He was a small-town kid brought up to work hard and tell the truth. He was transplanted into a town where lies and manipulation and greed are the order of the day, where crooks are honored, given the Order of Canada just like decent people. It eventually wore him down. He just got tired. But he'd written this story, the best story of his life. He wanted it to be noticed. He wanted to give it legs. He wanted to introduce it in a blaze of publicity."

"How would committing suicide accomplish that?"

"Because it wouldn't be seen as suicide. It would be seen as the murder of Gerry Steadman. And Dougie had left evidence that would make the cops suspect Cliff Ernhardt as well as tip them off to some of the bribery that was going on. And then Dougie's editor would run his story, and the rest of the bribery and the influence peddling and the political manipulation and the intimidation of the bureaucracy would be exposed. The Committee, the modern-day Family Compact that runs Ottawa, would be destroyed."

Oshie sighed into the side of my neck. "So what went wrong?"

"Two things. Dougie's editor was Ernhardt's stooge, and he killed the story. And the detective in charge of the case ran a leakproof operation, so none of the evidence that Dougie had manufactured ever became public. Any other jurisdiction in the world and that information would have been all over the front page."

Oshie sighed again, and I felt tears on my neck. "Such a waste. Such a waste."

We were quiet for a while and then I said I had to phone Stala. When I told him what I'd figured out, he said, "It wasn't suicide. There was no muzzle burn or contact powder on your friend's shirt."

I was patient. "Here's how Dougie did it. He spent months practicing with a paintball gun, shooting himself in the heart. I assume he wore padding under his shirt, or it would have been painful. He got so he could hold a gun away from his body in his left hand—it was his left-hand prints on the gun barrel, right?" Stala grunted. "Then Dougie pushed the trigger with the index finger of his right hand. You may remember there was a bandage on that finger but no wound. Dougie didn't want to leave his finger-print on the trigger."

Stala interrupted, "But the gun was found twelve feet away from the body. How did your friend manage that?"

"You remember that exercise equipment on the wall to the right of the door? Dougie used that rubber tubing. He stretched it out to where he stood in the middle of the room, placed the D-shaped handle over the butt of the gun and shot himself. The tubing recoiled and pulled the gun away from him before the handle slipped off the gunstock."

"But it would have pulled the gun toward the exercise

apparatus—to the right of the door. The gun was found directly in front of the door."

"That took me awhile to figure out, but it's simple. Dougie took about two feet of the tubing, measuring from where it was attached to the weight rack, made a little bight and held it on the top of the door with the door open, then closed the door so that the bight of tubing was pinched and held. Then he could stretch the rest of the tubing straight out from the door, and the tubing would pull the gun straight back toward the door. When the waiter opened the door in the morning, it released the tubing and it snapped back to its normal position."

"The waiter heard two voices arguing."

"That was just Dougie, doing an act."

Stala thought that over for a minute. "Well, that's complicated, but I can see how it would work. And your friend went to all that trouble, including faking his own death earlier, just so he could frame a bunch of sleazebags."

"He hated them, Stala. But he was tired and he thought he was losing the battle. Maybe he was right. Maybe we're all losing the battle."

Ever the detective, Stala had to clear up the last detail. "So when your friend faked his death at Canoe Lake, he left his vehicle there. How did he get back to town?"

"His dirt bike. It was in the back of the Jeep when he drove out there."

Stala said, "Well, at least I get to slam the door on someone. Three lowlifes who killed another lowlife. That's something, at least. We'll get the big boys next time. Thanks for your help, Swanson. You West-Coast boys have your own style, but it gets results."

When he hung up I looked at Oshie and said, "When the boys come home from school, let's take some food and go for a boat ride."

Which we did. The boys were thrilled to be cruising down the Fraser River on the *Ryu II*, passing seals and sea lions basking on the log booms, gulls and herons swooping in the afternoon breeze, and ospreys dive-bombing for fish.

We cruised out of the mouth of the Fraser and into the Strait of Georgia. Maybe three miles out, with the sun getting low over Vancouver Island, I shut off the engine and we drifted in silence. The four of us just sat on the hatch cover and existed for a while. Then I uncovered the barbecue and put some steaks on, along with foil-wrapped potatoes. We ate while the western sky brightened into yellow, then violet and red. The sun seemed to expand dangerously as it transformed into a fierce red globe at the edge of the world. The four of us sat shoulder to shoulder, leaning together just enough to feel each other's presence. We stared at the darkening horizon as the evening sky imagined our fate.

Nineteen

Daiki will graduate from high school this year. Ren has taken over his role as a normally troublesome teenager. We are fortunate that both of them have been able to vent their adolescent spleens on the rugby field, which has made home life pleasantly spleenless.

Oshie is still young, still beautiful, and still, apparently, in love with me. I no longer am—young, beautiful, or quite as much in love with me.

Dougie still lives in my thoughts, where he has upgraded himself from mere memory to *de facto* ghost. He is welcome there, because echoes of his words and thoughts have always bounced around my brain. I might as well have the whole personality, which exists quite independently and usually happier than he was in life. He had, after all, succeeded in severely discombobulating the activities of the Committee—with some help from me. But he was not happy this morning. He had read the newspaper with me, and he was not pleased.

"Ollie, what the hell's this all about? They're talking about running a pipeline into Kitimat and then loading supertankers to run down Douglas Channel. I thought you killed all that when you made your deal with the Chairman."

"Dougie, the Chairman died three years ago. I don't even know who these new people are. Tap Dickens is not part of it. He went into agriculture futures, sowbellies or something."

Dougie fumed, which was unfortunate because it always gave me a bit of a headache. "It's the same people, Ollie. It's always the same people. They clone each other, or reproduce through zombie sex or something. They never die!"

I tried to placate him. "I don't think they'll get regulatory approval. The tankers are just too much of a risk."

"Remember that bet I made with the Chairman?" Dougie said. "He guaranteed he could make the bureaucrats roll over and ignore all the risks. The Committee still rules Ottawa and they still control the bureaucrats."

Sadly, Dougie's ghost was as prescient as a good spirit should be. During the environmental review of what they were calling the Northern Gateway pipeline, the powers that be in Ottawa delivered a completely quiescent set of bureaucrats. Transport Canada signed off on a report that said of the proposed tanker route, "There are no charted obstructions that would pose a safety hazard to fully loaded oil tankers." Dougie was furious. "Have they looked at a fucking chart?"

Fisheries and Oceans Canada could see absolutely no "unmanageable" risk to critical fish habitat in the thousand or so miles the pipeline would cross, or in the thousands of square miles of highly productive ocean that the tankers would cross. Environment Canada chose what Dougie dubbed the Alfred E. Neuman approach. (What, me worry?)

As this depressing information dribbled out over the next few months, the arrangement of my synapses that Dougie had commandeered for his ghost became increasingly disturbed. Finally, I did as well. "I can't believe it," I said finally. "The bureaucrats delivered a report that was exactly what the oil companies wanted them to, thousands of pages of extremely expensive toilet paper. Were they stupid or just cowardly, or were they bribed?"

Dougie's rage threatened to materialize him, which would have been okay if he had been out of my head at the time. "Bewildered, bullied, or bought. Doesn't really matter. They failed."

Oshie came in and saw me moving my lips. "Talking to Dougie again?"

I sighed. "Remember when I blackmailed Tap Dickens and the Chairman into abandoning their pipeline plans? Well, someone has resurrected those plans."

"But that's ridiculous. It was a stupid plan then and it's stupider now. Aren't the bureaucrats going to stop it?"

I sighed again. It was the only reaction I was capable of. "The bureaucrats, for reasons unknown, have acquiesced."

Dougie spoke more calmly now. "You know what you have to do."

"What?"

"You have to write the story. All of it."

"Jesus, that'll mean months of two-fingered tapping away on my laptop. It'll take forever."

Dougie pointed out that there was no use in being able to type faster than you could think.

"Ha ha ha."

Oshie asked me what I was laughing at.

"That was an ironic response to Dougie's cheap sarcasm. But we've decided on an action plan. I'll have to write the story of the Committee's betrayal, all their betrayals, and get it published."

As you can see, I've done that, at great pains, which would have been greater without Dougie's help. But I could only write to the end of the past and the beginning of the present. The future remains unwritten, but not, I hope, unchangeable. Because if the future becomes the present that the Committee is lurching toward, slavering and blindly grasping, I fear for all of us. That was Dougie speaking. This is me. I am a little older and somewhat mellower, but I am still and ever mindful of the effectiveness of a good punch in the mouth.

And never mind the evening sky. Or imaginations. Or fate.

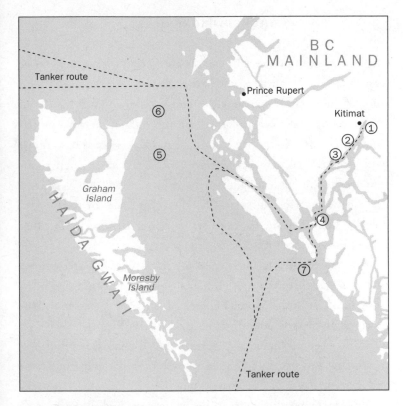

The map of "no charted obstructions that would pose a safety hazard to fully loaded oil tankers."

1. A freighter was obstructed by shallow water and went aground.
2. A freighter somewhere near here was obstructed by an "uncharted reef" and suffered a 12-inch gap in her hull.
3. Grant Point proved to be an obstruction to a freighter that veered sharply and hit it. This could happen anywhere along the route, which is as narrow as ⅘ of a mile in some places. The tankers can be more than a ¼-mile long.
4. Gil Island, which proved to be an obstruction to a BC Ferry. Two dead.
5. Shallows that would ground a loaded tanker.
6. More shallows that would ground a loaded tanker.
7. Caamaño Sound—a minefield of rocks and shallows.

Acknowledgments

This is a work of fiction, but what is not fiction is that there are at least three real live authors who have shed a great deal more light on some of the facets of this book. My cousin-in-law Donald Gutstein (*Not a Conspiracy Theory*) has written about the right-wing propaganda machine, the money behind it, and the effect it has on our lives. Andrew Nikiforek (*The Energy of Slaves*) has written about how the people who fought for the continuation of slavery used exactly the same arguments as do the oil pushers of today. And Stevie Cameron (*On the Take*) writes about the corruption that existed in Ottawa during the Mulroney era.

My first thank you must go to my publisher, because without the initial opportunity and then the ongoing encouragement of Ruth Linka at TouchWood Editions, this particular arrangement of words on paper would never have occurred.

I also need to thank my editor, Linda Richards, for dragging me kicking and screaming back across the boundaries of good taste and into the realm of decent writing.

Jim MacDougall, ex-Calgary detective, corrected all the errors (I hope) relating to police procedures, and my old friend John Sutcliffe corrected errors related to Ottawa. (Geography only—Ottawa-related errors in general are, unfortunately, impossible to correct.) Jeff Jones provided valuable legal advice, my daughter Carmen and granddaughter Carlee provided a Kaleva Road perspective, Robbie Boyes provided a Mitchell Bay perspective, and Stephanie Eakle provided a First Street halfway-between-the-library-and-the-breakwater perspective. And, finally, thanks to Heather Graham for the perspective of a local and very professional editor.

Vic Rhitamo has, over the years, told a number of fishing stories in the tradition of Paul Bunyan and Pecos Bill. I mashed several of them together to form the bedtime story that Ollie tells his kids. Perhaps one day Vic will write all his stories down. They would make a great book for anyone who has children or grandchildren or friends not totally committed to being grown up.

Most of the nicknames in this book belong to real people. I have changed their last names, however. In any case, the characters in the book are fictional and the real-life characters are only characters.

The quotations on pages 79–80 come from the following sources:

Norman Bethune, "Wounds," *Daily Worker*, February 19, 1940.

Randall Jarrell, "90 North," in *The Complete Poems* (New York: Farrar, Strauss and Giroux, 1969).

William Carlos Williams, "Asphodel, That Greeny Flower," in *Journey to Love* (New York: Random House, 1955).

BRUCE BURROWS is the mystery author of *The River Killers* and *The Fourth Betrayal*. Having spent years working as a fisherman, commercial diver, and, most recently, at-sea-observer, he is a true man of the sea. During his time as a fisherman, he wrote a weekly column called "Channel 78, Eh" about fishing on the West Coast. His collected columns can be found in *Blood on the Decks, Scales on the Rails*. Bruce lives on a small island off the northeast coast of Vancouver Island.